AMERICAN YAKUZA

AMERICAN YAKUZA

ISABELLA

SAPPHIRE BOOKS

SALINAS, CALIFORNIA

Cover Design: Sapphire Books Publishing
Interior Design: Sapphire Books Publishing

Sapphire Books
P.O. Box 8142
Salinas, CA 93912
www.sapphirebooks.com

Printed in the United States of America
First Edition – May 2012

Acknowledgements

First, let me thank the beta readers, you are the gems that make the writing shine. Lee Fitzsimmons, you've been with me since the start and I can't thank you enough for sticking it out, thank you. Terry Baker, whose feedback is always valued and appreciated. A big thanks to Brenda T., who was willing to share her gang and law enforcement expertise and answer tons of questions. Finally, Sue Hilliker, for your great eyes. You saw what most of us missed.

To Lisa, who found out that the other side of this endeavor is often tougher than we imagined. Thanks for checking, rechecking, and then checking just one more time. I appreciate the help, the support, and the friendship.

The journey couldn't be made without the love and support of one woman, Schileen.

Mi Amor, Schileen!

Chapter One

Her razor sharp stiletto buried between his eyes. The blade's mirrored finish reflected the faint light in the dimly lit booth. Pure luck had driven the lethal point to that perfect spot, but Luce would take what little satisfaction that provided. Luce squeezed harder, feeling the pain in her heart intensify as the blade bit into her palm. Her hand slipped off the handle and slid partway down the finely honed metal. No matter how tightly she grasped the edge, it didn't keep her from falling into the dark pit that held her heart.

"Kaida." The urgent whisper pulled Luce from her haze. *"Nye."*

"Kaida, your hand." Luce opened her eyes and stared down at the scattered photos on the table, blood pooling on the face of her father.

"Too bad it isn't for real," Luce whispered.

"Your hand, it bleeds. Please." The waitress reached for Luce's bloody hand, wrapping a rag around the cut, clucking like a mother hen at her chick. "Why did you do this? Who hurt you so bad you want to hurt yourself?"

"Stop mothering me, Auntie." Luce looked up at the older Korean woman, thinking of her mother.

She wasn't really Luce's aunt, but the woman had been her mother's best friend. Therefore, Luce gave her the respect of an aunt.

"Someone has to look out for you."

"I have my grandfather. He watches."

"How is the Oyabun?"

"Shall I send your respects?"

"Bah, he already knows how I feel about him."

"Yes, I'm sure he does." Luce examined her hand. The cut wasn't so bad, nothing a couple of stitches wouldn't fix. Later. "Auntie, bring me some Soju and a few napkins." The waitress raised her eyebrows and scowled. "Please?"

"Of course, Kaida."

"Thank you."

Examining the photos, Luce extracted the bloody one and tossed it aside. She didn't want it corrupting the beautiful memories the others invoked. Luce's heart ached as she looked at the young smile of her mother. She barely saw it anymore when she closed her eyes. Twenty-five years had a way of *etching new memories over old ones if you aren't careful,* her grandfather had said when she was young.

"She will always live here, Kaida. Always." She felt his fingers thumping her chest even now as she remembered that day.

Her nose tingled as tears filled her eyes. Blinking several times, she tried to stop the watery tribute to her mother's memory, but the photos brought back fresh pain. One day her father would pay for her mother's death, family or not. She would make sure of it.

"*Sa bum nim.*"

"*Nye.*"

A different waitress approached the table. She bowed before placing a frosted glass in front of Luce and poured her drink. Luce made a cutting signal and downed the drink in one gulp. The burn of the alcohol couldn't erase the pain in her chest, but would assuage it temporarily. Nodding her head towards the waitress, Luce waited as her glass was refilled, then watched her leave.

"How is your hand, Kaida?"

"Auntie, don't spend your time worrying about me. I'll be fine. Sit." Luce pounded the bench next to her and commanded, "Tell me, do you remember these photos?"

Luce hoped that the old woman would be able to give her some history or at least add to her dwindling memories of her mother. Watching her aunt pull out reading glasses and squint at the photos, she remembered a time when she would listen to her mother and auntie speak in Korean.

"*I'm practicing, honey.*" *Luce's mom said, patting her head.*

The hypnotic sounds rolled around her head as she tried to pick out words her mother had taught her, but the two women spoke so fast that the best Luce could manage was one or two words. Luce closed her eyes and smiled, trying to remember the sound of her mother's melodic voice. A Korean children's song filtered through her mind, its soft melody caressed the memory and then was gone.

"Your mother was beautiful. You look exactly like her." Her aunt's smile faded. "Except for the eyes, you have his eyes."

Her grandfather had nicknamed her his little Jade Kaida or jade little dragon, because of her eyes. They were the one thing that singled out her Caucasian heritage and a constant reminder of *him.* A gift she couldn't return even if she tried.

"I know, Auntie. I know." Luce swallowed another

mouthful of the burning liquid, hoping it would finally dull her brain to the point of forgetting, if even for a few hours.

After spreading the photos around, Luce's aunt picked through them and finally pulled a few out. She held up a photo in front of Luce. "This one was taken when we were in downtown. The bonsai festival. Oh, she loved bonsai trees. The way they were trained, the discipline and time it took to get the miniature tree to look like its bigger brothers." As her aunt flipped to the next photo, Luce squinted her eyes and smiled. "This one—this one was when you were only four years old. Every time she took you out, the old women of the park would stop and point. I think it bothered her, but she never complained."

Luce pulled the photo from her aunt's hand and studied it. Her heart ached for her mother. If she could hold her mother's hand or kiss her goodnight one more time. Her body relaxed as memories enveloped her. The nightly ritual of brushing her hair before Luce went to bed or the conversations they shared while sitting alone in her grandfather's garden would stay with her long after her mother's death. Luce's shoulders sagged under the weight of her emotional memories. Like the photos, they were all she had now.

She closed her eyes and took another long pull of her Soju. The rawness of the alcohol burned as she swallowed it down, and in another stinging gulp she had finished the bottle. Nodding for more, she grabbed at the stabbing pain in her palm, now another painful memory courtesy of her father.

The aroma of bulgolgi, the sweet Korean BBQ meat, filled the room as a hot, cast-iron plate was placed on the edge of the table.

"More Soju," Luce ordered. Her aunt raised her eyebrows in disapproval. "Please," Luce said. Her head bowed slightly at the request.

"Kaida."

"Auntie."

"Kaida."

Luce paused a moment before she responded again, weighing her options. Honor, respect and duty were all lessons she had learned early in life. Now that she was the one in command she rarely backed down, but for her aunt she would show respect.

"You must not dishonor your mother, Kaida. She loved you so much."

"Nye. I'm sorry if I have dishonored her in anyway, Auntie." Luce cast her eyes down and bowed her head. She felt a quick thump to her head and held her place. Suddenly, her aunt pulled Luce tightly into her arms and said softly, "You must let go of your anger, Kaida. You are like a daughter to me and it would wound my heart if something happened to you."

Luce leaned her head on her aunt's shoulder and reached around to hug her aging body. It had been so long since a woman like her mother had hugged her that she almost wept. Her body rocked slightly back and forth in comfort. Luce tried to swallow, but the lump in her throat almost choked her. Clearing her throat, she pulled away from her aunt and patted the woman's hands.

"I'll be okay, Auntie." Luce smiled, but she knew the smile didn't reach her eyes. It was only for her aunt's benefit. The tepid reassurance was all she could give at the moment without lying.

"I need to get back to work." She motioned to the pictures. "Bring them with you when you come back and I'll look at them again. Perhaps this old mind will remember more by then."

Luce smiled. Her aunt's mind was sharp as a tack, but perhaps the photos were hard for her to look at, too.

"I will, Auntie." Luce maneuvered her chopsticks, grabbing some kimchi and dropping it onto her rice. "Next time, you'll sit and eat with me. Right?"

"Of course, Kaida. Of course."

After a motherly pat on the head, Luce was left with a steaming skillet of beef, a table full of kimchi, memories, and a searing pain in her hand that almost numbed her heart.

Chapter Two

Sliding into the turn, the tires provided just enough traction to keep Brooke from losing control. She loved her new Mercedes Roadster, but she loved pushing it through its paces even more. The classes at the driving school in Laguna Seca had probably done less to harness her enthusiasm for speed and more to push her limits. Adrenaline pulsed through her veins as she braked briefly for the stop sign at the bottom of the hill. She made a quick check to her left—all clear. An even quicker glance to her right showed an empty curve. Punching it, she peeled out of the stop and fishtailed on to the rising grade. Her arms tingled as she gripped the steering wheel, white knuckles pulling the hundred thousand dollar car back onto to the pavement. Music blared through the expensive speakers and reverberated through her body, adding to the excitement she already felt.

Out of the corner of her eye a flash in the rearview mirror caught her attention. A motorcycle streaked within inches of her door. The driver hugged the metal monster, now sliding sideways in front of her car. Brooke slammed on her brakes and gasped when the back wheel of the bike bucked into the air, like a horse trying to dislodge its rider. Miraculously, the driver rode the front tire a few more feet and dropped the back tire solidly on the ground. She was amazed when the bike finally stopped in the middle of the road.

Brooke's car jerked to a stop only a few feet from where the driver straddled the raging machine. The engine issued a throaty protest as its rider gunned the throttle then turned it off.

Brooke sat stunned as the long body of the driver unfolded off the bike and dropped the kickstand. The tall, sinewy figure looked as though it had been dipped in black leather, the bodysuit conforming to every ridge and muscle on the rider's body. When the rider turned Brooke got her first view of a very feminine form stomping towards her. She cringed as the woman punched her hand into her palm with each step, moving closer.

"Oh fuck." Brooke gripped the steering wheel tighter trying to control the fear coursing through her body. Had she missed seeing the motorcycle at the last turn? Did she cut the rider off and was she now going to have to endure a tongue-lashing from the clearly angry motorcyclist? Her day had been going so well and now this. Slowly, without taking her eyes off the angry woman, she reached over and blindly reached for her purse. She wanted her cell phone close in case anything happened. No purse. Brooke eyed the passenger seat. The wayward bag was now on the floorboard.

"Fuck, fuck, fuck."

She glanced back at the driver, shocked when the woman took out a cell phone and snapped her picture.

"What the hell?" Brooke flipped up her sunglasses to see the rider better.

The driver slipped the cell phone back into her motorcycle boot and approached the driver's door. Brooke hit the door locks and sealed herself in the car. Desperate for an escape, she briefly contemplated sideswiping the motorcycle to make her exit, but she was damned if she was going to let this lunatic intimidate her.

She glared at the helmeted face as the driver motioned for her to roll down the window. Brooke shook her head. No way she was going to do anything of the kind. The rider nodded and tossed up her tinted visor, displaying only dark sunglasses and a perspiring upper lip. Once more the rider motioned for Brooke to roll down the window, and once again Brooke said no. In a split second, Brooke was covered in chunks of safety glass. She sat frozen in her seat. *What the hell?* Her breathing quickened and her fight or flight response kicked in. She focused on the motorcycle again and heard a low voice trembling with anger.

"Don't even think about it. You almost killed me back there and if you hit my bike, you'll most certainly be sorry."

Before she could do anything, the woman reached in and grabbed her keys. Still stunned from the smashed window, Brooke was too afraid to move. If the woman could punch the window out of her brand new car, god only knew what else she would do if pushed.

"Stupid little rich bitches like you get people killed. Daddy bought you a new car and you have to take it out and drive like a maniac. You were probably texting all your little girlfriends about your new ride and couldn't wait to show it off."

The low, menacing tone vibrated through Brooke as she realized the rider stood practically next to her. A chill crawled down her back and she thought she might wet herself. *All that's missing is a redneck tow truck driver and banjo music,* she thought. For the first time Brooke feared for her life, but she was damned if she was going to give this woman the courtesy of seeing it.

"I didn't see you," Brooke whispered.

"You didn't see me because you were too busy playing with your new toy."

Brooke tried to ignore her body's response, but she was starting to shake as she held on to the steering wheel. Releasing the death grip she had on the wheel, she dropped her hands to her lap hoping to control the trembling.

She whispered again, "I'm really sorry. I honestly didn't see you back there."

"Hmm."

Brooke stared, wishing she were anywhere but here, as the woman walked to the front and then back to the driver's door looking the car over. She flinched when she saw the woman reach for something else in her boot. "Relax. You're going to get that glass replaced and a tow truck."

"A tow truck? Why do I need a tow…?"

Before Brooke could finish her sentence, the lanky woman tossed her keys over the embankment on the side of the road.

"Because I don't want to see you in my rearview mirror when I leave. Consider it my gift to you. Otherwise, I might have to take you out of that car and spank your ass." A slight smile peaked up at the corner of her helmet opening. Shrugging, she handed Brooke two cards: A card for the auto club and a business card. "In case you want to sue me, I want you to spell my name correctly. Have a good afternoon, Miss."

Brooke released the breath she was holding and watched as the rider slammed her visor down, straddled her bike, and started the raging machine. Pulling the throttle, the woman made a point of leaving a tire slick in the middle of the road as she popped the front tire off the ground and rode the wheelie up the grade for a short distance.

"Arrogant bitch," Brooke said. Willing her body to relax, she dropped her chin to her chest and took a deep breath. She couldn't remember a time when she had been so scared. Picking up the cards in her lap, Brooke flicked the corners and studied them.

"Great, just great."

Chapter Three

Luce turned onto a dirt road and skidded to a stop. She dropped the kickstand and slid off her bike. Her body shook violently causing her to fall to her knees. Pulling the quick snap on her helmet, she tossed it off and gasped for breath. Cold, hard fear seized her heart and squeezed it tighter and tighter. Her lungs felt bottomless as she tried to catch her breath, leaning over farther and clutching at the loose dirt. Oxygen barely filtered from her lungs to her brain, so her grasp on reality was starting to wane. Bright reds and blues dotted her vision, a sure sign she was going to pass out if she didn't get control. She tried to calm herself taking slow, methodical breaths.

Sitting back on her feet, Luce couldn't believe her luck. She had dodged cars before, but never had she come that close to losing her life. Her body's visceral reaction to the near collision made her break out in a sweat. She wiped at the wet wisps of hair that stuck to her face. Her leathers did a great job protecting her body from possible road rash, but it did little to keep her cool. Looking around to make sure prying eyes wouldn't be a problem, she unzipped the top of her leathers and peeled them down to her waist, exposing her bra. Tossing off her gloves, Luce flexed her right hand and studied the bruise starting to form on her knuckles. She shook her head wondering how she could lose her temper so quickly. She was trained to control her emotions no matter the situation, but her temper had gotten the best of her on occasion. Today it flared—no, spiked out of control. Without thinking she had broken out the window of the car that nearly killed her, and then tossed the woman's keys down the embankment. What would her grandfather have to say about it all, assuming she even told him?

Luce wondered if the woman would call the police. No matter, she had a "relationship" with a few officers who would let her know if something came through channels. Still, replaying the situation over in her head, Luce was surprised she was even alive. Closing her eyes she relived the vivid memory of coming around the corner to find the red Mercedes right in front of her. Only a couple of yards separated them and the way Luce was eating up pavement, she was sure she would hit the damn thing. Her reaction was instinctive. She had stepped on the back brake first and then leaned left, pointing her front tire right at the car, and sending her into a sideways skid. If she was going to hit the car she wanted to hit it broadside and not head on. At least she had a chance of surviving the crash that way. Lucky for Luce, the woman punched the gas when she peeled out of the stop and probably saved Luce's life. Anger replaced fear as she remembered going around the red roadster. She recalled seeing the woman as she went by. Luce recognized the driver as a reporter who had been hounding her for a story on her company, Kaida Enterprise. She had turned the reporter down and now here she was, practically making her road kill.

Leaning against the seat of her bike, Luce reached down and pulled her phone from her boot. She thumbed through it and brought up the pictures she had taken of the car and the woman. Spreading her fingers cross the screen brought the woman's face into focus. *What was her name?* Luce thought. Grinding her teeth, she squinted at the face and tried to remember. It was no use, she couldn't remember the woman's name, but she always remembered a face. In her business she couldn't afford to forget the face of an enemy. While this woman wasn't an enemy, she'd almost taken the one thing her grandfather had always told her to protect.

My Jade Kaida," he said looking into her green eyes. "You have only one treasure you must always protect. Trust it to no one and don't lose sight of it."

"What's that grandfather?" a young Luce questioned. She looked down at their intertwined fingers as he led her around his manicured gardens. It had become their ritual after having tea.

"You're life, my young Kaida."

Luce smiled at the memory of the only family she had remaining—the only family she recognized. She would see her grandfather on Sunday, as she had for the last few years. He was her mentor, her friend, and only connection to a mother she had lost many years ago. Likewise, she was his connection to her mother. They shared a bond like no other and she cherished it.

She raised her eyes to the sun beating down upon her, sweat still dripping down inside her leathers. It was time to get home and take a shower. She had a meeting with the chiefs in her organization tonight and the events of the day had primed her.

Chapter Four

Brooke stalked into her editor's office and tossed her purse across the room onto the plush leather sofa with a thud. Slamming herself down on the cool surface of the sofa, she threw her arm across her mouth and stifled a scream. Investigative journalism had taken on a new slant: *How to get the interviewee to sit for an interview with the reporter who almost killed her. News at eleven,* she thought. A scowl replaced her usually calm exterior. Closing her eyes, she wished she could crawl back under her covers and start her week all over again. The new Mercedes was in the shop, and a crappy loaner sat parked in its spot in the parking garage. Sitting up Brooke pulled the business card out of her purse and flicked its edges. *Life wasn't fair,* she thought for the twentieth time that day.

She had traded the glamorous life of investigative journalism for the more stable life of a journalist stateside. Mucking through the countryside in Europe to follow leads on the new gangster elite had been tougher than she'd imagined. The rise of capitalism in the dregs of the fallen Soviet Union, and other communist countries, had created a subculture of American-style gangsters. Living the fast life, throwing money around like prepubescent teenagers with their first paychecks, driving fast cars and carrying big guns all made for an interesting story, for a while. However, it had quickly lost its appeal when her photographer Mike Waters was shot and killed behind the Orsha Linen Mill in Orsha, Belarus. Brooke had no idea what she was stepping into when she had started the investigation and now wished she hadn't heard of Kolenka Petrov.

Too afraid of the eyes and ears in and around Moscow, their informant requested that they meet at the linen factory in Orsha. The town was considered the gateway between Western Europe and Moscow. Orsha was an easy in and out for anyone traveling by train. The informant said he could provide them with names and information on the new transnational organized crime groups establishing themselves outside of Moscow. Petrov's money allowed the groups to set up operations in places like San Francisco, Los Angeles, Chicago, Manhattan, Cyprus, Canada and a host of other foreign countries. Establishing legitimate businesses like trucking, import-export and oil and gas operations, the bigger crime groups were able to send out the younger thugs who wanted to make a name for themselves to do their dirty work. Trafficking in prostitution, car theft, contract killings and extortion, their notorious reputations preceded them. Follow the money, Brooke had been told, and she did, all the way to Orsha. She had a bad feeling about the meeting, but Mike had persuaded her to go. They'd invested so many hours and months on the story that he didn't want her to blow a great opportunity at a Pulitzer Prize.

Brooke felt a chill descend on her just as she did the night Mike was killed. She rubbed her arms and tried not to think about that night, but it played in her mind like an old movie looping the same scene over and over again. They'd arrived at the meeting point behind the factory, making sure they weren't followed, as instructed. Why they couldn't meet at a hotel was beyond her, and probably the cause of her anxiety. Someone whispered her name and when she looked up it all played out like a black and white movie in slow motion, except the red blood that covered Mike and the snow around him. A shot had come from somewhere to her right. Then Mike fell without a sound. Dropping to her knees, she turned, trying to peer into the surrounding darkness. She tried to reach down and touch Mike but was stopped. The sound of a gun being cocked made her hesitate just long enough that her arm was jerked up.

"Go, you must go. Now, run to the train," a wiry man said. He pulled her toward the train platform. As they moved he searched the empty streets, for whom she wasn't sure. Fear gripped her when she saw the small revolver in his hand. He had shot Mike.

"I didn't shoot your friend," he said. "Now, you must go. Hurry, they will kill you too if you don't get on that train."

"Mike, I can't leave Mike here. He's an American. I need to call the embassy. Stop" She jerked her arm from his grasp to stop their progress.

His wide eyes looked back into her frightened ones, studying her. He looked more like a homeless man than an informant—whatever that looked like. He pushed her towards the train station and then shoved the revolver under her nose.

"If you don't get on that train, you will die, too. Do you understand me?" He pushed her backpack at her.

"My friend?"

"I'll take care of it. Now run and don't look back. Hurry."

Brooke grabbed the pack and ran towards the station.

The memories faded to black and she started to cry. She had left the only friend she had in Europe lying dead in the snow. Brooke had contacted the United States Embassy, but they offered little help, explaining that Belarus was corrupt with a capital C. They would check out her story and get back to her. That was six months ago and she still hadn't heard anything. It wasn't for a lack of trying, in fact she was sure the U.S. Embassy was sick of her phone calls by now. They exchanged pleasantries and then gave her the same answer, "We have no new information. Try again next week."

"Hey Pumpkin." A jovial voice broke the memory into tiny shards, scattering them in her mind. "I know, sexual harassment or something similar, but maybe I'm making a comment about your weight? No, that wouldn't work now would it. You're so rail thin."

John Chambers was her editor at the Financial Times. She had taken a leave of absence from her assignment after Europe, but couldn't sit around the house a minute more. When he found out she was stateside, he called and made an offer her bills couldn't refuse. The promise of easier work, writing up articles on the wealthy and famous, sounded easier than her past life, so she snatched it up.

"Hi John," she said, trying to muster up some enthusiasm. She was about to confess how she almost killed her next big story, knowing he would chastise her for being careless. "I'm afraid I have some bad news."

"Hmm…" He continued staring at the paperwork piled on his desk.

"I almost killed the owner of Kaida Enterprises today?"

"Really," he said, nonplussed.

"It was an accident, really. I thought you should

hear it from me before the lawyers. I'm sure she'll sue."

"I'm sure it was." Still not paying attention, he riffled through a stack of papers and then plopped back into his chair, almost missing it completely when he realized what Brooke had said. "Are you fucking crazy?" He leaned over the desk and stared at her.

"I'm afraid I am."

"Obviously. What the hell happened, and don't leave out one detail. The lawyers will tell me her version, so it's best if you tell me yours first. Jesus, Brooke."

John shoved her legs to the floor and pulled her upright. He was so close she could smell his cheap aftershave dripping off him. He must have had a lunch date. She knew it was the only time he wore the stuff during the day.

"I took the roadster out for a drive in the foothills. The next thing I knew there was this motorcycle honking at me driving all wild and stuff. It looked like she was riding one of those mechanical bulls. The way it tried to buck her off when she skidded around me. God, you should have seen the way she handled all that metal and speed. It was amazing."

Brooke blushed as she realized she was enthralled at the sight of the woman controlling the metal beast. At least she had the decency to blush; she didn't want to tell John how she really felt at the time. A hard ass reporter like her had a mystique to keep firmly in place and he knew little about what happened in Europe. What she had told him was only a smattering of information. She planned to go back at some time to find out what happened to Mike, so telling John anything would be fruitless.

"And?"

"Long story short, she busted out my window, tossed her business and insurance cards in my lap, and threw my keys over the side of the road. She said if I wanted to sue her at least I could spell her name right. That was the end of it."

"Geez, Brooke." John rested his head in his hands and sighed. "She's the fastest growing company on the west coast and you nearly killed her. How do you expect to get the interview with her now?"

"She didn't ask for my name."

"What?'

"She didn't ask me for my name," Brooke stated matter-of-factly.

"Oh, I see. You think because she doesn't know your name, you're good." He slapped his hands on his knees before dropping back against the couch with a groan. "How much investigating have you done on Kaida Enterprises, Brooke?"

"Some, but not a whole lot. There isn't a whole lot to investigate. Why?"

"I thought you were an investigative journalist?"

"Are you questioning my abilities, John? Seriously?" Brooke's anger boiled under the surface as she continued. "You act like I'm some kind of hack. I've been through the books. I've researched her and Kaida enterprises."

"Look, calm down. I'm saying that if you think she doesn't know who you are, trust me, she knows." John ran his fingers through his short, sandy blond hair. Worry creased his youthful appearance, adding years he hadn't lived yet. "The word on the streets is Luce Potter is involved in organized crime. Ask any crime beat reporter and the story is always the same. Her name comes up but no one can confirm any of it."

Reaching for his pen, he wrote a name and number on slip of paper and handed it to her. "Call this guy. He's a cop and knows Luce Potter."

Brooke's felt a chill slice through her. Did he say organized crime?

"Organized crime as in the mafia? Did I miss something, she doesn't look the type and trust me I know the look." Brooke ventured back in to her memories and remembered the thugs that worked for the Russians. Luce Potter wasn't even close.

"She took over for her grandfather, Tamiko Yoshida. She has a different last name, but trust me if you dig a little deeper you'll find the connection. Word is he made her the boss a few years ago. There was a bit of a dust up that was purposely kept under wraps. From what I understand he's still in the picture, but only in the background. The inner workings of the organization are not my area of expertise. One thing is certain, though: A woman at the head of a patriarchal organization like the Yakuza is big news somewhere."

Brooke pulled her notepad from her purse and started jotting down everything John was telling her. She never would have guessed Luce Potter was connected to organized crime. The Yakuza were a different animal than the Russian mob. They were more secretive about their business dealings. The fact that they integrated themselves into businesses and politics in Japan, mostly through illegal means, was the extent of Brooke's knowledge about the organizational structure of the Yakuza.

Brooke looked down at the name and number John had handed her. "Okay, but why all the cloak and dagger, John?" John fidgeted with something on his desk. She was tired of chasing her tail and secret meetings when it came to writing her stories. The very idea of meeting with a third person to get a lead on a story was starting to remind her of Orsha and that wasn't a good thing. "John?'

Chapter Five

Luce centered herself in front of the ceiling to floor mirrors. Rising on her toes, she paused, took a deep breath, and then lowered her heels down into the spongy floor of the training mat. Assessing her appearance in the mirror, she adjusted her black belt making sure it was centered directly below the black v-neck collar. It was the only color on her stark white uniform with the exceptions of the five gold stripes on the tip of the belt. The knot centered on her belly button she could feel its presence as she took a deep breath and held it for a ten count. After one last pull on the end of her *dobak* top, she released her breath and stood ramrod straight.

"*Cha ryuht,*" she whispered, snapping her feet together and clenching her fists against her thighs.

"*Kyung nae.*" Closing her eyes and bowing deeply to each of the three flags hanging in their place of honor above her head. She straightened once again looking forward.

"*Choon bi.*" She assumed the ready stance. Hands into fists, palm up at her belt. Her feet shoulder width apart. She had done this very thing at the start of every class for the past fifteen years and it had become rote for her. Moving without thinking, drilling and preparing while the mind was silent. It was her "zone time" as she liked to call it. The precious time in the day when she thought about everything and yet nothing.

Her body felt like a bow stretched tight with every muscle taut. One tweak and she was ready to release all of her pent up energy. Yet, she would slowly work through her forms, pushing each muscle to perfection. The artful lines of the forms veiled their true intent of self-defense and attack. A kick, a punch, a block, rhythmically practiced to perfection over the years with a snapping sound its final calling card. The force behind the snap could break a bone, injure an unprotected assailant, or break the window of a car. A well-placed blow could do enough damage that the unsuspecting attacker wouldn't know how badly he was injured until days later, when bruises formed or death ensued far away from the deliverer.

Staring straight ahead she pulled the blindfold from her belt and covered her eyes, tying it tightly around her head. She liked the challenge of being blindfolded when she fought, but today she would work through her forms, bottom to top, ending with her highest black belt form without the advantage of sight. It was a common practice at higher levels and was often used to encourage younger belts to practice, especially when the blindfolded person ended in the exact spot they had begun.

Returning to her ready stance, *choon bi,* she announced the form and stood for a brief second. Then as if getting a silent acknowledgement from her former master, she began. She readied her body for the simulated four-way attack that the form was designed to emulate. Pivoting to her left, she sliced the air with a downward block and then moved forward with a back-leg front kick. The snap of her uniform was a testament to the power of the kick. Moving through her forms, she felt fluid, slicing the air with razor sharp crispness, hearing her uniform snapping repeatedly at the controlled momentum. Luce could feel her muscles tense, release and then tense again as she delivered a bone breaking knife hand or spear hand to her opponent's chest. Trying to keep her mind clear as she moved through the forms was proving to be harder than she thought as the events of the day flitted through her consciousness. She finished her last form, held her position, took a deep breath, and then returned to what she hoped would be her starting point. Before she could remove her blindfold, the frightened expression of the woman from her earlier encounter flashed in her mind. Goosebumps popped all over her body, followed by a by a well-deserved blush. She had embarrassed herself, dishonored herself, and her family when she lost her temper and now she realized that she needed to somehow make amends. Frustrated, she tossed the blindfold to the floor and looked down at her feet. She had finished exactly where she had begun. It provided little condolence to how she was feeling, though. Biting her lower lip, she bowed her head and sighed. Her grandfather's words of praise echoed in her head, as they had done many time before when she had successfully completed her forms. Yet she didn't feel deserving of that praise, not this time.

Her success depended on her ability to maintain complete control, even when things went badly. Her employees, her company, and others depended on her discipline. Luce had worked hard building her companies' holdings. Starting with a business degree, she had managed to incorporate many of her grandfather's holdings into a substantial empire. At the time she had no idea what she had helped build until one night her grandfather took her aside and explained the family business.

"*Aw, my little, Jade Kaida. Sit,*" *he said, motioning for her to sit beside him. A nod of his head meant the waitress should pour another cup of hot tea. She then respectfully left the two alone.*

"*Grandfather.*" *Luce kissed her grandfather's cheek and waited until he sipped his tea before she raised hers to her lips. "I'm not so little anymore." She sipped gingerly, watching her grandfather.*

"*Yes I know, but humor an old man.*"

The respect she had for her grandfather was on two levels. The first being familial, he was family and her elder. Respect was given without question, but her grandfather had earned it tenfold. He had taken over as surrogate parent after her mother's death. His tenderness, his caring, and his devotion kept her grounded and focused when she had lost so much. He had provided a stable life, taking her to school and being there when she got out. They walked home together every day. As she grew older they talked of school and sports. He often tried to talk about boys, but Luce wasn't interested. She wondered when she would be interested, but the attraction never materialized, so she never questioned it.

The second level of respect she had for her grandfather involved the life lessons he imparted to her. They discussed culture, duty, and honor. He schooled her on how she should conduct herself when men from his business came over, which was rare. He influenced her college choices, pushing for one that would provide her the education he felt she needed. It was important not only for success in life, but to prepare Luce to take over his business.

"*Grandfather, you look ill, are you all right?*"

Patting her hand, he smiled lovingly at her. "Kaida, I am an old man, I always look ill." Laughing at his own joke, he continued. "The time is coming for you to make some decisions concerning your future. College is over and your future lies ahead of you."

"I'm not sure I understand."

Concerned, Luce grasped both of her grandfather's hands hoping what that whatever bad news he had to tell her she could handle.

"Grandfather, whatever is wrong we can deal with it. I'm sure it will pass and if it doesn't, we'll come up with a plan to solve it. I'm sure of it."

If Luce had known how much her life would change that day, would she still accept the responsibility she was about to shoulder? Smiling, she knew the answer, of course. She wondered why she ever had doubts about her ability to lead. Looking back she realized that everything her grandfather taught her had lead to that very moment. He would go against tradition that night, knowing that if she failed it would reflect on his decision to pass everything on to her.

"I don't understand." She watched as her grandfather began to take his shirt off. Not knowing what to do she stood and helped him slip the long sleeve dress shirt off, then asked, "Are you feeling ill, Grandfather? Shall I call Frank?"

"Kaida, please I think you will understand when you see..." Pointing to the tattoos she had never seen before, he continued, "These tell the story of my life, of who I am outside of my home. I am Yakuza, Kaida. I am Oyabun of our clan."

The colorful ink etched patterns of fish, women, and other things that she couldn't recognize from his wrists, up his arms and disappeared underneath his undershirt.

She had never seen her grandfather without his shirt on and now she knew why. But what did this have to do with her and what was an Obyabun, she wondered.

"I don't understand."

Slowly and methodically he explained all the things he had kept from her for her protection. Luce's grandfather, Tamiko Yoshida, never married after his wife died giving birth to Luce's mother. He adored his wife, Hyun. They had met when Tamiko was serving in the United States Army and stationed in Korea. Luce smiled as she remembered how he talked about his one true love. His eyes sparkled and his wide smile still lit up his face when he talked about Hyun. Luce had only heard the story a couple of times, but she had committed it to memory. The typical, strong American GI travels the world and meets his wife overseas in a foreign country. Only this story was real and marriage had caused dishonor for Hyun's family. Bad blood still existed because of the Japanese occupation of Korea and two young people in love wouldn't change a centuries old feud.

He had served his country with honor and distinction, but when he came home with his new bride, he returned to a family in decline. Their pride would never allow them to tell Tamiko how bad things had gotten. Tamiko had worked hard to rebuild the floundering family business when he returned from overseas duty. His hard work and reputation had earned the respect of his community, but it had come with a price. His dealings had made him the target of rival "businesses" and he knew that sometimes things would need to be done to protect what he had built. Therefore, he did them without apology, or second thought.

"Your grandmother would be so proud of you,

Kaida,"

"*I wish I had known her.*" *Her chest tightened, grieving the loss, knowing that she would never know her grandmother and in turn would never experience the loving comfort only a grandmother afforded their grandchild.*

"*She was a wonderful woman. She had a passion for life. I was lucky to have her, even for the little time we were together.*"

"*Let's sit and talk about what's on your mind.*"

Quietly, the waitress brought a new pot of tea and small dishes of food were placed on the low table. Luce sat opposite her grandfather and waited as he spoke to the woman serving them. A quick command from the woman brought hot sake and two cups to the table. Dismissing the server, Luce began to fill his plate, poured his sake then filled her own plate. As respect dictated, she waited to eat until he started. However, he didn't. Instead he cleared his throat and looked at her.

"*So, now we come to the reason we are having dinner here. The lines of succession are traditionally handed down to the men of our culture, but you Kaida, you straddle three cultures: your Korean culture, your Japanese culture, and your American culture. All of these make for a difficult path for you to follow in your life.*" *He cupped his sake and took a small sip.*

So began her formal history of her grandfather's business, his culture, and his life.

Luce found herself hypnotized by his tattoos and wondered why she never noticed them before. The intricate designs were beautiful. The colors vibrant and strong like her grandfather. Suddenly she realized the weight of what he had told her. He was essentially part of an illegal organization—not part—he was the head of the organization. Her mind swirled with questions, and yet out of respect she would wait for him to tell her what he wanted her to know.

"I want you to take over my position in the organization when I'm ready to step down."

Her face flush, Luce sputtered as she choked down the swallow of warm sake. "I'm sorry? What did you say?"

"You heard me, you're more than ready. I wouldn't give you such responsibility if I didn't think you could handle it." He reached for her hand and gave it a squeeze. "Relax, I'm not stepping down for a while, but I want you to be ready for the time I do. So—"

"Grandfather, I don't know the first thing about... about..." Trying to be delicate, she stammered looking for the right words. "I mean...I don't know anything about," she said shrugging her shoulders. "Yakuza."

"First, let me explain how I earned what I am about to pass on to you. As I said before, my family struggled when I returned from my service in the Army. As I grew the business, I made decisions that hopefully you will never have to make, but if you do know I've had to do things only a boss can do," he said looking down at his hands.

"What kind of decisions are we talking about?"

"A few years ago, a group of businessmen came to me. Another family was squeezing them so tightly that they were looking at going out of business. I had taken great pains to make us a legitimate part of the growing businesses around us. This family was killing off not only the businesses, but murdering those who didn't comply with his orders. He eliminated anyone who was getting in his way, including his own men who were giving him guidance. This looks bad for all of us if one family is out *of control, so I had a choice to make. I called for a meeting to try and reason with him. His family was small but it was destroying the Yakuza organization from within, like a cancer. How do you get rid of cancer?" he asked rhetorically.*

Luce shook her head. "I'm sorry grandfather." She could guess what was coming.

"You cut it out, Kaida. I knew that as the bigger family I had to make a clear statement to the smaller families. No one defies Tamiko Yoshida. I killed him. It had to be done. After that, I offered to take in those that were part of his family. Most came, but a few joined other families. We became the largest family in the state. The reason I tell you this is because you must be willing to cut the head off a snake if it threatens to bite. It is your job as Oyabun."

"I understand," Luce said bowing her head.

"Sometimes you must be ruthless, Kaida, it must be done and never apologize for being the boss."

"I understand."

"You'll learn the business from the middle up. I want you to work for me, learn it from the inside. Otherwise, you will not earn the respect from the men."

"Of course."

With that the deal was done. An offer had been extended and accepted. The details were negotiated that dictated Luce work her way from the middle to the top. Now, she sat at the head of an organized business plan that included both legal and illegal business dealings. She took the profits from the card rooms, alcohol sales, and protection dealings, and built Kaida enterprises. Downsizing the illegal side turn by turn, she reduced her possible risks of exposure and arrest, realizing it would take years to divest herself of the illegal dealings she had taken over. When she had presented the plan to her grandfather he smiled, patted her on the head, and walked away. She felt like a child being humored. Steamed, she threw all of the hard work in the garbage and drank until she couldn't stand. By the time she sobered up, she had punched a hole in the wall of her new house, busted out a window in her solarium, and her hand was in a cast. Three broken bones all in payment for the time and energy she'd spent developing what she thought was a workable idea. Pulling the papers out of the waste bin, she smoothed them out on her desk and studied them again. Luce looked at every event, every business, and every person involved, ensuring everyone and everything had been taken care of. They were family and she had a duty to protect her "family". She pounded her fist on the table before she swept her arm and scattered the wrinkled sheets of her life across the floor. She slumped against the wall defeated. All she wanted, no needed, was her grandfather's approval. Luce had been desperate to show him he had made the right decision in selecting her to take over the organization. She checked and rechecked, looking at every scenario, timing the withdrawal of certain operations to coincide with the opening of legitimate businesses and finally she lifted up her hands in resignation, she had done all she could do. *Let the pieces fall where they may,* she thought. She had done her best.

It took Tamiko weeks to see the bigger plan, but once it unfolded before him, Luce had earned his approval. Now, ten years later, she wanted to finalize the elimination of the last of the illegal operations, but the arrival of new competition and the hint of white slavery kept her firmly at a standstill.

Her temper spiked again as she untied the knot

in her belt. The Russians were coming to town and she knew trouble followed close behind. If they continued on their current path, it would throw a wrench into her plans. Now that she'd come so close to remaking the business end of criminal enterprise, she wasn't about to let Petrov and his gang stop her. After the charity ball she would deal with the Russian. He would be sorry he hadn't taken her advice and left town sooner. Now he would see how business was really done—Asian style.

Chapter Six

Luce pulled, exposing a fashionable view of her French cuff beyond the tuxedo sleeve. The charity dinner had been on her calendar for months and she still hadn't come up with an acceptable excuse to get out of it. Oh, she supposed if she had really wanted to, she could have made a sizeable donation and that would have handled the matter. However, according to her grandfather she needed to be more approachable. *Eliminate the mystic that swirls around you and Kaida Enterprises,* he had told her recently. He was worried that she spent too much time in the office and not enough time with people. Making an appearance here and there would hopefully put the rumor mills to rest. Nevertheless, she knew what people said and they weren't rumors, so much as unsubstantiated truths.

She played her cards pretty close to the vest and only a chosen few knew about the darker side of her business dealings. Those operations she had taken over from her grandfather with his blessings and guidance. She had been groomed to take over without knowing it. No matter, duty to family was a tenant that she held on to firmly. Her grandfather had mentored her well as she grew-up. When she had come of age, he made it clear that it was her choice to help run his "business dealings." Her ties to her family were tightly bound around her heart and she was thankful for her grandfather's guidance and love after her mother died.

Her culture demanded she follow tradition, even if she thought otherwise. Therefore, it was a choice she'd made willingly. Family was everything.

Truth be told, Luce enjoyed the social scene. Beautiful women of the upper crust of society could be counted on to be sexually frustrated and lonely. Their husbands spent too much time wheeling and dealing and not enough time on their wives. Throwing money at them was an easier alternative than the precious commodity of time they needed to seal the next deal.

A stray piece of lint caught her eye as she adjusted the collar of her shirt. The mirror reflected the crisp lines of her slacks, the slim, long line of her jacket. Tonight's benefit was for Luce's favorite charity, the cancer wing of the pediatric hospital. A playroom had been named after her grandfather and Luce's mother, Hyun Chu. Luce never turned down an opportunity to help, but she did turn down all opportunities for the recognition her donations garnered. What she donated was a private matter. It had taken more than a few reminders to the head of the cancer wing, when he had repeatedly suggested that they set a plaque honoring her. Her grandfather was surprised by the honor Luce had bestowed on him. In fact, he almost had the hospital convinced that it would be in their best interest if the playroom was named for his daughter instead, but Luce had intervened just in time. Luce smiled as she remembered the day they dedicated the playroom.

"Grandfather, please. Allow me this honor. It's only a playroom for children who have so little. Besides, you and mother have given me so much and you rarely allow me to do anything for you and there is nothing I can do for her now."

Luce looked lovingly at her grandfather. The years

had been gentle to his mind, but hard on his body. His hands showed the wear of decades of hard work, his body bowed from the same stress. Yet, he always had time for lessons, as he liked to call them, for Luce. Honor, respect, and duty were daily reminders when she was with her grandfather.

"Kaida, you must remember that you are from different cultures. All three expect something out of you, but you must expect more from yourself," Tamiko would tell his granddaughter. "You mother knew this and wanted more for you as well."

His gentle pat on her head made her smile as she bowed before him to pour his tea. Their "tea time" was really his time to impart wisdom that she knew he hoped would stick with her throughout her life. She valued his advice and still consulted him when she was pressed with a problem she couldn't solve. She felt her chest tighten, remembering she hadn't talked to him in a few days and at his age, days might be all he had.

The ringing of the phone pulled her from thoughts of her grandfather.

"Yes. Good, I'll be right out."

Luce checked the mirror one last time to adjust anything that might be off, then picked up her overcoat and gloves and strode to the limo waiting outside.

John had asked Brooke to be his date for the charity ball, and she begrudgingly accepted when he reminded her that she owed him a favor for saving her ass from the legal department. While Brooke didn't mind playing dress-up, she hated when it involved business, too. This wouldn't be a relaxing night for

Brooke. Keeping her ears open and her eyes moving made for a long night. She felt her shoulders tighten as she thought about the grilling John would give her on the way home.

"What did you hear? Whom did you talk to? Why didn't you talk to so-and-so?" It would all end with something like, "Oh my god, did you see what, Mrs. What's-her-name was wearing? Girl, she is not twenty-five anymore. I'm saying." Then they would laugh all the way home when John started doing his impressions of whatever socialite had caught his eye. For a gay man John had no boundaries when it came to gossiping.

Brooke held two pairs of shoes against her dress and tried to decide on comfortable flats or sexy pumps that would kill her feet by the end of the evening. Being a slave to fashion Brooke went with the heels. *Besides, maybe I'll meet Ms. Right-now tonight,* she thought as she walked into the front room of her quaint bungalow. The Craftsman-style home had been up for short sale, making it a nightmare to get, but Brooke had persevered. She had waited out the bank and two other couples who had finally given up after eight months. The only thing that didn't need repairs was the stone exterior. *Thank God,* she thought as she remembered the months of sanding, painting, and plumbing. The final touches were almost done and she couldn't be happier. Christmas in her new home would be overwhelming with the size of her family, but they had made her promise to host it this year. Smiling, she slid the leaded glass French doors closed, running her fingers over the stained oak, the last rubbing of the stain had taken her long into the night, but now they looked fantastic. She jumped when she heard someone clear their throat behind her.

Without a hesitation, she swung wide and clocked

whoever was behind her square in the jaw, nearly knocking him to the floor. Lifting her skirt, she curled her toes back kicked his shin sending him to the floor.

"Ow. Holy shit, Brooke. I rang the bell, but I guess it doesn't work."

"Fuck, John. You could get yourself killed sneaking up on a girl like that." Brooke watched as John rubbed his face and his throbbing shin at the same time. "Geez, let me get some ice for your face. That's gonna leave a mark."

"Damn, Brooke. You got a wicked left."

"Next time make some noise when you enter a house. Besides, why didn't you knock?"

"I did, sorta. You wouldn't have heard me anyway. It looked like you were doing some weird thing with your doors. Mooning over them and all."

"I wasn't mooning over them. I was admiring all the hard work it took to bring them back to life." Brooke laid a baggie of ice on John's face. "Quit lying down on the job, John."

"Hey, you're the one that assaulted me, remember?"

Rolling her eyes, she grabbed her wrap and purse, murmuring, "Wuss."

"Hey, I heard that. It's not my fault, I'm a lover and not a fighter. Good thing though 'cause I might of decked you back there."

"Try it. Wuss."

"Keep it up, Brooke. We'll see who's a wuss tonight. I didn't want to have to tell you this," he said, shutting the car door behind her. Brooke watched him limp to the driver's side and slide into the practically horizontal sports car.

"Okay, don't keep me in suspense John, what's

the big secret about tonight? I thought you said we were going to a charity ball." The little car weaved in and out of traffic, making her glad she hadn't eaten anything before the jaunt to the ball. Otherwise, she might puke on John to round out the night's events.

"Remember, ears open, eyes moving and…" Looking at her pert lips, he made a squeezing motion with his index finger and thumb. "Mouth shut."

"John."

"Brooke."

"I don't like this game we're playing. Spill it, now."

John rubbed his thigh and watched the traffic. His left leg steered while his right hand held the ice pack on his face. She watched him move his jaw back and forth, trying to loosen the tightening muscles.

"John."

"Patience. You're my best reporter and I want you to pay attention tonight, especially tonight," he said.

Brooke grabbed her stomach as he continued to weave through traffic. This was payback for the slap, she was sure of it. "Luce Potter is going to be the guest of honor at the charity ball. Seems she donated all the money for the children's cancer wing at the hospital and named it after her grandfather and her mother. Therefore, this is a big "taa-do" tonight. She rarely makes appearances and so I am dropping your story right in your lap. Don't blow it." John pointed his finger at Brooke, shaking it for emphasis. "Keep your ears open and listen to what people are saying about the guest of honor. Be a fly on the wall." Looking her over he continued, "But I guess with that dress on, you're the one who's going to be attracting flies. Because Honey, you look good." John's low whistle made Brooke roll her eyes. "What no thank you, John? I drop you right into Luce Potters lap and you don't have anything to say?"

Brooke watched as John gave her his best puppy dog eyes, as he liked to call them. Slouching back into the leather seat, she let her head loll to one side. She'd been set-up and now she knew it. Looking down at her stinging hand, she wondered if she could slap him again and survive the impending crash she knew would come from such an impetuous action. Watching license plates whiz past her at breakneck speed, she nixed the idea for something a little more controlled.

"I quit."

"What?" John swerved into oncoming traffic.

Brooke grabbed the steering wheel. Her heart practically jumped out of her mouth as they narrowly missed being impaled by lumber hanging off a construction truck.

"Watch the road, John or it won't matter that I quit."

"You can't quit."

"I can quit and I just did. Now take me home."

"No, I won't take you home and you can't quit. This is ridiculous, besides you have to quit in writing. So, why don't you wait? Go to the charity ball, do the story and then..." The ringing of John's phone stopped him in mid-lecture.

"There, I quit. It's on your phone. I think that constitutes 'in writing'." Brooke smiled, proud of the cunning idea of texting him her resignation.

"Let me see that." John wrestled with his phone, practically tearing his tuxedo jacket to get at the buzzing machinery.

"Hey, eyes on the road." Brooke slapped at his

elbow and put a hand on the steering wheel again. "Eyes. On. The. Road. Damn it. You suck as a driver," she said. Slapping at the elbow that was now in her line of sight she pushed it down in time to see their certain demise. "John!" Brooke screamed as he stomped on the brakes and skidded to a stop inches from an open manhole cover. The construction worker, who had been trying to flag them down, ran towards them shouting something interspersed with a few well-chosen curse words was now thumping the trunk of John's car.

Brooke clutched her chest, sure she was having a heart attack as sweat rolled down between her breasts. She reached for the door handle and John grabbed her arm with a sweaty hand.

"Brooke, please. Hear me out," John begged.

Brooke lurched as he threw the car in reverse and then sped around the barrier surrounding the manhole. Pulling into an open parking space, John grabbed her arm again and held her.

"Look, I didn't think this was going to be such a big deal. I thought I was doing you a favor getting you close to Luce Potter. Obviously, I over estimated your dedication to your job." John looked down sheepishly at his nails and pretended to pick at one.

"Don't even, John."

"What?"

"Don't even pull that bullshit with me. It won't work. I don't do guilt."

"What? Me, try and guilt you? No way, I'm trying to appeal to your sense of duty, Brooke."

"I don't think you understand how pissed off that woman was when she punched out my window. She frightens me, John." There. She admitted what she didn't want to believe. Luce Potter was a powerful, imposing, dark woman who scared the shit out of her.

"You, the woman who's been to the jungles of Columbia, interviewed drug lords and lived to report it? The reporter who sneaked across the border, and back into the United States so you could write an in depth article on Coyotes, who traffic in human cargo? The woman who investigated the Russian mafia and barely made it out of Eastern Europe alive is afraid of Luce Potter? Granted if half of the rumors about how she makes her money are true, she's an imposing story, but Brooke you don't do scared."

The grey gloom of the day had made the night darker, more shadowy, giving it an air of foreboding that echoed Brooke's mood. She couldn't tell if the visceral reaction she was having was from the memory of Luce Potter's fist inches from her face or from the thought of seeing her again so soon.

"You didn't see her that day, John. She's intimidating in every way." Brooke said. "She has a way about her that's...I mean...I don't know if there are words to describe her adequately."

Brooked looked at John and wondered if he had ever gone out on assignment. Some editors were that, editors. They weren't reporters. They were micromanagers who worked with deadlines, cranky staff writers with bylines, and reporters who often thought so highly of themselves that they should be banned from ever mixing with real people. She had to give him credit though, he was good at his job. He didn't play favorites, he honored his word, and he rarely forced her to do things if she objected. When she left her last position, he sent her a personal note in writing, asking her if she would consider joining the *Financial Times*. He knew she wasn't a business writer, but she was a damn good reporter he'd told her, clearly playing to her ego. It didn't matter, she needed to get out of investigative journalism, and this opportunity presented itself at the right time. She didn't have to guess that her salary alone could pay for three staff reporters. She knew he had gone out on a limb with his bosses when he suggested they hire her, so she owed him and now he was going to remind her of that fact. She steeled herself for the impending doom and gloom story she heard a thousand times from other editors she worked with.

"Brooke," John said. The timber of his voice so low, that she craned her neck towards him to hear it. "I don't know what happened in Orsha. I've heard stories and seen the reports, but I wasn't there and I have no way of understanding how awful it must have been to lose Mike. To see him shot or the fear you must have felt for your life. I do know that you're a good reporter and we are lucky to have you. So, if you think your safety is at risk tonight then we don't go. I'll call Steve Johnson and send him. He's always itching to do some covert research."

She felt the thin veneer she had been hiding behind being peeled back as John exposed her fear, smartly tracing it back to that night in Orsha. Her emotions lay at the surface, not buried deep like they used to be. Brooke didn't need to confirm John's suspicions about Orsha. She didn't want to because it would make them more real than they already were. She needed to insulate herself from the fear that kept her awake at night. The night terrors had subsided, but they weren't gone. They were more like bouts of post-traumatic stress. She could only wonder if what she was experiencing was similar to what soldiers went through when they came back from war. She felt as though she lost her ability to be impartial with a tough story. Death had a way of doing that to people. She saw it in the people she wrote about.

Violence changed people, snuffing out that light that lit one's soul and made them compassionate, made them human. Once it was gone they turned into animals fighting for survival. They turned on each other and took what they needed or wanted without fear of the consequences. Violence was the currency that they all used to get what they wanted, and what they wanted was money and power. She was sure Luce Potter traded in that commodity. She witnessed it firsthand that day on the roadside.

Thinking about what John said, Brooke knew she had two choices, fight or be swallowed up in her wallowing guilt and fear. If she quit, word would circulate about her in twisted strands of the truth. No matter what she said, editors and other journalist would come to their own conclusions about her ability to get a story out and her career would be over. The world was a small place when it came to reporters and you were either on top or trying to claw your way back on top. Either way, Brooke knew she wasn't quite ready to quit on her career. Swallowing her fear wasn't easy, but as John had said, she did have a fierce need to see things through to the bitter end.

"I'll go."

"What?"

"I said, I'll go."

"Are you sure? I can call Steve." His cell phone sat open, his finger hovering over the button that she knew would speed dial Steve.

"He'll just drool all over, Ms. Potter, besides I've done the research already. Sorta."

"Sorta?"

"There isn't much. The only thing I can figure is she keeps it close to the vest. No outsiders in and no insiders get out."

"Go with your gut on this." John paused and then countered, "I mean if you're sure about tonight, go with your gut. Watch her, don't engage her. We'll send a formal request again for an interview and see what happens." Patting her hand for reassurance, he smiled and dipped his head, still watching her. "Okay?"

"Okay."

Chapter Seven

The mass of people milling about in front of the civic center looked more like a movie premier than a charity event. The society reporters with their photographers were pouncing on the top echelon of the wealthy. There was a pecking order amongst the wealthy elite and interviewing someone beneath them first would kill a reporters chance to get an exclusive in the future. Brooke knew that the young moneyed always showed up first, hoping to get their shot in the society pages, while the old money was respectably late, but not so late as to hold up the event. It was charity after all.

Brooke and John elbowed their way to the bar to make their way past the snobbish banter. A stiff drink would do much to improve her confidence and help her screw her courage back into place.

"Cape Cod," she said.

"Vodka and tonic," John said. He looked at Brooke and smiled. "I learned early on that vodka doesn't leave your breath smelling like shit."

"We must have had the same journalism teacher. Cheers."

"Cheers."

The room swelled as people, mostly men, made their way to the bar. Being an observer of human nature, it wasn't hard for Brooke to notice that, while they served champagne at these events, the men usually needed something a bit stronger to indulge their wives' charitable giving.

"See her yet?"

"Nope." Brooke visibly relaxed as she finished the last of her drink.

"That was quick."

"I don't like to walk around holding a drink. I'm good for one, maybe two and that's my limit. I'm not a big drinker."

"If Jay were here I might have a few, but since I'm driving I'll nurse this one all night. Besides, it's my job to protect you tonight, remember?" John winked at Brooke.

Brooke was nudged from behind by two women making their way to the bar. She couldn't help but overhear the high-pitched murmur dotted with excited undertones of their conversation. "Did you see her? She's wearing a tuxedo. Dashing. Absolutely striking."

"She could put her boots under my bed anytime. Anytime Bob isn't home that is."

"I know what you mean. God, if I wasn't married, I would rethink men for her."

It didn't take a rocket scientist to figure out whom the women were cooing over. Luce Potter was here somewhere, now all Brooke had to do was find her.

"Let's walk back over there and see if she notices us."

Problem solved. Brooke slid her arm through John's, jostling his drink. "Come on, these young ladies are going to lead us right to our story."

"Huh?"

"Oh, come on."

Pulling John along, Brooke watched the women weave their way through the crowd faster than a hungry man to a burger. Slowing down she scanned the crowd that seemed to ebb and flow like the ocean, each woman cutting a path right to their intended target. Luce Potter.

"There she is." John pointed. "See her, over there."

Pulling his hand down, Brooke whispered. "I see her, don't point. It's not polite."

"Right." John stuck his hand in his pants pocket and casually sipped his drink. "Sorry."

The tight confines of the room were starting to overwhelm her so she slipped to the perimeter of the growing crowd, putting a good group of people between her and Luce Potter. She didn't want a showdown and she definitely didn't want to engage Luce. The easiest thing to do, she surmised, *was to place yourself outside your enemy's grasp and hide in plain sight.* Watching Luce, she realized there was no need to be so deliberate in her plan. If power was an aphrodisiac then Luce Potter was catnip to all these pussycats. Women hovered around Luce, jockeying for position and changing places as a husband retrieved his wayward wife.

Luce's nonchalant attitude hid any aggravation she might have felt being swarmed by the privileged class of women. Brooke's reporter side couldn't help but study her from a safe vantage point. Stunning in a tuxedo, with the exception of the long black hair and conservative makeup Luce wore, her look was androgynous. She couldn't see the green eyes, but could imagine it was one of the qualities that drew the women to her. Each woman probably romanticized getting lost in them, as if she were the only person that mattered to the successful and powerful executive. Little did they know that she probably could have anyone here, including the men, with the snap of her fingers. The way Luce moved amongst the women reminded her of a jungle feline stalking its prey. Long, sleek lines that exuded power and strength lay under the surface of her tuxedo jacket as Brooke remembered the body dipped in leather. A sudden warmth in the pit of her stomach snaked its way through Brooke's body as she realized she too was attracted to Luce Potter. She ran her fingers through her hair, shaking a few tendrils loose to cover the furious blush that had burned its way to the tips of her ears and down her neck. She was embarrassed to realize she wished she were standing with the women experiencing Luce's charisma. Maybe Brooke was romanticizing the affect the elegant and gorgeous woman was having on these admirers, or maybe she was falling victim to the dangerous effects of Luce Potter.

"Vodka. Chilled, no ice"

Recognition spiked through Brooke as she focused on the command being given by the man standing behind her at the bar.

"Make that two."

"*Dah*, I need something to get me through this horrible American food tonight. Do you think they would give us a bottle for the table?"

"*Nyet*. We'll have to endure the crappy wine they're serving. I don't think they believe in decent Vodka. Take this crap for instance, it's from Sweden. What the fuck do the Swede's know about Vodka? Volvo's maybe, but Vodka, nyet."

Resisting the temptation to turn around for confirmation of her fears, Brooke listened more intently as the two men continued their rant, moving on to flavored Vodkas. Her pulse raced, beads of sweat broke out on her upper lip, and she was paralyzed. She looked out of the corner of her eye at the two men standing only an arm's length away from her. The taller man with the thicker accent wasn't someone she had seen before, but the shorter, heavy man was Kolenka Petrov, the head of one of the biggest Russian Mafia organizations in the world. The last she had heard was he was moving around the world checking up on his businesses. The hairs on her arm stood when she realized he was looking around the room and turning towards her. Like a pair of synchronized swimmers they both turned and looked in different directions, Brooke deliberately placing her face completely out of his view.

"Come on, let's sit and talk about that piece of shit who's trying to drive a wedge between us. Luce Potter might think she's the smartest woman in the room, but I have news for her, she still isn't Kolenka Petrov." He thumped his chest as a throaty laugh bellowed out of his fat body.

"Grab that bottle. We can finish it then talk how to get rid of Luce Potter and her chink family business."

Brooke's head spun as she gasped for breath, her knees starting to buckle.

"Hey, you all right? You look pale."

"Yeah, I'm...fine," she said, working to focus on John's voice.

"Why don't I help you get some fresh air?" he said.

"No, I...I'm fine...I need to get out of here."

She wasn't claustrophobic, but she started feeling the room spin and her breathing sped up. Pulling on John's elbow, she whispered her need for fresh air and begged off his offer again to go with her. Threading her way through the crowd, she pushed through the crushing mass, the bodies feeling like walls suddenly closing in on her. With the stabbing pain of a migraine headache coming on, she moved faster. Tunnel vision took over and she squinted, barely able to focus on the blurry exit sign.

Brooke forced herself through the doors, gulping in the smoke-filled open air, but glad for the space it afforded her. She had never been afraid of tight spaces and wondered if it was part of her new world of PTSD. Thinking about the circumstances again, she realized this wasn't PTSD—it was full on terror. She hadn't expected to ever see Petrov again, let alone here in the city at a charity function. The veiled threats he made against Luce surprised her, too. What kind of business was Luce in and what did it have to do with Petrov? She needed to dig deeper on Luce Potter. Clearly, anything she found was only surface stuff. The kind of information businesses wanted you to know, but when the Russian mafia wants you, there's something more to your business.

Leaning her head against a cool wall, far away from the cloud of second hand smoke wafting in the air, Brooke ran her fingers through her hair and massaged her temples. Her body felt like a knot of tension. Her thoughts were like horses on stampede running wild in her head. Grappling with a returning demon tonight was not on her list of things to accomplish.

"Are you alright?" The question was whispered in her ear. She felt a body close to hers, its warmth wrapping around her, offering security for the briefest of moments. The low vibration and the tickle of breath on her neck fired up nerves, as her body responded to the intimate contact.

Without turning, she offered a meek response, "I'm fine. Why do you ask?"

"I've been watching you all night and...you looked like you'd seen a ghost."

"Really?"

"I know fear when I see it, Ms. Erickson, trust me."

"Yes, I'm sure you've seen it on my face before, but I assure you I'm fine."

She turned and placed her hands on Luce, pushing her away slightly, putting space between them. Luce captured Brooke's hands, trapping them tightly against her very feminine chest. The tension between the two women was palpable, but Brooke wasn't about to confirm Luce's suspicions. Why bother? She didn't owe this woman anything and what she'd heard earlier only made her more suspicious. Standing this close, Brooke worried she would be engulfed in the waves of danger emanating from Luce Potter.

"Ms. Erickson, I want to apologize for the other day. I've rarely seen my life flash before my eyes like I did that day, and I'm afraid I let my temper get the best of me. I trust my insurance company is handling your car." The low timber of Luce's voice washed over Brooke and she wished she were anywhere but here standing in front of a woman who scared her almost as much as Kolenka Petrov.

And yet, Brooke wondered if Luce Potter had any idea of how much sexual energy she gave off. The woman was a walking aphrodisiac. The way she smiled or the way her low gravelly voice sounded when it was bedroom soft. She was a walking contradiction of power and sex, of fear and pleasure. A heavy silence fell between the two women as neither moved. Brooke felt herself fall into Luce's beautiful green eyes, captured by the unwavering stare. She shook herself, breaking the hypnotic gaze and answered the question.

"Yes, they've been nice enough to loan me a car while mine is being repaired." She noticed the way a man behind Luce assumed a position blocking Luce from the small crowd of smokers.

"Are you cold?"

"Excuse me."

"Are you cold? I felt you shiver." Luce pulled off her tuxedo jacket and began wrapping it around Brooke's shoulders. "There's a bit of a chill in the air and...your dress is..." She watched Luce's eyes trace a forbidden path over her body, stopping to take in the tight fabric pulled across her breasts. "I mean you're lacking a jacket. Please, take mine."

The sudden act of chivalry took Brooke by surprise. The woman standing before her was nothing like the brazen, angry maniac who had busted out her window and she was having a hard time reckoning the two diametrically opposed images.

She felt Luce's arm tug her closer as she tried to shrug off the jacket and step away from the intoxicating warmth.

"Now about that interview you keep hounding my secretary for, shall we say tomorrow?"

Luce Potter was full of surprises tonight. Brooke knew Luce was probably offering up the interview out of guilt. Something in her gut wouldn't let her trust the woman was doing it out of the goodness of her heart. Clearly, if she didn't pounce on the opportunity, she may not get another.

"What time?"

"I have an appointment at noon, so let's say one-fifteen. Does that work with your schedule? I know it's short notice, but I'd like to repay you for being without your prized Mercedes."

Brooke couldn't ignore the slight smirk that broke across the porcelain skin. Luce knew exactly what she was doing. It would leave little time for Brooke to do a thorough prep for the interview and limit the questions she would be able to ask. *Smart*, Brooke thought, *very smart.*

"One-fifteen works for me. How long do I have for the interview?"

"Let's play it by ear shall we? I'll free up a couple of hours, that way you won't feel rushed."

"Okay."

"By the way, there won't be a follow-up, so make sure you have all your questions ready."

"I see. I'll try and do the best I can to be —"

Before she could say anything else, Petrov's voice cracked through her fragile shell.

"Aw, we can have a smoke out here, finally." His voice sliced through the cool air like a knife directly to her gut.

Brooke quickly dipped her head, resting it against Luce's chest. She pulled the jacket tighter around as if it would offer some sort of protection against an advancing enemy. She felt herself slowly moved backwards away from the sound of Petrov's voice and further into the darkness. Luce pulled Brooke's chin up. Now Brooke stared into Luce's knowing brown eyes.

"Do you know him?"

Brooke asked, "Do you know him?"

Luce's body tensed at the accusation. "Why would I know him?"

Brooke continued her reporter's line of questioning, "Because I overheard him say that you were driving a wedge between him and someone or something else. That doesn't sound like he doesn't know you, now does it?"

Brooke knew she had said too much when Luce's eyes narrowed. An aura of darkness clouded her features. This was the woman Brooke had met that day on the road. *This* was the real Luce Potter.

"Ms. Erickson—"

"Ms. Potter, please don't play me a fool. I've been doing my job long enough to know when someone's about to blow smoke up my butt. So save it."

"I was just about to make an observation, Ms. Erickson. It seems you had a reaction to Mr. Petrov's close proximity. Am I mistaken about your behavior?"

Brooke looked over Luce's shoulder at the man she believed had Mike killed. She took a long breath and held it. How much should she tell? Nothing, she surmised. Luce Potter was her story, and she wasn't about to give anything away, especially not after Petrov had referred to Luce in his conversation. There was more to this story and she was going to find out what it was.

"I'm afraid you are, Ms. Potter. Now, if you'll excuse me my date is waiting inside. I'll see you tomorrow then." Pulling the jacket off she handed it to Luce and extended her hand, hoping it would some how seal the deal they had made for the interview.

"Tomorrow."

Chapter Eight

L uce watched Petrov suck on the fat cigar. His bulging lips practically swallowed the slim taper. He was a disgusting fellow, scum of the earth type that had no boundaries in his business dealings. His short, greasy appearance made Luce cringe. Drugs, banking, import-export, and garbage were all avenues of business Petrov had his pudgy fingers in and he wanted more. He took advantage of the most basic of human emotions: the urge to survive at all costs, and peddled his brand of business to animals that traded in human flesh, too. White slavery was suddenly thriving in town, no longer relegated to Asian flesh. The new import was of the fresh, young, and pink kind.

It curdled Luce's stomach when she found out he was trying to work his way into her clubs and promote his "business" venture to some of the local businesses. The promise of quick money and no questions had tempted a few, but she had squashed the temptation when she personally visited the business owners. A visit from Luce wasn't an honor, it was a reminder that she had a strong organization behind her. A friendly reminder that "family" was rule number one in their world and she was the mother of the family, now that she had taken over for her grandfather.

Pulling on the cuff of her sleeve, she readjusted the jacket, the small .380 firmly concealed again in the small of her back. She had forgotten the gun was there when she offered her jacket to Brooke and now mental chastised herself for it. Lucky for her, Frank was off her shoulder blocking everyone's view.

"Luce, my friend, how are you?" Petrov approached Luce before she could slip past the fat bastard. His grubby hand slapped Luce on the back practically pushing her over. Righting herself she pursed her lips, grinding her teeth. A slap and then the click of a gun echoed through the air as she turned towards Petrov.

"Frank, no."

Frank had Petrov's in a wristlock twisting it to the point that Petrov was practically on his knees, his face grimacing in pain. Frank pointed the silencer of his gun dead center at Petrov's companion's forehead.

"Call off your dog, Luce before you're sorry."

Frank applied more pressure to the wrist driving Petrov to his knees. Luce bent down to the Russian's level and patted his sweating face. "You're not exactly in a position to make snide remarks Petrov. What are you doing here, anyway?"

"Fuck you. You should be in a whorehouse."

Frank's polished loafer smacked Petrov in the face, bloodying his lip. A screech of pain slipped from his bleeding mouth before he bit his lip and muttered something in Russian. Luce was sure he was cursing, but it didn't matter, sooner or later he would learn some respect and she was happy to be the teacher in his much needed lesson.

"That was a tap, next time he's going to knock your teeth out. Let me give you a little advice since we're on a first name basis. I've told you not to show your fat little face around here. This is my town and if you don't find your way out of it, I'll be happy to offer some assistance. Now, let's try this again. What are you doing here?"

Luce looked up at Frank who still stared directly at Petrov's companion. He tossed his chin at the man, challenging him to make a move. Frank was trained to stand between her and any threat and right now she could feel the raw energy flowing off of him. His body wound tight like a coiled snake ready to strike, all she had to do was nod in his direction and it would be over.

The people who had been milling about earlier had gone inside for the start of dinner, so there would be no witnesses if she decided to snuff out Petrov's cigar, so to speak. Reaching behind her, Luce drew the concealed Government Pocket .380, pulled the slide back and chambered a round. The hair on Luce's neck stood, she liked conflict. Grabbing Petrov's hair, she pulled his head up so he could see her face better.

"Now." Pushing the tip of the gun barrel between his lips, she opened her mouth as if it would help Petrov open his own mouth. "I'm not in the mood for your shit tonight. Therefore, I'm going to ask one more time and then I'm going to let Frank shoot your friend. Then, if you still don't talk I'm going to send you back to your comrades in a bag. Trust me, I can get ten pounds of shit in a five pound bag, minus an arm or two." Luce stared at Petrov. She knew he didn't intimidate easily, therefore she must be willing to go through with her threats. No problem.

"Frank."

A shot rang out, whizzing past Petrov's friend, dropping him to his knees.

"Fine. I'll tell you, I'll tell you, you slant-eyed bitch." Petrov cringed and threw his hands up in defeat. "I'm looking to expand my import-export business and

I was in town looking for warehouse space."

"What are you doing here? Tonight."

"I'm here with the banker I'm doing business with."

"Hmm." The smell of cordite wafted in the air, then a click broke the silence as Frank pulled the hammer back on the gun and pointed at the man laying on the ground. "You're going to get back in your car tonight and go back to that cave you live in. If I ever see you again, I'm not going to give you a warning. I'm going to kill you on sight. Did you hear me Frank?"

"Yes, Kaida."

"If Frank sees you he's going to shoot you. Right, Frank?"

"Yes, Ma'am."

"Now take your flesh peddling ass out of my city and tell your associates they'll be shot on sight. Dah?"

"Dah."

"Good, I'm so glad we had this talk Petrov. Aren't you?"

"Bitch." Another snap kick and Petrov spit out a tooth. "You fucking asshole, you broke my tooth. You'll pay for that, asshole."

"You really should learn some manners. Didn't your mother ever tell you that honey attracts more bees than vinegar?" Luce nodded her head at Frank, but never took her eyes of Petrov. "Now get up and get your ass out of here."

Luce pushed Petrov backwards and continued, "That way." She pointed towards the back of the building. "I'll let your banker friend know you had to leave. Now get the fuck out of here before I do something you're going to regret."

Luce slipped the cold metal in the small of her

back and adjusted her tuxedo jacket to hide the slight bulge. She wiped sweat from her forehead while keeping her gaze fixed on the departing duo.

"Have Luen follow them. Make sure they get out of town. In fact, I want to know where they go when they leave."

"You got it, Kaida." Frank said, deconstructing the gun. He slipped the silencer in his pocket and re-holstered it.

"We have another problem, boss." Frank chewed the inside of his mouth, a sure sign he was worried.

Thump, thump, *umph*. Thump, thump, *umph*. Thump, *umph*, thump, *umph*. The sounds barely echoed in the cold, dark warehouse. The old wooden walls absorbed what they could and rejected what they couldn't hold onto. Another round of punches landing firmly against the solid bag ringing out in the damp space.

"Boss, let me do this." A deep throaty voice pleaded.

"This is my mistake, I'll carry my own water, Frankie."

"Boss, please."

"Frankie."

"Yes, boss."

"You were my grandfather's second, now you're mine. Would you take over for him or would you allow him to mete out his own justice?"

"But it's different. I mean, you're different."

"I'd shut my mouth if I were you. If you know what's good for you."

Luce could feel her muscles twitching at the workout. Her punches had landed solid on the man hanging from the rafters. Her long sleeves rolled up gave her some room to move, but sweat made her button-down shirt stick to her back. Steam rolled off her overheated body, a direct contrast to the freezing cold in the warehouse. She had divested herself of her gun in case she felt the need to shoot him instead of wasting her energy on the beating. The pistol sat waiting for its owner's guidance on the rickety table, along with her dress coat. Twisting her head to the right she felt a pop, twisting it to the left she felt a tight muscle keep her from releasing the kink in her neck.

"Cut him down."

Frankie unceremoniously dumped the scumbag on the dirty floor, kicking up a puff of dust as he hit the solid concrete. Walking to the guy, she twisted his face so he was looking directly at her.

"Listen, and listen carefully, you piece of shit. I run a clean operation. Did you think I wouldn't find out about your skimming off the top? Did you think the dancers wouldn't tell me you were hustling them for protection? Huh?" The sound of her palm smacking his cheek snapped in the frigid air. "I might be a second generation Yakuza, but my business is out there for all to see. I don't hide behind anyone and I run a clean operation, legit gambling, legit bars and no two-bit hustler is gonna come in and fuck-up my legitimate businesses. You fuck." Luce kicked Marcus squarely in the rib she'd tenderized.

"What else has he been doing?" Luce despised the uncertainty in Frankie's expression.

"I'm not sure, Kaida. He was working with Jojo."

"What do you mean you don't know? You're

supposed to know everything, Frankie. Jojo works under you. You manage his business, don't you?"

"Yes, Boss."

Examining her fingernails and clearing some phantom dirt from under them, she said, "I heard Marcus and my father are close friends."

"No shit?"

"No shit."

"How do you know?"

"The same way I found out about Marcus. You pay attention long enough and people start to make mistakes. He met my dad at one of my bars and passed him an envelope."

"You saw him do it?"

"Yeah, I saw him do it."

"Fuck, let me kill him, Boss."

"What?"

She gave Frankie a puzzled look. Did he actually think she would let him kill her father? Was he crazy? Her father was blood and if anyone were going take his pathetic life it would be his daughter. She would have the honor of watching the life flicker out of his green eyes. The same green eyes she looked at with shame every day.

"Let me take care of this piece of shit." Frankie kicked the moaning man at his feet.

Luce felt her blood pressure rising. Frankie didn't screw-up like this. He was her grandfather's second in command, and when her grandfather stepped down Frankie had the option to walk away or become her second. She would have hated to lose him because he knew everything in the business, but she was starting to get rid of some of the "old school" establishment and moving into operations that were more legitimate. Ones she controlled and with people, she had handpicked to run them. They answered only to her. She didn't have to worry about loyalty, honor, or being stabbed in the back by some overachiever wanting to prove himself to her grandfather. She was starting to wonder if she should have picked her own second, too.

Pain started to stiffen her knuckles and she rubbed them as she stared down at the only Caucasian she had in her operation—which should have been her first clue. Thinking back, she couldn't remember how Marcus Freeman had come into the organization. Likely through the back door, a way some guys piggybacked on an already established member who could vouch for them. His misfortune was assuming Luce didn't monitor her businesses.

"I want to know who brought him in, who spoke on his behalf. That guy you can get rid of, Frankie. Send him home for a visit. I don't ever want to hear from him again."

Nodding, Frankie pulled his cell phone out and spoke Japanese to someone. The call was heated and short.

"I'll have it taken care of by tomorrow night, Kaida."

Marcus was still on the floor, wheezing to pull in a breath and Luce knew she wanted to kill him. However, beating him would serve a higher purpose and send a message to her father. She picked up his chin and stared into his dazed eyes, daring the man to say something. She hadn't touched his face, she didn't want to leave visible evidence of his betrayal, but she knew every time he moved he would curse her. She knew she had transposed her hatred for her father to this man although he deserved everything he got tonight and then some.

"Good, now give me that pen." She reached for the permanent marker and ripped open Marcus's shirt. Across his hairless chest she wrote in big letters: *You're next, Dad. Your loving daughter, Luce.* Tossing the pen to her second, she muttered, *"Asshole,"* wishing she had killed her sperm donor a long, long time ago.

The cold metal of her pistol gave her a start when she returned the .380 to her waistband holster. She hated bodyguards following her around, so the gun was an easy compromise for her grandfather. Strumming her fingers on the table she felt restless, nights like tonight always left her keyed up and edgy. Quickly she mentally ticked off her list of things that would relax her. A quick list, but there was one sure way Luce relaxed when she was this keyed up. Women. *Should I call one of my regular women to come to the house for some midnight recreation? Maybe Mandy needed attention.* Flipping her cell phone open, she hit a number that went to speed dial.

"Hey Frankie." The cold warehouse made her shiver so she pulled her jacket on and instantly regretted it. Her body was still sweaty and the jacket felt like a smothering blanket. "Send him to my father, alive. I'm going home. I suggest you go home and visit your wife, tell her I said hi." She covered the phone with her hand and continued, "Call me in the morning and let me know what you find out about this asshole."

"You got it, Kaida. Try and relax, huh?"

Luce nodded and waved at Frankie as she left the building for her car.

"Dr. Williams are you busy tonight? I think I need a treatment." She checked her watch. "Perfect, I'll see you then."

Chapter Nine

Brooke arrived early for her meeting with Luce Potter. After a lengthy conversation with John, which came with a warning, Brooke went back and tried to do more research. What few things she could find were mere press clippings and society page stuff that left Brooke more frustrated than when she had begun. Did the woman have something to hide or did she simply value her privacy? She'd been given the name of a police officer who might be able to provide her with some information, but hadn't had time to call. She dialed the number and waited. After a few rings it went to voice mail and Brooke hung-up. She had already left one message and didn't want to seem like a pain-in-the-ass cub reporter.

Opening the file sitting in her lap her skin tingled as she stared at the black and white promo shot of Luce Potter. The photo didn't do the woman justice.

"There's something about this woman. I don't know what it is, but no one wants to talk about her or to her. So, you get the job of finding out what makes her tick. Dig and don't stop until you have something. Got it?" John had said. "Don't let those pretty eyes tell you differently, Brooke. My gut tells me something's going on at Kaida Enterprises."

"So you want me to go with your gut on this?" Brooke smiled at his implication. "Maybe it's indigestion, John."

"Cute, Brooke. Just figure out how she keeps the investors happy and how she makes her money. Got it?"

"You got it."

Brooke couldn't help but be drawn in by the exotic beauty in the photo. Luce's Asian heritage was clearly on display, her eyes almost translucent, as if she could look right through a person. A shiver sliced through Brooke and she closed the folder.

"Interesting," she muttered. Tossing the folder and her cell phone in her briefcase, she decided that being early and waiting inside would be more comfortable than sitting in her rental car. Outside the car Brooke sniffed her jacket, worried it smelled like an ashtray. The rancid cigarette odor assaulted her senses every time she got into the car, reminding her why she had it in the first place. A week, the dealer had promised her a week, and now here she was almost two weeks later and still no Mercedes. Brooke breathed deeply. No, it wasn't the car making her nervous. It was finally sitting down with the woman everyone was scrambling to land an interview with, the elusive Ms. Potter.

Calmly, she put her reporter's hat back on and took in her surroundings. Manicured lawns spread out around the mansion like perfectly colored green carpet. The pea gravel under her stilettos made it hard to walk, scrunching with every step she took. Rising up on the balls of her feet, she took small quick steps to the stucco tile walkway. She noticed tiny boxwood hedges, each one the exact same size and shape, were perfectly spaced along the walkway, forming an edging between the tiles and lawn.

"Holy shit, someone's anal," she said, admiring the artistry of the gardens to her right. More pea gravel formed walkways through a well-thought-out floral garden. Their pungent odor wafted in the warm breeze and wrapped around Brooke like a fragrant intoxicating blanket. Each flower in the garden had it's own marker. Perfect lettering announcing the geographical region each flora came from with the date. Brooke knew she could spend hours in a garden like this. Her love of all things green made her small home a burgeoning tropical forest.

Brooke admired the mansion before her with its simplistic lines of glass and stucco. Two huge ornate doors stood out in stark contrast to the architecture. At least ten feet tall, each door displayed a massive carved dragon replete with exposed claws, imposing eyes, and dagger shaped teeth. The mirror images faced each other looking as though they would spring to life any second and tear the unsuspecting visitor to pieces. Moving closer, Brooke traced her finger along one of the tendrils that flared from the nostril of the huge dragon. She felt a visceral reaction as the tip of her finger ran along the rough-hewn edges of the mythical beast. It was almost as if she could feel the strength and power flowing off its scales. A chill rolled through Brooke as her gaze wandered back up the doors and stopped at the jade inlay for the eyes. Clearly, the owner was making a statement with the imposing figures whose eyes seemed to have a life of their own. Perhaps they protected the secrets that lay behind the massive doors or perhaps the dragons were meant to scare visitors. If so, Brooke was sufficiently intimidated. *What other surprises did Luce Potter have?*

Clutching her briefcase tightly, Brooke took a deep breath and raised her free hand to announce her arrival. Before she could knock, the door opened slowly. Behind the massive panel stood a woman in something that barely passed as an apron, with nothing on behind the shear fabric. Brooke blushed when she was greeted by a low bow and down cast eyes. As the woman stood, she made a motion for Brooke to enter and then addressed her.

"You're early, Ms. Erickson." Laying her hands out for Brooke's briefcase and jacket, she kept her eyes down, submissively.

Oh brother, what have I gotten myself into? Brooke wondered as she handed her things to the petite woman. Brooke assessed her. Average height, brown hair, but her beauty was striking and Brooke felt her body reacting to the nude woman—almost nude. Brooke quickly turned away, trying to replace the image of the woman with something less stimulating.

"I know I'm early, but I thought traffic would be worse than it was, my apologies." Brooke said. Without realizing it she was returning the bow, putting her at eye level with pink nipples. A blush heated Brooke's face and she once again tried to divert her eyes. This time her gaze landed on the rather simple "fuck-me" pumps the woman was wearing. *Oh my god, Ms. Potter is a dog.* "Aren't those rather uncomfortable to wear for work?" Brooke closed her eyes and wished she had kept her mouth shut and her reporter mind in check, but it was too late. The last thing she wanted to do was engage the naked woman in any way. It would only prolong her contact in what could only be called a delicate encounter.

"Ms. Potter is in another meeting and wasn't expecting you for another twenty minutes. Please, follow me and I'll show you to the library."

Oh thank god, she isn't one for small talk,

Brooke thought, looking around the marble entryway. Now her curiosity was piqued and a ton of questions floated around in Brooke's mind. Why would a woman work for someone when being naked was part of the job description? Why would someone require their employees to be naked? What kind of pervert does that? What other oddities would Brooke find? Who was Luce Potter?

Brooke waited while the woman deposited her briefcase and jacket on a settee in the entryway. The soft click of heels kept Brooke's eyes glued to the long, slim legs guiding her down the hall. *So much for finding something less stimulating,* Brooke pleaded as she watched the perfect ass walk in front of her leading her deeper into the mansion. As she passed further down the hall, Brooke admired the beautiful artwork hanging on the walls. Each lit piece reflected a Japanese simplistic style of art. Birds, gardens, and flowers lined the walls until they reached the end. There hung a glass case with a beautiful Japanese kimono laid out for display. Brooked paused for a moment to admire the beautiful work of art on the kimono. *Breathtaking.* Brooke barely had time to look at it as she was gently ushered into the library.

"Ms. Potter will be with you when her appointment is finished. Please let me know if there is anything you need." With that, she backed out, closing the doors as she left.

"I can't believe this. My host is a pervert."

The only furniture was a large, comfortable couch facing a ceiling to floor window that didn't have curtains. Sitting on the couch gave Brooke a view of the atrium, as she was sure it was meant to be seen by an outsider. A small gentle waterfall flowed off to her right, the water breaking on black lava rocks that slipped gently into the pond, stood in stark contrast to the greenery around the pond. The calming effect wasn't lost on her. Just listening to the waterfall caused her to relax into slow, deep breaths. She noticed movement at the other end of the pond. Barely under the surface, gentle ripples broke the smooth glass reflection. Standing to get a better view, she had to step on the tips of her toes and press her nose against the warm glass to get a better look. She watched white and gold Koi fish swim from her view, hiding under strategically placed water plants to avoid her gaze. *Elusive like their owner.* Looking again around the atrium, she marveled at how it looked almost exactly like the manicured lawns and gardens in front of the mansion. A meditation bench and a forest of bamboo that edged the back of the pond were the only differences added to the miniature, tightly clipped boxwoods. Peering up she felt the sun shining through the glazing, she was sure this gave the room an illusion of a warm summer day in the doldrums of winter.

"Oh, how the rich live," said Brooke.

She turned back to admire the room behind her, impressed by the order of everything in it. Volumes of leather bound books sorted by size and author lined the wall to her right. Beyond the bookshelves, a lit glass case sat displaying carved ivory statues. Looking closer, Brooke felt a blush creep up her neck and warm her face when she realized each statue was an erotic carving of women in various sexual positions. The detail was amazing and she felt her body warm looking at one particular couple engaged in a position she had never tried. Its grotesque beauty pulled at Brooke and soon shame over enjoying the display replaced her embarrassment. She quickly moved away from the glass case in hopes she wouldn't continue her perverted gawking.

Photos lined another wall. Here were mostly old black and white photos of people in Asian clothing. One shot of an Asian man in a U.S. Army uniform standing with a beautiful Asian woman stuck out from the old photographs. A young couple in love, a broad smile for her husband, but pain etched the woman's eyes. Brooke could feel her sadness, and something else hidden behind the ancient eyes. A few color photos interspersed throughout the collection caught Brooke's eye. One in particular drew her in. The picture was of a man with his arm around the shoulders of younger woman holding a baby. A Caucasian man definitely seemed to be the odd person out in the photo. The woman holding the baby looked almost like Luce, perhaps her mother, but the Caucasian man was definitely not a welcome addition to the photograph. One feature stood out about him, his eyes. The green eyes gave away Luce's father, but without confirmation, Brooke was only guessing.

Suddenly, the rest of the pictures were only of Luce and the older man. Her mind worked to catalog everything she was seeing, the family resemblance, the happiness, and the sadness that seemed to be in many of the more recent photographs. Something had happened in between the photos. A solemn look on Luce's young face never seemed to disappear at about the same time her father was absent in the new photos. Reaching down, she felt for her slim notebook she carried around with her, but realized it sat in her briefcase.

"Damn," she whispered.

She glanced around unsuccessfully for something else to take notes on. Her phone, it had a camera in it. Brooke pulled it out and quickly moved around the room snapping pictures.

"It's probably not ethical, but hey, they left me here to my own devices, what do you expect?"

Finally finished with her photo exposé, she realized she needed access to a bathroom. Opening the door, she expected to see the young woman from earlier, but there was an eerie silence in the house. Peering back down the hall in the direction she had come, she couldn't make out much. Across from her location were three doors, one of which was ajar.

"One of 'ems got to be a bathroom," she surmised.

Slipping out of the room, she walked towards the three doors praying one was a much-needed bathroom. Curiosity got the best of her as she noticed one door ajar. Nervously, she peeked around it. Startled, she jerked her head back, afraid that the person on the other side of the door would see her. Her pulse pounded in her neck as her heart rate sped up. She slowly stepped back and tried to control her irregular breathing. Fear of certain discovery caused a cold sweat to break out across her body. Cemented to her place outside the door, Brooke scanned around her once again, certain she'd be seen by the help Luce employed. She closed her eyes and replayed the brief scene out again in her mind. Surely she was dreaming, there was no way this could be happening right here, right now.

No way. This is not happening.

Unable to resist the temptation, Brooke leaned back into the room. Her body's reaction betrayed her as she stood transfixed by the sight before her. "No fucking way," she whispered again.

The allure of what she saw on the other side of the door enticed Brooke closer as she peered again into the room. Curiosity had her firmly in its grasp and it kept her rooted to where she stood. Her mind tried to wrap itself around what she was witnessing, but she had never been exposed to this world. Although she had heard of it, never in her wildest dreams would she imagine being a witness to something so intimate, so kinky, and so powerful. Energy surged through Brooke's body as she committed every detail to memory.

In the center of what appeared to be a bedroom, sat a woman on her knees, blindfolded and bound. Her elbows were pulled back almost touching, tied with a thick, red, fibrous rope. Brooke noticed that it forced her breasts up and jutted forward, each breast bound tightly, so tight in fact that they had a reddish purple sheen to them, their nipples standing erect. She noticed how the rope bit into the woman's porcelain skin as it made small knot patterns over her torso. The rope work was intricate and detailed. Each side symmetrical, crisscrossing in the same way at each interval down her back, the same pattern repeated across her front and then spilt as it went between her legs and back around, caressing each firm cheek of her ass. If the beautiful woman was in pain, she didn't demonstrate it. She wasn't struggling against her restraints; in fact, she seemed almost at peace with her situation.

A long black braid hanging down the back of the blindfolded woman gave Brooke her first clue as to who the woman was. "Luce?" she whispered. Her gaze remained glued to the woman as Luce sat back on her heals and dropped her head.

Brooke bit her bottom lip in an attempt to control the surge of energy pulsating with every beat of her heart. As much as she wanted to, she couldn't take her eyes off the bound and beautiful woman. Edging slightly closer and squinting, she noticed a tattoo on Luce's left arm and upper body. A dragon.

The tail of the dragon began the journey above Luce's wrist and then made its way around her arm, with the talons of a back foot digging into her bicep. The other talon griped Luce's back as if it was climbing over the slender, athletic body. The body of the dragon covered her shoulder and made its way over the top and down the front of her chest. The dragon's neck and head descended to her chest. The mouth of the powerful beast opened and seemed ready to devour Luce's breast. The forked tongue wrapped around the nipple and razor sharp teeth on either side of the left breast sent a chill through Brooke. She could almost feel the slippery tongue on her own nipple that twitched in commiseration. She shuddered as goose bumps crawled all over her body and tendrils of nervous energy fingered through her. She wasn't a reporter right now; she was an accidental observer of this intimate encounter that was playing out right before her eyes, a voyeur of sorts.

A drop of sweat slid down her neck and between her breasts. Her fight or flight response had deserted her long ago. Now she had to see how this little vignette played out. She didn't have to wait long. A woman entered the room wielding a leather whip. To Brooke it didn't look impressive, but when the woman swung the instrument, she could hear it cutting the air. Brooke's quick assessment of the woman put her at about five feet tall, almost a foot shorter than Luce, she suspected. The woman's own attire was simple leather pants, boots and a bustier of some type. The powerful way she swung the whip kept Brooke more focused on the woman's wide sweeping arc than anything else.

"Are you ready?"

Luce's bowed head nodded gently, but she didn't speak.

"Good. Up."

Luce rose up to her knees and raised her blindfolded head. A swishing sound followed by a swack and it was all Brooke could do not to rush into the room. The leather whip had landed against Luce's nipples, and then another, and another. This time the woman stepped in front of Luce and alternated blows to her breasts. Brooke couldn't help herself as she counted out the ten lashes to each side before the woman stopped. The leather thongs then dragged gently across Luce's nipples and brushed up and down across her breasts. The woman bent down and whispered something in Luce's ear. Luce nodded again and this time the woman slid her hand between Luce's legs, rubbing her. Brooke backed away from the door and took a slow, deep breath, still unable to believe what she was witnessing. Again, the reporter side of her said run, but her body screamed for more. Before she could make a decision, a slap against naked flesh pulled Brooke back to the display. Expecting to see a red mark on Luce's face, she was shocked when she saw the woman rub, then slap Luce's bare pussy. Again, the woman bent down to whisper something in Luce's ear, and again Luce nodded her head. Dropping the whip to the ground, the woman began stroking Luce's pussy with one hand and twisting a nipple with her other. Luce remained rigid and the woman continued her assault on the taut body. Finally, she moaned as Brooke watched an orgasm spear its way through Luce's cool demeanor. Shaking, Luce tried to remain upright, but she finally leaned against her torturer, her body jerking as each tremor passed through her. A fine sheen of sweat covered Luce's tight body and Brooke wondered how much more Luce could take. Watching the intimate display between the two women had Brooke's own body aching for release.

Remembering her phone in her pocket, she pulled it out and briefly considered taking a picture of Luce in this compromising position. It would be worth a fortune, but then what would that say about her? She had already treaded where she wasn't supposed to be. The ultimate betrayal to her profession would be to snap sleazy pictures of one of the most powerful women in business. No, this was something no one would see or hear about, not from her. Her reputation would be shredded as an investigative journalist if she stooped that low and she did have standards, at least she liked to think she did.

Brooke's pulse raced and she walked quickly back to the room she had come from. She needed to leave and fast. She was in no condition to interview Luce Potter now, not after what she had witnessed. Her own body was betraying her as she felt her panties rubbing against her hard clit and a slight wetness seeping down her leg. No, she needed to make an excuse and leave before Luce even knew she was here. She paused and tried to control her breathing.

Slow, deep breaths, she told herself, *count one, two, three, four...ten.*

Finally, she had regained enough composure to walk back out the door and into the hall. Automatically she raced back the way she had come in earlier. Clearing her throat, she looked around expecting to see the half-naked woman from earlier. She coughed louder when she finally reached the entryway. Just as she was grabbing her jacket and briefcase, the scantily clad woman appeared from nowhere.

"I'm sorry, are you leaving?"

"Yes." Brooke cleared her throat again. "I'm feeling a little under the weather. Please make my apologies to Ms. Potter and…"

"I'm sure she'll be right with you. It seems her appointment has run longer than she anticipated," the woman said. Once more, her eyes barely made contact with Brooke's.

"Yes, that's fine. I think I need to go…I mean I'm not…."

Brooke made a show of feeling her forehead and then her throat, coughing again.

"I'm sure Ms. Potter will be with your shortly, please let me go and find her."

"NO, I mean that's all right. I'm sure she's a busy woman." Brooke grabbed the woman's forearm, stopping her progress. "I'm going to go, I'll call her office and reschedule. Really, it's no big deal."

Nervous energy poured off Brooke as she slid into her jacket. Smiling, she nodded and pointed to the door. "I think I'll just—"

"Ms. Erickson. My apologies. My appointment ran longer than I expected."

Brooke watched as Luce Potter arrived, tightened the belt to her silk robe, and extended her hand towards her. The slick black silk pajamas hugged Luce's body and gave little evidence to what lay underneath. That was until Luce extended her hand. Brooke flinched when she saw slight bruising on Luce's knuckles. She wondered if these were part of the day's activities she hadn't seen. Without hesitation, Brooke took Luce's warm hand and this time looked down at her wrist. Obvious red marks snaked their way out from under the silk sleeve and made Brooke blush. It was as if she was following the rope marks up Luce's arm when she finally met Luce's gaze.

"Ms. Potter, I was explaining that I'm feeling a bit under the weather."

Brooke tried to pull her hand from Luce's grasp, but realized that Luce had both her hands around hers, pulling her closer. The tail of the dragon peeked out of her sleeve and Brooke's blush deepened.

"Ms. Erickson, you are looking rather warm. Perhaps you should lie down for a moment?"

"No, no I'm fine really." Trying to pull her hand from the warmth of Luce's, Brooke reminded herself not to panic. Luce placed the cool back of her hand against her forehead causing a quick exchange of energy between them.

"You feel a little warm, Ms Erickson. Please, I insist."

"No, really I'll be fine. I think I need to get home and into bed."

"I have a bed you're more than welcome to use until you feel better," Luce persisted.

Brooke practically moaned when she thought about the bedroom scene again. The dizzying explosion of feelings crashed down around her. She could feel the blood pounding in her ears, as the first thing she remembered was Luce's bare breasts. The thought of leather slapping at the erect nipples made her inwardly throb. Heat flowed through her body, resting at her swollen clit. Closing her eyes briefly, she bit the inside of her cheek. The pain pulled her back into the moment, but did little to dull the ache of her own nipples pressing against her lace bra.

"That's not necessary. I know we were scheduled to meet today for an interview, but would it be possible to reschedule? I apologize for any imposition," Brooke said.

Standing in front of Luce, she felt her nerves getting the best of her as she fidgeted with the handle of her briefcase. The urge to run hadn't abated and now she felt like a caged animal mentally pacing the entryway looking for a quick way out. Her anxiety rose with each passing minute, sure that Luce knew that she was outside the door.

The dispassionate reporter she used to be was gone, in her place was a raw, anxious woman who had witnessed her first, and hopefully last, bondage scenario. Her palms were sweaty and her heart felt as if it would stop beating any minute if she was exposed as an interloper on Luce's private moment. *Was it the sexuality of the event or the idea that a woman like Luce Potter let herself be tied up and beaten?* Thoughts flashed around her mind as she tried to corral them into one lucid moment.

Less than half-an-hour ago, she thought she knew everything about one of the most powerful women in corporate America. Now it all had to be re-evaluated and re-written, but what would she write? Headlines flashed in Brookes mind, "Top executive has kinky side," a mental shake and another headline popped in "Luce Potter, provocateur in the boardroom and the bedroom," another mental shake, "Will the real Luce Potter please stand up?" She knew she would never use such racy stuff to sell newspapers, but she wasn't sure how low her editor would stoop. If she wasn't careful, she knew she could easily become part of the story.

"So, Ms. Erickson, how did you feel when you realized Ms. Potter was a pervert?" The non-descript interviewer would ask. "Ms. Erickson let me ask you this." She could see him now raising his eyebrows. "What was going through your mind as you watched all of this unfold right before you?" The innuendo hung like a wet t-shirt on her naked emotions. There was no way she would write about what she had witnessed. After her encounter on the road, Brooke's inner voice reminded her of how violent Luce Potter could be. There was no way she would poke that tiger, no matter how beautiful the tiger was.

How would she explain the pleasurable warmth that coursed through her body as she became a voyeur and not a reporter? Her guilt was palpable. The act had a strange pull on her. It was something she could neither explain nor rationalize. A shame descended on her and for a brief moment, she wanted to rid herself of it and confess her sins to the woman before her. Even now, standing in silk pajamas, Luce Potter had an aura of strength and elegance that Brooke found intimidating.

Brooke slipped her slender hand from Luce's firm grip, worried it would transmit her emotional shame with the simple touch. She clutched her briefcase tighter with both hands, holding on to it much like a child's death grip on their security blanket. Yet it offered none of the serenity a child would find clutching their prized possession.

"I'm sorry to take up so much of your time. I really should be going if I'm going to beat the traffic home."

Luce clapped her hands once and Marcy appeared holding a leather bound book. "Please have the car brought around front. Ms Erickson isn't feeling well enough to drive."

"No, that's alright. I...I mean, I'm —"

"Ms. Erickson, you're quite pale, in fact the only

other time I've seen someone this pale was before they hit the floor." Luce took the leather book from Marcy and jotted something down. "If something should happen to you on your way home I would feel responsible. End of discussion. You can come back and get your car tomorrow when you interview me, unless of course you would rather meet in my office?"

Brooke watched as Luce made it a point of looking in Marcy's direction then back at her giving her a questioning glance.

Feeling trapped, she knew there wasn't anything she could do if she wanted to get this interview. She could press her luck and request the meeting at the office, but she would have to figure a way to get her clunker back home.

"You're being very generous, Ms Potter. Tomorrow will be fine. Thank you."

The tension was snapped when a soft voice interrupted.

"Ms. Potter, I'm sorry, I heard you say that this young lady isn't feeling well. Would you like me to take a look?" The woman from the bedroom stood before Brooke, dressed in a business suit and carrying a small bag offering her hand. "Hi, I'm Dr. Williams. I didn't mean to eavesdrop, but I heard you weren't feeling well. Perhaps, there's something I can do?"

Brooke froze. Here she was sandwiched between the two women she had seen in a tête-à-tête a few moments ago. She felt as if she would faint if one more unexpected thing happened. Pulling herself together she choked back the lump in her throat and smiled, then gave a brief nod.

"Dr. Williams." She briskly shook the doctor's hand—the hand that had delivered lashings to Luce

Potter's breasts. *Focus,* she thought, *you've got this.*
"My pleasure, but I'm fine really. Now if you'll excuse
me. Ms. Potter, may I reschedule our meeting? At your
convince of course," she said giving a slight bow. *Now
that was stupid. I'm not one of her concubines.*

"Ms. Erickson, if you won't stay I must insist that
you let me make accommodations for your ride home.
You may pick up your vehicle tomorrow when you
return for our interview."

The smile Luce gave Brooke unsettled her. The
woman was rescheduling the appointment on the spot
and Brooke really didn't have a choice. Her boss had
made it clear, get the interview or else.

"I'm off, Ms. Potter. Ms Erickson, if you're sure,
I'll say my goodbyes and leave you two to work things
out between you. I have another appointment I'm late
for, Ms. Potter." Dr. Williams said.

With that, Dr. Williams was gone and Brooke was
left standing in the entryway with a barely presentable
version of Luce Potter in her silk pajamas. Fingering
the handle of her security blanket, she looked Luce up
and down and then cleared her throat. Clearly sensing
the appraisal, Luce offered, "I'm sorry, I was in such
a hurry for our interview, and I didn't have time to
change after my appointment."

Brooke once again studied the outfit that Luce
wore and wondered if the woman actually thought
Brooke would buy her excuse. The silk pajamas hung
on the muscular frame. If it wasn't for the fact that
she had seen this woman naked, her mind wouldn't be
wondering if the ropes left any permanent damage and
would instead be focused on her interview. Her gaze
wandered up the extended hand and noticed the tail of
the dragon tattoo exposed above her wrist. Following it

up, she imagined she could see the impressive beast as it reached around and grabbed the soft breast with its teeth. She wondered if Luce's breast were firm and soft or if the illusion of them standing taunt was because of the tight situation they were in. Taking a deep breath and exhaling slowly, she took the hand Luce offered and begged off the interview.

"No apologies necessary. I'm not feeling well. Perhaps it was the chicken salad I had for lunch" Patting her stomach, hoping it would somehow give her the strength to walk away from what could be the biggest story of her career. That was if she added the whole bondage angle. *Why wouldn't she?* Brooke wondered. Because it was something so private that it could not only damage Luce Potter's reputation, but could make her a potential target for the woman's anger and she had already experienced that once. Not some place she wanted to go again, she was sure. "Is it possible to reschedule?"

"Marcy, could you please get Ms. Erickson a glass of water."

"Of course, Ms. Potter." Marcy bowed and walked to the back of the house.

Brooke watched the firm ass and bit her lip briefly before she realized the woman was having an effect on her libido.

"Beautiful, isn't she?"

Startled that she had been caught, Brooke rocked on her heels and looked down at her briefcase, nope it wasn't working to shield her from the powerful Luce Potter. It was as if Luce could read her thoughts.

"She's easy on the eyes and is very efficient at her job."

"I didn't realize you actually had her work." The

snarky comment escaped Brooke before she could think. "I'm sorry, I wasn't —"

"Ms. Erickson, you obviously don't know me and so I'll let that slide." Luce thumbed open the journal. "Now, when would be a good time for you to meet me tomorrow? Perhaps at my office would be better for you." Luce looked at Marcy and smiled, winked and tossed her head to her left. Clearly, it was a silent command as Marcy bowed slightly and left the entryway with the glass of water.

"Again, please accept my apologies, I didn't mean anything by the comment."

"Apology accepted, now when is a good time for you to meet, Ms Erickson?"

Brooke deserved the all business tone and so she wasn't surprised by it.

"Since I'm canceling on you, I'm free anytime you'd like to meet, Ms. Potter."

"Fine, how about two tomorrow?" Luce jotted some notes in the journal and closed it with a snap. "I'll call if something comes up and we'll reschedule."

"Of course." Brooke extended her hand but Luce didn't take the offering. Withdrawing it she continued, "Again, I apologize for my insensitive comment, Ms. Potter."

"I'll see you tomorrow, Ms Erickson."

"Goodbye then."

"Goodbye. I'm sure you can see yourself out."

With that, Brooke was dismissed. Walking towards the limo, she shook her head and wondered how she could have made such a careless comment. It was one thing to think it, but to give it voice, Brooke knew better. Looking back at the mansion Brooke played out the last hour. Her body vibrated remembering the scene that had played out before her. *What woman allowed herself to be tied-up and beaten, especially one of the most powerful women in business?* Flipping her phone open, she called her assistant and asked for a list of psychologists and a list of bondage clubs. It wouldn't do her reputation any good to be seen in a club like that, so she instructed her assistant to find one outside the city, way outside.

She snapped the phone shut, tossed everything in the passenger seat of the limo, and looked back at the mansion one last time. *What secrets did it hold and would she ever find out?* Her internal voice asked, while her head laid out her next step in the researching of the powerful woman. If she wasn't drawn to the story before, now she felt compelled to learn everything she could about the mysterious Luce Potter.

Chapter Ten

The sound of fingers tapping keyboards echoed throughout the empty corridors. Brooke had been in the office for an hour and watched as people trickled in. It was a weekday, but the building never seemed to be empty, someone was always working, even on the weekends. Deadlines had to be met, production went on, and the financial market was unstable, so that meant more news than usual.

"Morning, Brooke."

"Hey Stella."

"Coffee?"

"Naw, I'm good. Hey did you find that information I was looking for?" Brooke thumbed through the file she had started on Luce Potter.

"Yeah, but you never said why you wanted a listing of local bondage clubs."

"Not local."

"No, no local clubs, but you never said what you wanted with the list."

"Didn't I?"

"No, you didn't. Is there something you want to tell me? You got a kinky side?"

"No, I'm not that kinky!"

"Really? How kinky are you?"

Brooke paused and looked at her assistant. She knew this conversation was going in a direction she didn't want, but she had been stupid enough to ask

Stella for the information. She still wasn't sure what she would do with what she had seen, but she had to admit she was intrigued to find out why a woman like Luce Potter did what she did in the bedroom. Luce was beautiful, sexy, and powerful, but she liked being tied up and beaten. This was a world Brooke knew nothing about and she needed to educate herself. That involved research and she loved doing research.

"Earth to Brooke, earth to Brooke."

"Sorry."

"Hmm, sorry, right."

"What?"

"You know what. The question was, how kinky are you? Something you want to share? New hobby maybe?"

"Nope."

"Awe, come on. You call me, frantic, asking me to get you the phone numbers of bondage clubs, but 'not any in the city', and you don't want to tell me what's going on? Come on." Stella was pouting, but Brooke wasn't sharing, she knew when to keep her mouth shut.

"Begging isn't becoming on a woman of your age, Stella."

"What? How old do you think I am?"

"Old enough to know better."

"Hmm, well," Stella said. She stuck a page of yellow ruled paper under Brooke's nose, blocking her view of her monitor. "There aren't many, but here's the list. Oh, and I got the names of a few sex-shrinks who specialize in these types of lifestyles. It's a lifestyle, did you know that?"

Brooke looked down the list of clubs, noticing names like "The Cave", "The Bunker", "The De Sade", and a few other names that conjured up images of leather-clad natives humping whips and chains. If they were anything close to what she had seen the other night, she was almost positive the research would be interesting at best. Looking further down the yellow paper at the names listed one stuck out immediately: Dr. Williams.

"No shit," Brooke whispered.

"No shit, what?"

"Huh, nothing. No shit nothing." Brooke smiled before folding the list in half and slipping it in her pocket. She didn't want someone finding the list for bondage clubs and sex-therapists in the same folder as Luce Potter's information. It wouldn't take a brain surgeon to figure out there might be a connection.

"So when ya going?"

"Going where?"

"Really? Clearly, *my* short-term memory isn't as bad as yours is. At your age, you should be able to remember what you wore yesterday and not wear it again today. At least not the same top."

Brooke clenched her teeth. Stella was the epitome of a fashion slave. She never wore the same outfit more than once in the month and everything matched, disgustingly so.

"Yes, I was distracted this morning." Why was she engaging Stella in this stupid conversation she wondered.

"I'm sure you were. You investigative journalist types are *so busy* with the next *big* story..." Stella's dramatic facial gestures were starting to wear thin on Brooke, so she ignored the next dramatic emphasis she knew as coming. "that I'm surprised you can even remember us lowly ol' assistants."

"Is this about me forgetting your birthday, again? Jeez, let it go, Stella." Brooke slapped her forehead and threw herself prostrate across Stella's desk. A firm slap on her ass made her jump off the desk and glare at her assistant.

"Oh, kinky, huh? Maybe, that's what momma likes?" Stella wiggled her eyebrows at Brooke giggling.

"Is there something you want to tell me, Stella?"

"Huh, *now* you want to know the down and dirty details, huh?"

Did she want to know what Stella did in her free time? Not really, but she needed some background before her interview this afternoon with Luce Potter. She felt her body amp up at the memory of the bondage scene, but knew she wouldn't bring up the bondage encounter. However she did want to know what kind of woman let herself be tied up and beaten with a leather "thingy". Heck, she didn't even know what the name was, but it had made a visible impression on her, *obviously.* Pulling out a drawing of the leather whip from her purse, she handed it to Stella.

"Have you ever seen one of these, Stella?"

Stella gave a lecherous smile as she studied the rough pencil sketch. Running her fingers over it, she closed her eyes and gave a slight moan of pleasure. Handing the picture back to Brooke, she said, "Nope."

"Really? Cause I could've sworn you were moaning." Brooke raised a dubious eyebrow.

The smile returned, splitting the chubby cheeks of her secretary. "Of course I've seen one of these. I think I might even have one or two at home."

Brooke flopped her head back and closed her eyes. *God, shoot me now.* She was learning more about her secretary than she wanted, but she also suspected that she would soon know as much about Luce Potter too, if she played her cards right.

"So, Stella, tell me, what kind of person likes to get tied up?"

"Depends."

"On what?"

"On what you get off on."

"Okay, so let's say that I like to get tied up and slapped with one of these things?" Brooke waved the paper in front of Stella's face. "And I like to...well...I like to have...you know." Brooke stammered hoping Stella got what she was implying.

"You like to what?"

Clearly, Stella wasn't going to let Brooke off that easily, so she needed to try a different tactic.

"What kind of person likes to get tied up?"

"Depends?"

"Stella."

"Okay, okay. Jeez, I'm just trying to have a little fun with my vanilla wafer sister."

Brooke rubbed her temples, trying to stave off the headache she knew was coming.

"A bottom."

"A what?"

"A bottom. From what you've described, the person who likes to be tied up and spanked is a bottom. They like to submit, not think, to be subservient to their master." Stella twirled a lock of hair around her finger, looking more like a little girl than a forty-two-year-old woman.

"I see."

"No, I don't think you do. I can see it in your eyes. You're judging."

"You're right, I don't know how someone

can allow themselves to be 'spanked' like that. It's degrading."

"In you're world it's degrading. In his world it's a release from the confines that bind him. He probably has power and makes million dollar decisions during the day, but at night, he wants someone else to take control. To take power over him and this is the way he does it. It's a total mind fuck really."

Stella still twirled her hair, but now she alternately ran it through her mouth and licked the ends. Something was going on inside Stella as she talked about the control issues, but Brooke didn't want to delve into whatever was running through Stella's mind ever, not after seeing her like this.

"Actually, a bottom is in total control. They call the shots. It stops when they want it to stop, they tell their master how far they want the action to go. If it goes too far, they pull out their safe word. Bam, it stops," Stella said hitting her palm on the desk.

"What's a safe word?"

"Oh for gods sake. Here," she said, tapping the keyboard on the desk. "You can find out almost everything you want to know at this website. Let me know if you have any questions. I have work I need to do or John will have my ass."

Brooke was surprised by Stella's change in attitude. One minute she was ready to take Brooke to the local bondage club, the next she was cold as a fish. Shaking her head, she knew she would never figure out the volatile woman. In fact, she was surprised she had kept Stella on as long as she had, usually she would have talked to the editor and gotten a replacement. She didn't have time to try and figure out what her issues were now. Looking down at her watch, she realized she only had a few hours before her interview with Luce. Time was ticking, and she needed to be ready for what she knew would be one of the toughest interviews she would have in a few years.

After a few keyboard strokes the black screen jumped to life with an image of a woman tied almost identical to the way she had seen Luce the day before. Brooke felt embarrassed that the image sent a jolt of stimulation to her toes and made her tingle. Navigating through the website, she found more pictures of women being hog-tied, metal braces spreading them open, clamps in places she thought surely must be hurting the women. Others were in compromising positions, usually with a man standing menacingly over them. Not finding what she wanted, she clicked on several of the links that lead her deeper and deeper into the bowels of the bondage scene. Each website darker and more demeaning than the last. Finally she found one that had directions on tying knots, how to achieve the most erotic look on a body when knot tying, and other instructional advice on bondage. Bookmarking the website, Brooke shut the monitor off, closed her notebook, and tucked the drawing back into her purse. She would look for the leather whip when she got back from her interview, but right now she needed to wash the images from her mind. Walking to the bathroom, she shivered as she remembered how some of the women looked, strung up like meat and the pleasurable looks on the men's faces. She wondered if that was how she looked watching Luce's bondage scene.

Chapter Eleven

So what do you have for me, Frank?" Luce watched Frank fidget with his teacup. She was certain the events of the last few days were weighing on his position as her second. The Russians had come into the city without anyone knowing, but more importantly, they had shown up at the charity ball without *her* knowing and it was Frank's job to protect her.

"I don't have anything yet, Kaida."

Clearing her throat, she knew it showed her disapproval. "That's not what I want to hear."

"I'm sorry."

"Don't be sorry." She slammed her fist on the table. "Find out what Petrov is doing here. I don't want to find out that he's suddenly set up shop in my city and I didn't know about it. If you can't do your job, I'll find someone who can, Frank."

Frank rolled the cup between his hands as Luce followed the small bead of sweat rolling down his temple before he wiped it away. Her doubts about Frank's abilities were nagging at her again. He had been dedicated to her grandfather, but now he had to buck tradition to follow her as Oyabun and she was sure it was a cause of great stress for the older man.

"What did you find out about that asshole from the warehouse?"

"Um." Frank cleared his throat then stretched his neck. "He works for your father, Kaida."

"And?"

"Your father's working for the Russians." Frank gently put the fragile porcelain cup on the table and pushed himself away from Luce's reach.

The silence is the room was deafening. Her father had always been a thorn in her side. The minute Luce's mother died he had disavowed Luce's very existence. To shun her would have been one thing. Completely disavowing her very existence was something else. She and her grandfather had never spoken about her father after the death of Luce's mother. It was plainly clear at the funeral how her grandfather felt about him.

As her mother lay in her coffin, John Potter, JP to his friends, sat stubbornly refusing to pay any respect to his dead wife. Instead, he glared at Tamiko, almost daring a confrontation between the two men. Luce gripped her grandfather's hand tighter. She studied the man who was responsible for part of her biological make up, but was still too young to understand exactly what was going on. Even now, Luce could still feel the rage from her grandfather as he stood up to the challenge John Potter was throwing down.

"You did this you bastard. You killed her," Tamiko choked out, tears threatening to fall.

The smug satisfaction on John's face turned to fear as Tamiko advanced on his arrogant son-in-law. The ever-present cool demeanor of the Oyabun snapped when John waved his hand off at her grandfather.

"Please, old man. She was unstable, a nut-case."

"You fucking little bastard. She would never leave Luce behind in your hands. You killed her. I know it."

"Those are the ramblings of an old man. Prove it." The challenge had been thrown down. "As for Luce, I never wanted the brat. Look at her, she looks like her

mother. Besides, why would I want to saddle myself with another slant-eyed bitch in my life?"

Her head spun as the words rocked Luce's world out of its orbit. Perhaps she had heard her father wrong. Was he actually saying he didn't want her? Luce grabbed at her chest, her small fragile world lay in pieces before her. To have the man she adored disown her was devastating. She buried her face in her hands, sobbing. How could he talk about her as if she was yesterday's garbage? Was that all she was, a meaningless object to be tossed aside without a care? What would she do now that her mother was gone? Reaching for her grandfather's hand, she felt it slip from her grasp before Luce could tether herself to the only family she had left. She watched as her grandfather threw himself at her father. Sitting on top of the prone form, her grandfather's hands firmly around his neck he began choking the life out of JP. Stunned Luce looked around for help hopping from face to face at the men sitting around the brawl, but no one moved. No one stepped up to help her father and not one single man looked in their directions. The struggling men were suddenly invisible to those around them.

"Grandfather." The tiny plea for her father's life fell on deaf ears. Standing on shaky legs she softly touched his shoulder and felt the Oyabun stiffen. "Please, he's my dad."

Luce heard a final thump as Tamiko slammed his head on the carpeted floor and slightly released his hold on JP's neck.

"You owe your daughter your life, JP. One day it's my hope she'll collect that debt. I'll make sure if it."

Through tears, Luce watched as her father was escorted out of the temple. She could still smell incense and flowers of a day she wished she could forget. It would

be one of the few times she would see her father in the
next twenty years. She would often wonder about her
father when her birthday or a holiday came and went
with no word from him, but eventually she realized that
she couldn't miss what she never had in the first place.

For Luce, the heartbreak of that day was still with
her, and now looking back she wished her grandfather
had killed JP.

"Luce? Are you all right?" Luce was pulled back
in to the present by her Frank's question.

"How do you know?"

"Sammy saw JP with the Russian at one of the
clubs on the eastside. They weren't hiding, sitting right
out in the open drinking and laughing it up."

"And I'm just now finding this out. Why?"

"We took that bastard out and beat the crap out
of him before we took him back to your father." Frank
fidgeted some more before he continued. "There's
more Luce. Seems your father promised the Russian he
would get to you."

"Get to me, how?" Luce felt her pulse speed-up
and her skin prickle thinking about what JP might have
promised the Russians. She knew the arrogance of the
man who called himself her father when the situation
served itself. She steeled herself for what was about to
assault her last good memory of her father, as if she had
any left. "How?"

"Seems, JP told the Russians he could bring you
to their side and if he couldn't you would be dead. I'm
sorry, Kaida, I should have killed that bastard."

Thinking about the situation, she had made
the right decision to deposit the man at her father's
doorstep. The message she scrawled on his chest had
been right on target, "Next time it's you", would serve

her now. Her father would think she knew about his plan all along and now he would panic and do something stupid, she hoped.

"Do we know where JP is now?"

"No."

"Find him and put someone on his ass. I'm not directing a hit, so if someone kills him, they die, too. I'll take that pleasure myself."

"Understood."

"This makes things worse for Sammy. Doesn't it?"

The lull in the conversation continued as Luce studied Frank. His silence was wearing on Luce and she felt herself getting more agitated as Frank dodged the questions. Running a tight ship required those who worked for her to be on their A game all the time. If they weren't then it was time for her to bring about the ship and find a few new deckhands.

"Call Sammy in, I need to talk to him."

"Sure Kaida, but—"

"But what, Frank? Are you questioning my orders?"

"No."

"Good. Tell Sammy to meet me at the warehouse. Bring the bosses, too. It's time we had a little restructuring." Luce closed the lid of a black lacquer box and placed it on her desk. She would need the ceremonial knife later when Sammy did the honorable duty and offered her the first digit of the pinkie on his sword hand, otherwise known as yubitsume. She planned to make his fealty an example to those who might question her leadership, but more importantly she was sending a message to the heads of her organization—don't screwup.

Frank still stood in front of her, his questioning glance at the box and back to her clearly expressed his own fears.

"Don't worry Frank, this isn't for you. Make sure that there is a comfortable chair for my grandfather. He'll be in attendance."

"Yes, Kaida."

Luce opened the lacquer box and pulled the ceremonial knife from its snug satin confines. After thumbing the blade, she replaced it and passed the box to Frank.

"Make sure this gets sharpened. I want it to be a clean cut."

If Frank wasn't worried before she was sure he was now that he knew the Oyabun would be in attendance. She returned Frank's low bow and waited, knowing after his quick retreat he was going to be calling Sammy with the bad news. Rubbing her forehead she tried to smooth out the worry lines she knew were beginning to etch their hereditary paths. Now she knew how her grandfather had acquired his, concern over his "family".

Flicking open her cell phone she hit the key that would put her in touch with the only man in her life that mattered.

"Good morning, Grandfather. How are you?"

"Aw, my Kaida. How is my favorite granddaughter?"

"I'm your only granddaughter, Oyabun."

"Yes, but you're still my favorite." His voice was light with humor.

"I see. I'm good, but I have a problem I think you should be aware of and I would like your counsel on how I plan to handle it."

"Okay."

"JP is in talks with the Russians."

"Hmm." Luce knew her grandfather was reaching for his bonsai trimming shears. He always gardened when a problem presented itself. Even though she ran the company now, she always kept him informed of any possible issues that could affect him. "Are you sure?"

"Frank informed me that Sammy saw them both drinking in one of our clubs on the eastside."

"That's pretty brazen to flaunt himself right under our nose."

"I agree."

"When did he get in town?"

"I don't know. Seems none of the men were watching out. I first saw Petrov at the charity ball and gave him some "friendly" advice. If I had known he brought JP with him I would have been a bit more persuasive."

"How did Petrov get so close, Luce?" Now, she knew her grandfather was worried. His tone was no longer light and he had used her given name, which he only did when he was upset. Her guts churned and she got a sick feeling in her stomach. She knew what he would ask next. "How did this get past Frank?"

"He's been busy watching my ass, Grandfather." Luce had wondered the same thing, but stating the obvious wasn't going to help matters.

"Bullshit. He's paid to know everything. It's his responsibility to protect you and know where everyone is at all times." Luce suddenly regretted the phone call, but knew she had an obligation to her grandfather and to the empire he had built and entrusted to her. "Have you called a meeting of the bosses?"

"Yes."

"Good, let them know I'll be there. I want them to know you have my full trust and authority. If there are any stragglers left that think you can't be Oyabun, it's time to end their misconceptions, now." The tension he put on the final word scared even Luce. Her grandfather was not one to be disobeyed and he had little time for those who might question his orders, even if they came from his granddaughter. To disrespect Luce was to show Tamiko disrespect and that wouldn't be allowed.

"I can handle it grandfather. I don't want you getting your hands dirty."

"Stop, Kaida. I put every trust I have in you, but I know these men, and traditions are hard to break some times. I want to make it very clear that you are the head of the organization and a public display of that will only solidify it. Then I can go back to my retirement secure in the knowledge that I don't have to worry about the only treasure in my life that matters."

Luce blushed at the inference. She idolized her grandfather and the thought that it was mutual gave her a warm feeling that she rarely got from anything else.

"I understand, grandfather. I apologize for not seeing the logic in your actions."

"No apology necessary, Kaida. Where are we meeting?"

"The warehouse on Water Street."

"Good. Now, when are you going to find a nice man and give me great-grandchildren?"

"Grandfather!"

"I know, I know. You don't like men. I get it."

"Grandfather."

"Kaida, I want you to be happy. I want you to find the kind of love your grandmother and I had together.

Is that too much to ask for an old fool like me?"

"You are hardly an old fool, grandfather."

"No, and you are hardly a nun. So, I expect to see a beautiful woman on your arm soon, but be careful, Kaida. You will have many who want you for the things you can give them and it won't be love they're after. Lead with your head and then your heart. Love follows easily enough if given good guidance."

"I know grandfather, I know."

"Tonight then."

"Tonight."

Chapter Twelve

Brooke once again stared at the massive mansion before her, marveling at the symmetry of the gardens and architecture.

"Let's get this show on the road."

Nervously, she pulled her briefcase from the passenger side. With a soft push, she shut the door to the Mercedes. She had finally gotten the car back that morning, going over every inch of it to make sure the dealer hadn't missed anything. It was only a broken window, but never-the-less it only had one hundred and fifteen miles on it and was her baby so she wanted it kept in pristine condition. After buffing a smudge on the door with her shirtsleeve, she stood back and marveled at her reflection in the glossy finish. The reflection showed a confident, self-assured woman, but what she felt inside was inadequate. A second interview with Luce Potter hadn't been in the cards, at least not the hand Brooke had dealt herself. Now she found herself going into the interview with more questions about Luce Potter's personal life than Luce's professional life. They were questions Brooke knew she would never ask, but they would be nestled in the back of her mind begging for answers.

Smoothing down a crease in her skirt, she stood confidently and pushed the doorbell. The massive carvings on the door were imposing. Brooke was certain now they were a veiled warning of the dangerous woman who lived behind them.

"Ms. Erickson. Please come in."

Brooke noticed a new woman behind the gossamer thin apron before she could avert her eyes. This one was a tall, striking blond with similar features to the last woman who welcomed her. *She must have a thing for beautiful women. Oh!* The realization hit Brooke. Luce Potter was a lesbian, she had to be. Why else would a woman have naked women walking around her home? Brooke had a hard time controlling the impish grin threatening to bust loose.

"Thank you."

"Not at all. I'll let Ms. Potter know you've arrived. Please, follow me."

Brooke's highly trained reporter's mind had suddenly taken a vacation as she watched another perfect set of high heels lead her gaze right up to the nicest ass she had seen in a long time. Mentally slapping herself, she looked up at the blond head bobbing in front of her. *Please let this be the last time I have to endure such torture,* she prayed.

"If you'll wait here I'll get Ms. Potter."

"Thank you."

After a low bow, the beautiful woman was gone. Brooke closed her eyes and let her head fall back against the wall. This was starting to be an exercise in denial. The kind of denial that made Brooke go home and have an in-depth conversation with her right hand so her body could stop protesting its lack of intimacy. The sooner she was done with this interview the quicker she could forget everything about Luce Potter, the handsome woman whom she was sure commanded women to do her bidding in the bedroom—if only she were *that* woman. *Where did that come from?* Brooke wondered.

Oh, this job was getting to her and bad. Pulling out her cell phone she texted John, requesting a few days off. His reply was swift and short.

"Why?"

"I'm sitting here watching naked women walk around me and I can't seem to stay focused."

"What? You're supposed to be at Potter's doing an interview."

"I am at Potter's."

"What?"

"Yep."

"Have you been drinking?"

"Nope."

"Are you sure?"

"No, I don't drink during the day."

"No, I meant are you sure you're at Luce Potter' house?"

"Yep."

"And she has naked women walking around."

"Not exactly."

"Oh good. For a minute there I thought you were serious."

"They're wearing see through aprons."

"Shut-up!"

"Seriously."

Brooke heard the door open and watch as Luce's assistant came back in. "Ms. Potter will be with you shortly. Would you like some tea?"

Startled, Brooke stammered, "Thank you, that would be nice." She worked to collect her thoughts.

"Milk and sugar or lemon?"

"Milk and sugar, please."

As the woman turned to leave, Brooke pointed her cell phone at the retreating naked ass and snapped a picture, sending it off to John. A second later her cell phone vibrated.

"Holy shit."

"Told you."

"That is some kinky shit."

"If you only knew." Brooke hit send before she realized she had given voice to the thought. She knew what was coming next.

"What do you mean?"

"Nothing."

"Brooke."

Brooke turned the phone off and slipped it into her briefcase in time to see the door open and Luce Potter step through.

"Ms. Erickson."

She stood and smoothed her skirt, then took Luce's hand. A surge charged through her body. Brooke couldn't deny she was attracted to the "bad girl" of finance as she was called in the few magazine articles she had found. Being so close to Luce and knowing how she lived her personal life was more than a turn-on. The sexual energy around Luce Potter made her charisma that much more enticing. Brooke understood how this Pied Piper could get women of different stripes to follow her every command. If she hadn't seen the real Luce Potter the other day, she wouldn't have believed it herself. Pulling her hand from the sensual stroking Brooke imagined Luce was doing in her mind she finally replied. "Ms. Potter. How are you?"

"Thank you for asking." Luce motioned to the couch for Brooke to sit, and took the chair to her right, facing the door. Motioning to the couch Luce sat down. "Ah, tea has arrived."

Brooke watched Luce's expression as she took the

serving tray from her assistant.

"Thank you Audrey. Do we have any of those sandwiches from the bakery? Perhaps our guest is hungry."

"Yes, Ma'am. I'll put a tray together. Would you like anything else other than the sandwiches?"

"Ms. Erickson?"

"No, no I'm fine. Thank you."

"That'll be fine, Audrey. Thank you."

Brooke watched the exchange and blushed as Luce patted the woman on the butt, causing Audrey to smoother a giggle.

"Beautiful isn't she?"

"Ah…yes…she's…" Brooke nodded her head wondering what to say that didn't sound perverted. "She seems very adept at her job." She hoped the professional response sounded believable. Suddenly, Brooke felt as though she had a mouthful of cotton, her tongue sticking to the roof of her mouth.

"Yes, well Audrey is very adept at her job, as you say. So, Ms. Erickson, it seems I owe you an interview." Slapping her legs as she sat down, Luce turned towards Brooke looking her straight in the eyes. "I hope you came prepared."

Brooke couldn't help but let her mind wonder about the statement, she hoped her face didn't betrayed the internal blush her body was reeling from. Squeezing her thighs tighter she tried to stop the wetness she was sure was peppering her underwear. *Prepared to be seduced, prepared to be ravished, prepared for a mind fuck.*

"Yes…yes, I did. Thank you for the offer to reschedule. I know you're a busy woman so I'll try not to take up much of your time."

Audrey returned with a tray of sandwiches and plates, setting them on the corner of the table closest to Luce. Serving Luce first, Audrey placed a napkin on Luce's lap and then a small plate with even smaller sandwiches.

"Tea?"

"Thank you, Audrey." Luce said. Brooke noticed Luce run her hands up Audrey's leg and then cup the woman's firm ass, eliciting a brief smile before Audrey returned her attention to Brooke.

"Ms. Erickson." Brooke was vaguely aware of Audrey passing a plate, but was transfixed on Luce's hand. "Ms. Erickson." The second mention of her name brought Brooke around. The intimate touching between the two women would play with her mind the rest of the interview. She was sure Luce Potter could be responsible for running a small city with all the energy flowing off her and Audrey. Her tortured body rebelled against the tight confines of her clothing. Squeezing her thighs tighter, she hoped her nipples only felt erect and didn't show through her padded bra. *Please God give me strength.*

"Oh, forgive me I wasn't...I mean I was just..." Brooke felt like a fool as both women smiled knowingly. "Thank you," she mumbled and took the offered plate.

Fidgeting with her napkin, she placed it on her lap. A moment later she shifted and repositioned it lengthwise across her lap. Finally, she set her plate on it, willing herself to be still.

"Tea?"

"Oh, thank you." She practically spilled the plate on the floor, reaching for the cup and saucer. Luce grabbed it before the contents met a nasty fate.

"Ms. Erickson. Why don't we take a moment and

have a cup of tea to settle our nerves?" Luce said, sitting back down.

"Oh, I'm not nervous."

"I need a moment. If that's all right?" Luce placed the plate back on the coffee table and took a sip of her tea.

"Of course."

So far, the interview was a flop and Brooke knew Luce was giving her some much-needed time to compose herself. A long, deep breath, a slow sip of tea, and a deep shallow exhale kept Brooke focused on one thought: Finish the interview.

"Do I make you nervous, Ms. Erickson?"

"No, no, not at all. Why do you ask?"

"The last time you were here you became ill. Now you seem a bit flustered again. So one has to assume that either you are quite high strung or I make you nervous."

For some reason the stinging honesty of the remark made Brooke angry. *Would she concede to Luce that she found her intimidating, that her beauty was disconcerting? Would she have to admit that the scene she'd witnessed on her last visit had left her with dreams so wild and out of control that she hadn't slept well since?* Slowly, she slipped back into her reporter façade and smiled politely.

"Neither."

"Neither?"

"Neither. I've been anticipating this interview and would prefer to get started. I hate to admit I get a bit clumsy when I'm focused on something I really want."

Brooke couldn't ignore the smug smile that broke across Luce's face. She rolled her eyes, certain she had played into the woman's ego, but nothing could be done about it now.

Luce's hand glided along the silky leg of her assistant and stopped once again at the top of her firm ass. Her hand rested there momentarily before sliding back down to her calf. The long slow strokes were starting to have an affect on Brooke, so she turned back to take another sip of her hot tea, practically burning her tongue as she gulped down a mouthful.

"Let's get started then. Shall we?"

Brooke placed everything on the table and pulled out her digital recorder and her reporter's notebook and pen.

"You don't mind do you?" She said holding up the digital recorder.

A moment passed while Brooke opened the new notebook and scribbled the date and time at the top of the page. Hearing no answer, she glanced up to see Luce purse her lips and bite the inside of her mouth. Clearly, she was wrestling with whether Brooke could tape the conversation. It was standard operating procedure and Brooke would simply have to explain that she often couldn't take notes fast enough once things got rolling. Besides, the paper was more for writing questions than for taking notes.

"That's fine."

"Are you sure? You seem apprehensive. It's just that—"

"It's fine. I only ask that you run the quotes by me first so I can make sure we're both on the same page. How you write the article is up to you."

"Okay. Shall we get started?"

###

After twenty minutes of basic questions about Luce's background, stuff everyone knew, it was time to move onto what Brooke considered the meat of the interview. First, she would start off with the things she couldn't find any information about—Luce's family. Reading her notes, she wondered how she should approach the subject. Her editor had warned her off, but the family dynamic was too important to the story to ignore.

"So let me ask you about your family." Brooke watched Luce over her notebook and saw her jaw flinch as the question took residence. "I see that your mother is deceased and that your father is still alive."

"That's correct."

"I have John Potter as your dad."

"That's correct."

Luce's stilted, abrupt answers felt like a warning Brooke should heed, but she didn't get to be a top reporter by avoiding difficult situations. She pretended to jot something down, buying time to rethink her strategy.

"Are you close to your father?"

"Define close?" Without waiting for a response Luce continued. "If by close you mean do I see him, the answer is no. If by close do you mean we talk? The answer is still no. Next question."

"Why?" Brooke's curiosity was now peaked.

"Why what?"

"I have a few more questions about your dad."

"If you want to continue this interview, you'll drop the questions about my father. Otherwise…" Luce clapped her hands and Audrey appeared at the door.

"Yes Ms. Potter?"

"Audrey—"

"No wait. Fine. No more questions about your father. I apologize if I overstepped."

Brooke looked from Luce to Audrey, then back to Luce hoping she once again hadn't blown her chance at another interview.

"Audrey, would you please bring us more hot tea?"

Luce sat back down and stretched her legs out in front of her. The relaxed pose looked more like a tiger studying the angles, preparing to pounce on its unsuspecting prey. That feeling made Brooke uncomfortable, realizing she had pushed when she perhaps should have pulled. Reviewing her notes, she stole another glance as Luce's hand slid up Audrey's leg again. This time the tips of Luce's fingers worked between the cleft of her front. *Oh fuck, she's copping a feel right here in front of me. Shit, shit, shit.* Brooke tried to write something, but only succeeded in scribbling gibberish on her notepad. She forced a breath through pursed lips and the two women looked at her in surprise.

"Oh, sorry, I was trying to figure out what I might ask next." Realizing she needed a break from the tension in the room, closed her notepad. "Do you mind if I use the ladies room?"

"Audrey, would you please show Ms. Erickson to the bathroom down the hall?"

"Of course. Follow me, Ms Erickson."

The course to the bathroom was the same path she had taken days before when she stumbled upon Luce tied up in her room. A sudden rush came over her as she glanced at the closed door. Audrey opened a door opposite Luce's room, then flipped the light on and reminded Brooke of the way back to the room they'd left.

"Thank you."

Brooke smiled and closed the door. Looking at her reflection in the mirror, she blew out another breath, braced herself on the marble counter, and dropped her head. If she believed in God, this would have been the time to say a prayer. It would take an act from the deity to get through the interview at this point. Adding to the already tense situation was the fact that Luce had naked women walking around, and Brooke was almost positive that she had seen Luce practically finger fucking Audrey in front of her. At a minimum, she was definitely caressing Audrey's genitals. The cold water she splashed on her face gave her system a momentary shock and forced her to suck in a breath. Holding the breath while she gently patted her face dry, Brooke tried to regain a modicum of composure. Wriggling her body, Brooke felt like an athlete getting ready for a big meet trying to shake off a bad case of nerves. Twisting her neck, she felt it pop and grind. She took a few more deep breaths and was ready to face Luce again.

"Oh shit," she said as she reached for the door. "Bathroom break, right." After flushing the toilet she waited, counted to five, and then ran the water again. She wanted to make sure they thought she was using the bathroom. She was going mad, she was sure of it.

Walking out of the bathroom, she glanced at the closed door, but this time she hesitated briefly. The memory of that day flashed in her mind again, only this time it was Brooke tied up on the floor and not Luce Potter. *Oh fuck, me. I am going crazy.* She bolted down the hall and to the sitting room. A sound pierced her consciousness as she pushed the door open and saw Luce give a resounding swat on Audrey's ass.

"Oh sorry, I didn't mean to interrupt anything. I mean...I can get my things... and..." Turning towards the couch, she finished, "go."

"My apologies Ms. Erickson, Audrey was leaving. Weren't you Audrey?"

"Yes Ms. Potter."

With that, Audrey was gone and the door firmly shut behind her. Brooke felt odd, standing in front of a woman who clearly patronized the female gender. In fact she was starting to become a little steamed at the way it seemed Luce Potter treated women in general. First her and the broken car window, and then the two women who were made to walk around naked for Luce's pleasure, or so it appeared. How degrading could Luce Potter be? Maybe that was the real story here, not how she had taken her grandfathers illegal holdings and turned them into an empire. No. Brooke was sure the real story was what happened behind the closed doors of her office and mansion. From what she had observed, it was perverted and kinky at best. At worst, the only word Brooke could come up with was depraved.

"Perhaps I should come back another time. It looks as if this is a bad time for you." Brooke said as she reached for her bag.

"Ms. Erickson, it's today or nothing. I'm a busy woman and unfortunately something has come up this week that will need my attention for the next few weeks. So, you must catch as catch can, as they say."

The realization suddenly dawned on Brooke that if she was going to interview Luce Potter, half the world's most sought after scoop, she needed to stay focused and do her job. Exhaling quickly she grabbed her pen and notepad out of her bag and tried to smile as sweetly as she could.

"You're right. I'm sorry. So where were we?"

"Ask me anything you like, but nothing about my father."

"Right. Anything."

Brooke noticed Luce was once again lounging comfortably. Her longs legs crossed at the ankles, and a smug smile greeted her. *Infuriating*, she thought.

"Anything."

"Why do the women who work for you have to do it naked?"

"Do 'it' naked?"

"You know what I mean. Why are they naked?"

"Are you offended by the female form Ms. Erickson?"

"No, of course not. I find it…" Brooke searched for a word that wouldn't offend Luce. Why she wasn't sure. "unsettling."

"Do you?"

"I do. Don't your other guests?"

"I don't have other guests, Ms. Erickson."

"That's not true. I saw Dr. Williams here the other day. She's a guest."

"True."

"Ms. Erickson, in my line of work people want to…hurt me. I've made a few enemies, but I need employees to run my house. So in exchange for excellent pay and benefits, I hire beautiful women who are good at what they do, housekeeping, errands, cooking, the things that keep my house a home."

"But why are they naked?"

"You can't conceal a weapon if you're naked. Can you? Besides, these women are as smart as they are beautiful. Take Audrey for instance. Audrey can you come in here please?"

Brooke couldn't believe what she was hearing. Luce was worried for her life so she made the women that worked for her do it naked, on the off chance they might want to kill her? It made no sense.

"Yes, Ms Potter."

"Audrey, can you please tell Ms. Erickson what you do when you aren't working for me."

"I'm a student at the university."

"Studying?"

"Molecular Biology. I hope to be a research scientist."

"Thank you, Dr. Audrey Wentworth."

Brooke wrote down Audrey's name. She was certain Luce was pulling her leg, but in case she wanted to make sure she had it for later, when she did a background check on the woman.

"W.E.N.T.W.O.R.T.H. Wentworth. You might know the family. The Wentworth's go way back in this part of the country, as I understand."

"*The* Wentworths. You want me to believe that Audrey is a Wentworth?"

"Would you like me to call her back in and you can interview her, too?"

"No." Brooke sighed. This was becoming an exercise in futility. "I believe you, until I can prove differently. So let me see if I get this. You make women work around you nude so they don't kill you?"

"I'm sure you find it hard to believe Ms. Erickson—"

"Please, call me Brooke. I think we're way past formality, don't you?"

"As you wish. As I was saying, Brooke, in my line of work you make a few enemies. My family's business comes with its own set of, shall we say, inherited enemies. The competition is brutal and they don't care who gets in the way of what they want. Money does that to people, but I suspect you already know that, don't you?"

"Why would you say that?"

"Brooke, you don't think you're the only one who does their homework before an interview?"

Brooke squirmed a bit on the couch. She hadn't anticipated Luce investigating her, which meant she had clearly underestimated Luce. The bigger question was what else did Luce know about her?

"You seem surprised? Like the other night at the charity ball when I told you I had been watching you. In my line of work, I don't get a second chance to make a mistake."

The implication wasn't lost on Brooke as she locked eyes with Luce. The look she gave Brooke lacked sincerity. Instead it was the cold, hard stare of someone who knew the harder side of life, the side that didn't take or make excuses. Feeling a chill settle on her, she broke the stare and thumbed through her notepad.

Chapter Thirteen

Luce smiled watching the reporter fidget with her notepad. She knew she made Brooke Erickson nervous, it was written all over the poor woman's face. Whatever agenda she had arrived with had evaporated the minute she sat down, Luce was sure of it. Brooke Erickson was just another hack reporter trying to write a fluff piece on the elusive "Luce Potter". Brooke didn't know shit about Luce's business and knew even less about her personal life. She had offered to sit for the interview with the hope that Brooke wouldn't sue for the little indiscretion out on the road last week, but she was almost at her limit with the woman. At least she's easy on the eyes, thought Luce.

"Can we come back to the whole naked worker thing later? I have a few other questions I'd like to ask you before you boot me out of your house."

"You surprise me Ms. Erickson." Suddenly, the familiarity of using Brooke's first name made Luce uncomfortable.

"In what way, Ms. Potter, and please I asked you to call me Brooke."

Luce didn't miss the smile and knowing look that was soon replaced with a veil of indifference.

"I've taken great pains at retooling the family business. My grandfather passed his holdings down to me and I've reestablished and built an empire of legal holdings and businesses. I dare you to find someone who says differently."

"Okay, you've diversified your holdings. Brooke flipped through the slender notebook and stopped. "You have a chain of martial arts schools and sponsor some mixed martial arts events."

"Yes."

"All legal businesses right?"

"Yes." She had perfected the art of subterfuge, but here she sat dethroned by what she would've consider only seconds ago to be a rank amateur at the game.

"So what about the illegal gambling that takes place at these events? You get a cut?"

"I've built a legal business venture around the up and coming market of mixed martial arts. I'm not involved in gambling. Next question."

"I see another divesture is your financial stake in a few banks. Are you involved in the drug money laundering that's seems to be taking place in the city?"

"I've invested legally in a few local banks. I believe they have boards and executives that run their operations. I don't know anything about illegal activities these banks might be involved in. If there is money-laundering happening at these institutions, I can assure you that I'll be pulling my interest in them. Next question."

"I see you own a few local clubs."

"Yes."

"I guess you don't know anything about their using bootlegged alcohol, non-taxed cigarettes, or the white slave trade happening in concert with some of the local establishments?"

Luce felt her temperature rising uncontrollably. It was one thing to deny gambling, loan sharking, and a few of the other business dealing, but to be associated with white slavery was crossing the line. She leaned in and aimed her steely gaze at Brooke.

"I don't traffic in women. I might be a lot of things, and I can see where you might even try to connect the dots between my employment of the women who work for me, but I can assure you I would never, I repeat never, treat women in such a demoralizing, demeaning way. I would never try to make money off the misery of women in such a way. Do you understand, me?"

Brooke raised an eyebrow and then cast a dubious glance in her directions. Clearly, she hadn't been intimidating enough to scare Brooke, yet.

"You make it easy to make that leap with naked women walking around your house. Don't think I didn't see the way you were touching Ms. Wentworth earlier."

"I see."

"Are you intimately involved with the women who work for you?"

The conversation had taken a right hand turn and Luce wasn't sure if that was a good thing, but she wasn't done with Brooke Erickson.

"Only if they want to be."

"What does that mean? You don't request favors from the women who work for you? I would assume that they wouldn't turn down your advances for fear of losing their job."

"I'm telling you, that I don't make any sexual advances towards the women who work for me. I pay them well, they have a great benefit package, and I have great fringe benefits. If you'd like to find out more about the fringe benefits, perhaps you'll consider working for me. Interested?"

Luce had volleyed and landed the ball back within

the grounds of what she was willing to talk about. She wasn't sure she had set the reporter straight, but she was definitely throwing her a lob that would take her time to handle if the growing blush on her face was any indication.

"I have a job, but thank you for the offer. I'm sure it's quite generous."

"It is and you should consider it. In this economy you never know when you might need a back-up plan. I hear I'm a pretty benevolent employer, but feel free to ask around."

"Oh, I will, you can be assured of that, so back to my question. I hear white slavery is trying to make its way into town via the massage parlors. Know anything about that?"

"It's not coming here if I have anything to say about it."

"So, you don't know anything about underage girls and prostitution at the massage parlors?"

"I don't have any business interests in massage parlors. Take a little advice. When I tell you I'm not involved in something you can take that to the bank. It's not a check that's going to bounce, trust me. You might want to turn over some other rock for that exclusive."

"Does the name Kolenka Petrov, ring a bell? Perhaps you remember him from the charity ball the other night? I do." The statement hung like a bell ready to be rung. The question wasn't said as a condemnation or an accusation, but like pulling a loose thread hoping to unravel the story to see where it led.

"Awe, Mr. Petrov. Perhaps he is where the real story is, Brooke."

"Why does he want you dead?"

"Dead? Is that what he said when you interviewed

him?"

"I haven't interviewed him, but he did say something to that affect at the charity ball. Now why would he want you out of the way?"

"We're business rivals. So, I guess he sees me more of a threat than I see him, but I guess you'll have to ask him."

"That's it?"

"As far as I'm concerned that's it. Next question or is the interview over."

"Not quite, if that's all right with you?"

"Your dime," Luce checked her watch. She wished time were moving faster. The anxieties of the events of the night before pulled on her mind. She wanted Brooke Erickson gone, but she made a promise and she was a woman of her word, unfortunately.

Thinking back to the hospital fundraiser, Luce remembered how scared Brooke looked when she heard Petrov's voice that night. Now, she had to wonder what would make a financial reporter so scared of a Russian gangster. Petrov had only been in town twice, and both times the visits were short and sweet, under the cover of darkness, so to speak. She doubted Brooke and Petrov's paths had crossed, but anything was possible. The palpable fear that rolled off Brooke that night wasn't from a few words heard at the charity ball, so she was sure there was more to the story and Luce was going to find out.

"Hobbies? Do you have any?"

The quick shift in topic practically gave Luce whiplash. "Hobbies?"

"Yeah, what does a powerful woman such as yourself do for relaxation, other than drive her motorcycle too fast?"

"You're serious?"

"Look, I want this to be a well-rounded interview. Surely, you have a hobby or something that you do to take the edge off such a fast-paced, stressful life."

Luce studied Brooke and wondered what angle she was aiming for now.

"Right now you're the story our readers want to read about. You're the most influential woman in the city, the state, perhaps the whole country and that intrigues people. They want to know who Luce Potter is and how did she become so powerful, so rich, so fast and what does she do for fun."

"Flattery will get you nowhere with me, Brooke."

"Ah, and here I thought it was my winning personality."

Luce leered at Brooke hoping it would throw her off her stride. "Actually."

"Don't even think about it. Look, the faster you answer my questions the faster I can get out of your hair."

"Sure, shoot." Brooke's eyes widened in surprise and Luce cocked an eyebrow. "Figuratively, of course."

"Of course. How long has your family been in organized crime?"

Luce choked on the mouthful of tea. Her stern gaze was met by Brooke's innocent one. Setting the cup and saucer back on the table, she crossed legs and thought about how she was going to answer the question. She had underestimated the reporter and now wasn't quite sure how to handle her.

"Define 'organized crime'."

"Ms. Potter, please don't play coy with me. You're so much better than that. I asked, how long has your family been in organized crime? I can only go back to your grandfather, Tamiko Yoshida, but surely, it goes back further than him. My research tells me that Yakuza organizations have their roots in Japan and all clans started there around the...let me see."

Luce had definitely underestimated Brooke's abilities. She was a worthy opponent and deserved the respect of an adversary. As far as she knew Brooke Erickson was a Financial Times reporter with her own by-line. Her own research had only told her a few things about the reporter and now she cursed herself for not being more thorough.

"Off the record." Luce pointed to the digital recorder on the table, its red light flashing.

Brooke reached down and shut the player off, then started to toss it in her bag.

"Give it here." Luce's held out her hand. "I'll give it back when we're done."

"Okay."

"How much do you think you know?"

Luce drummed her fingers and stared while Brooke recited what she knew about Luce, her grandfather, and their organization. Watching the way Brooke's lips moved suddenly made Luce want to run her fingers over them. The deep pink lines formed perfect syllables, occasionally flicking the tip of her tongue out to wet them, while she continued with the vague history of Luce's grandfather's life. She had considered Brooke attractive the day she almost ran over Luce, but anger and rage had colored her vision of the reporter. Now, sitting close to the woman, she could feel her pulse race as Brooke's soft, melodic voice recited Luce's college achievements, her work history, and her rise to the top in her grandfather's company. She was hypnotized by the way Brooke described Luce's eventual takeover of the organization. Brooke made it seem that her grandfather had started with so little, and yet Luce knew the actual truth about his empire.

"So, is that about right?"

"Hmm, I'm sorry did you say that my grandfather had a brothel?"

"No, I said that your grandfather had no brothers and no sons, so you were the logical choice to inherit the family business."

"I earned my grandfather's respect. I went to college, graduated at the top of my class, and then worked the business from the bottom up. Ten years later, here we are. You're asking me questions and I'm doing my best to dodge them."

Without an acknowledgement of Luce's answer, Brooke dove into the next question.

"According to my research, the Japanese Yakuza is a male dominated hierarchy. How do the men who work for you handle taking orders from a woman?"

Luce rested her lips on her steepled fingers and contemplated the question. She could go into a diatribe of duty, honor, and respect, but she was sure it would be lost on someone like Brooke, whose Anglo roots kept her firmly planted in a vastly different world and culture. How would she explain that her cultures were driven by doing what was best for the family, the organization, and for her grandfather? It was her job to instill loyalty in whatever way necessary for those under her. Her position and the way she demanded respect would be no different if she were a man. Her gender had little bearing on how she did her job or how she ran the business, at least it didn't to her. Reflecting back, she did often wonder if her appointment was out of the privilege she enjoyed being the Oyabun's granddaughter.

"Ms. Erickson, how do I explain duty, honor, and respect to an Anglo such as yourself?"

Brooke visibly flinched at the statement. Surely, Brooke could understand the cultural differences between her and Luce. The daggers shooting from Brooke's eyes almost made her break out in a laugh, but she held on to her reserved composure and leveled a stare at Brooke.

"I'm afraid your green eyes give away your Anglo roots, Ms. Potter, as does the Anglo name you go by. Therefore, before you try to one up me, I assure you I understand organizational behavior at its highest level. However, cultural traditions often trump an organization's business structure. Now, if you would be kind enough to answer the question...."

The silence that passed between the two made it clear that Luce had no intention of being baited. She had jousted with men far better equipped to throw the importance of cultural identity at her than Brooke Erickson, and she had walked away the lone victor in those exchanges.

"If you won't answer my questions, I'm sure JP Potter will be happy to fill me in on how his little girl became one of the richest, most powerful women around."

If Luce could spit fire, she was sure the flames rising from her belly would vomit out of her mouth and burn the smug smile off the reporters face. Twice, she had brought up her father. Once, Luce had offered to overlook the transgression, but she knew she couldn't do it a second time. Luce shot out of her chair, positioned herself over Brooke, and bent her back over the arm of the couch. Nose-to-nose with Brooke, Luce let out a long, controlled deep breath flaring her nostrils. Clenching her jaw with her molars grinding against each other, creating an awful sound that she was sure was like nails on a chalkboard, given Brooke's reaction. Goose bumps popped all over her arms.

"I've warned you about my father. I thought you were a smart woman, Ms. Erickson. Perhaps I need to readjust my thinking. JP Potter is the scum of the earth and if you want to interview that piece of shit, feel free, but don't say I didn't warn you. Let me pass on a piece of advice my grandfather imparted to me at a very young age, 'if you keep your distance from the devil he can do you no harm'. It's an old Japanese proverb that I think speaks for itself. However, if you want to know about him, I'll be happy to share how that bastard killed my mother, if you think it's relevant to the story. Otherwise, I'll let him tell you his version, but—and let me make this very clear, if you mention his name and my name in the same article—I'll own that magazine you call home. Then you will work for me. There is more than one way to skin a, pussycat, Ms. Erickson." As she slid her body across Brooke's, breast against breast, abdomen against abdomen, Luce whispered one last thing, "Then you'll get to find out what fringe benefits really are. Do I make myself clear?"

Brooke nodded and then sat up straight, blinking rapidly, looking as if she was trying to stop the tears that threatened to fall. Luce shifted herself to the end of the couch facing Brooke, her knee resting inches from the frightened reporter.

"Next question, and don't tell me you're all out of questions."

The gantlet had been thrown down and as far as Luce was concerned, she was going to see the damn interview finished, so Brooke Erickson didn't talk to her father.

Chapter Fourteen

Brooke sat stunned. If death had a face, she would swear Luce Potter was that image. It was as if she had been engulfed in a flash fire. Everything happened so quickly. Luce's anger, her own body's response, and then Luce's retreat, all done within a split second. Every nerve was firing throughout her body. If she didn't know better, she suspected Luce had deliberately forced her body against her own. Nothing about Luce Potter was predictable, nothing. Her reaction to the mere mention of JP Potter had been like setting a match to kindling. The explosion was... Brooke wasn't sure she could explain the hate she saw flash over in Luce's eyes. Fire was the only word Brooke could think of at the moment. Her body was raging, her mind was exploding, and Luce looked as though she would combust at any moment.

"Would it be possible to get a glass of water?" Brooke's voice shook.

"Of course."

As if on cue, Audrey entered the room, making Brooke wonder if the room had a camera or if it was mic'd. Oh, if it was then her last visit was all on tape somewhere in the house. Shit!

"Ms. Erickson would like some ice water, Audrey."

"Of course. Ms. Potter, Mr. Yoshida called and would like you to call him when you have a free moment."

"Thank you, Audrey."

"You know what? I'm fine." Brooke started grabbing up her things and shoving them into her briefcase.

"Ms. Erickson."

Brooke felt her hands stopped. The touch was almost more than she could bear so she looked any where but Luce's face. Afraid of the anger she would see, she kept her eyes down and her face expressionless.

"I'd like to apologize for my behavior. Once again, I was out of line. I let my temper get the best of me." Luce touched her hand under her chin, forcing Brooke's gaze up and towards Luce's face. Brooke resisted making eye contact. Luce pressed, "Look at me, please. I have no excuse for my behavior other than I hate my father with a passion."

"Oh, I think you've made that quite clear, trust me." Brooke had pressed for more information and knew she had probably compromised the only chance she would ever have to interview to Luce. She never suspected that she might worry for her own life. Now she could confirm that her editor was right, Luce Potter was not someone to be taken lightly. Nevertheless, Brooke wasn't someone who scared easily, not after what happened in Europe. She would get her story if it killed her, at least she used to think she would. She didn't think of Luce as that kind of person, not like Petrov. Then again, she would hate to be proven wrong.

"I don't expect you to understand how much I hate the man who killed my mother, but let's suffice it to say, I wouldn't lose any sleep if he suddenly disappeared." Brooke watched Luce raise a finger before she could say a word. "Before you say anything, if I wanted that to happen, we wouldn't even be talking about him. He would be a footnote in your article."

"I suspect that's true."

"Please, if you have any more questions please feel free to ask away. As long as they don't have anything to do with my father, I think we'll be fine."

Audrey's knock interrupted and she entered the room with a tray. As she set it on the table, Brooke noticed the knowing glance the two women shared. Brooke held the cold glass as Audrey filled it. The coldness of the crystal was distracting enough that Brooke could finally focus on what she needed to do, finish up the interview and get the heck out of there. She was determined not to let Luce influence how she did her job, no matter what Luce did to sabotage it. A long slow sip of the icy liquid not only quenched her thirst, but also gave her a minute to assess Luce. The woman sat back and waited as Audrey filled another glass and passed it to Luce. The smile the two shared was sickening to Brooke. There was definitely something going on between the two and she wondered if that was a safe topic to discuss. She had warned Luce she would revisit the question, maybe now was that time. *It isn't as it seems,* Luce had informed her.

"So Audrey, do you have sex with Ms. Potter?" The stunned look both women gave Brooke didn't push her off her task. "I mean Ms. Potter is an attractive woman and look at the way she has you dress. Don't you find it rather demeaning?"

Audrey looked from Brooke to Luce, who shrugged her shoulders, and then back to Brooke. Searching the woman's face, Brooke felt sorry for Audrey. Clearly, she surprised by the question, but Brooke didn't care. She was here to get the real story on Luce Potter and naked women walking around the house wasn't your usual soup de jour.

"I'm sorry I don't understand."

"You don't understand the question or you don't understand why it matters?" Brooke said.

"Both, I'm just an employee. I thought you were here to interview Ms. Potter?"

"I am here to interview Ms. Potter, the real Ms. Potter. I'm sure you can understand my curiosity when you're the second beautiful woman I've seen walking around the house naked."

"I don't see how that would matter, Ms. Erickson."

"Didn't you think it was odd that one of the requirements of working for your boss was to be naked during your time here?"

"I suppose at first, but when my friend, you met her the other day, told me about the job, I jumped at the chance. She loves it here and when I heard about the pay and benefits, as I said, I jumped at the chance."

"Really?"

"Really."

"Will that be all Ms. Potter?"

Brooke looked at Luce who shrugged and raised her hands. "Is that all, Brooke?"

"Not quite. Audrey you didn't answer my question. Okay, let me put it a different way, are you involved with Ms. Potter?"

"No, I'm...well I..."

"I think that answers your question. Don't you, Brooke?"

Frustrated with the circular answers, Brooke threw her hands up. "I guess."

Both women sighed as they watched Audrey

leave, one out of frustration and one out of gratitude.

"So, Ms. Potter, tell me why you have sex with your employees."

Brooke was like a dog with a bone, she never left something hanging, not if she knew someone was lying and both Luce and Audrey were lying. But why?

"Let's try this again Ms. Potter. Why do you require that the women who work for you do it without clothing?"

Brooke's hand shook as it hovered over the notepad, waiting for Luce's answers. Gripping the pen harder to stop the tremors wasn't working, so she rested her hand against the lined paper. If anxiety were a sport, she would be crossing the finish line right about now, having survived the onslaught from Luce. Looking back at Luce, what she saw wasn't what she expected. Luce fidgeted with some phantom lint on her pressed slacks. Her polished androgynous image, with her button-down, form-fitting white shirt hugging her ample breasts, the motorcycle cufflinks accenting the starched cuffs, was flawless. Yet, she looked frazzled and worn. Slipping a wisp of hair behind her ear, she looked at Brooke with something akin to bedroom eyes. The hooded lids covered eyes that now smoldered with desire. Whatever happened was like someone had flipped a switch between the raging woman to the sexy provocateur that now sat before her.

"I guess the easiest way to say this is...it's hard to hide a weapon on your person if you're naked. Isn't it?"

"Paranoid much?"

"Wouldn't you be if you got death threats on a regular basis?"

Surprised by the remark Brooke wondered what

kind of enemies a beautiful woman like Luce Potter created. "How often do you get death threats? Monthly, weekly, daily? Why would someone want you dead?"

"Sometimes monthly, lately it's been weekly. Ms. Erickson, I do business in a man's world and that comes with its own inherent dangers. You mentioned Petrov, he's one, but there are others. Some I suspect within my own organization who don't agree with idea of a woman being an Oyabun. My culture has deeply seeded ideas of where a woman's place is and isn't. All you have to do is look at the Middle East and I think you get a real sense of how culture affects beliefs."

"So they come to work in what? A trench coat?"

"I'm sure it seems silly to you, but the mental has as much to do with the physical. If they think they will be searched, then they are less likely to try bringing in any contraband. I have my ways of checking for things and it can be quite pleasurable, if you know what I mean."

"But you said that you don't require sex from your employee's."

"I don't, but that doesn't mean they don't find me irresistible." Brooke felt like she wanted to whip that broad smile off Luce's face. How arrogant could one woman be?

"So you want me to believe that these women throw themselves at you and you...accommodate them."

"History tells us that many great leaders slept with their men to gain their loyalty."

"So you're telling me that you ensure the loyalty of your employees by sleeping with them?"

"I'm telling you that there are those who would like to see me dead and I have safeguards in place that keep me secure. That's all, Ms. Erickson. You can read into that any way you want. Now, if you would like to come and work for me to find out what those safe guards are I would be happy to add you to my employ, assuming you can pass the background check."

"You are persistent aren't you?"

"I didn't get to the top of the food chain by waiting for an opportunity. You must create your own destiny or it will be created for you and it may not be one you want. Now, do you have any more questions for me?"

The apologetic woman who had sat before her minutes ago was replaced with a cocky facsimile of Luce Potter. Brooke assumed it was how Luce Potter stayed on top of her empire, the constant change didn't allow anyone to get a bead on her. How could they she was a constantly moving, morphing target.

"No, I think I have enough to get started. I'm sure you won't mind if I interview others for their perspective on you and your business."

"As long as you don't talk to JP Potter, I'm sure we'll be fine."

"Oh I got that loud and clear, trust me."

"Don't forget you promised to run the article by me, first."

"No, if I remember correctly I said I would run any quotes by you, for your approval."

"Of course, you're right. I look forward to hearing from you. Do you have any idea when the article will be released?"

"My deadline is two weeks. It should be in the next edition, which is in about six weeks." Standing Brooke finished shoving everything in her briefcase, extending her hand to Luce. "Thank you for your time and once again I apologize for any misunderstandings.

I'll send over a copy of the quotes I plan on using in the article. By the way, if it is still all right with you, I'd like to interview the women who work for you."

"Of course, I'll tell them to make themselves available to you."

"Thank you."

"Of course."

The silent, long walk to the door was painful in its lack of courtesy. Brooke knew she had a lot of research to do, and while Luce had told her JP Potter was off limits, Brooke knew she needed that part of the story to offer a complete image of Luce Potter.

"Good-bye, Ms. Erickson. Again, I hope you'll accept my deepest apologies for my earlier behavior."

Brooke nervously took the extended hand, giving it a quick shake afraid she might be pulled into whatever neurosis Luce was going through.

"Good-bye, Ms. Potter. I'll send the quotes and if you have any questions I'm sure you know how to get a hold of me."

With that, Brooke practically ran to her car, tossing her stuff inside and slamming the door, locking it. *What happened? Did she just imagine the naked women, the spilt personality of Luce Potter, or the threat that if she followed the lead on JP Potter something awful would befall her? Would this day never end?*

Chapter Fifteen

The steam that rolled off Luce gave evidence to how wired she was in anticipation of the night's event, while the damp chill of the night did its best to try to seep into her bones. It wasn't her wool driving coat that kept the dank weather at bay, her determination to prove her leadership had her amped and ready for the evening. Wringing her hands, she felt as if she were ready to spontaneously combust. Only the top bosses and a few underlings would be at this meeting. The fewer ears present the better. The bosses ran a tight ship and information was passed quietly down the ranks on a need to know basis. Her final attempt at reorganization would be to downsize to only a few individuals from the original Yakuza organization. She had informed her grandfather of her decision and was met with some skepticism, but eventually he agreed. To move forward would mean that some legitimacy was needed and that meant putting the old ways behind them.

She was the boss now and she needed to be in place and ready for what might come at her. As each man arrived, she personally greeted him, bowed and shook his hand firmly. She couldn't help but notice each boss had their own style of dress, most preferring the shiny suits, ties, polished boots, and sculpted hair. They looked more like comic book caricatures than menacing Yakuza bosses, but let someone challenge them and they would show their traditional roots within seconds. As she hugged one whom she had become fond of, she could feel his semi-auto tucked nicely under his armpit. Luce wished she had remembered to make it a no guns event, but her mind was on other business. Now she hoped it wasn't one transgression she would regret.

As a few of the men chatted in small circles, smoking cigarettes, she nodded in their direction acknowledging them again. She wasn't worried about how it looked, her meeting the bosses outside, she was trying to duck the tradition of the men coming to her for respect, so she was willing to meet them first. Waiting patiently, she paced back and forth outside the warehouse for her grandfather to arrive. Tradition had its place, but she was a non-traditional selection for Oyabun. Her decision tonight wouldn't reflect that change in tradition. She had decided that Sammy must prove his fealty in front of the bosses. If he couldn't then he would be replaced and out of the organization. The ceremony was important for two reasons, first the fact that her grandfather would be in attendance let everyone know he agreed with her decision. Second, it would solidify her position as leader, and any who questioned it could do so in front of her grandfather, but no one would be that disrespectful.

Peering around in the darkness, she wondered if anyone was watching and recording their meeting. The cops were the least of her worries. Now that the Russians were in town, she was sure they would be watching her every move until there was a confrontation or something worse. Pulling her jacket away from her body hoping it would cool her, she noticed steam rising off her. Yep, I'm going to spontaneously combust right here in front of the bosses, living up to my nickname,

Little Jade Dragon. All I need now is to spit fire. She forced a breath through her nose and watched the steam circle around her head. Taking another deep breath, she rolled her neck and shook her shoulders, hoping to release the tension that had settled in them.

A black sedan turned the corner around the warehouse and rolled up to where she was standing. The driver exited, but Luce waved him off. She would do the honors of walking in her grandfather herself. Centering herself, she reached for the door, waited a moment, exhaled and opened the door.

"Grandfather. Thanks for coming." Luce bowed, extended her hand and gripped his arm and elbow to assist him out of the car. Looking around inside she made sure no one else had accompanied him, and then waited for him to stand before placing a kiss on his cheek.

"Oh, stop that and give an old man a hug. I've missed you my Jade Kaida."

If anyone thought the years had been hard on Tamiko Yoshido, they didn't know her grandfather. He wrapped her in a hug so tight that it forced the breath out of her and stopped her from taking another. Finally, he released her and turned her around to get a better look at her.

"I see your packing." Tamiko patted Luce's back touching her constant companion, the .380 nestled in the small of her back."

"I'm always ready, Grandfather."

"I only wish it wasn't needed." Tamiko patted Luce's face as if she were a child.

"Me, too. Grandfather, you look good."

"I am good. I feel like a million bucks and I can't wait to see my Jade Kaida in action tonight." The smile

Tamiko gave was infectious and Luce beamed at the compliment. "So how is business?"

"Good, I think I'm going to squash that bastard Petrov once and for all, but it means I need to take care of JP." She looked at her grandfather for a reaction. His stoic features gave nothing away so she continued. "Tell me, oh wise one, what advice do you have for your prodigy?"

Luce felt him tap their clasped hands. "You do what you must do Kaida. I once told JP that his daughter would come for her own justice. If now is the time, his hourglass has run out of sand. However, once something is taken, it can never be given back. Whether that is something said in anger, an action done out of spite, or a promise made, it must all be done with great care and reverence. Age isn't an excuse for bad behavior. The old make just as many bad choices as the young, but time is not on the old man's side. He may not have time to fix what he has put in motion. Whereas, the young have time to smooth the rough edges of hate. I trust deep down inside that you know what must be done."

Luce was puzzled by her grandfather's answer. Was he condoning her decision to eliminate the Russian and by proxy her father or was he telling her that because she was young time would take away the pain of losing her mother? It didn't matter. JP Potter wouldn't be long for this world, especially if he had aligned himself with Petrov.

"As always, sage advice grandfather." Luce winked at Tamiko.

Another car pulled up as they were speaking. Frank and Sammy had finally arrived. Sammy carried himself as if he were going to his execution. The pale pallor of his skin and the light sheen of sweat reflected in the dim light. Luce almost felt sorry for the man, but too many mistakes had made this ceremony an inevitability.

"Oyabun." Both men said, bowing to her grandfather.

"Frank, Sammy." Tamiko said, shaking both men's hands.

"I'm sorry Kaida, I meant you, too." Frank said, bowing towards Luce.

"I understand Frank. Please go inside. Please make sure everyone is seated and ready. We'll join you in a minute."

"Poor Sammy," Luce said.

"Well, unfortunately you can't overlook his mistakes, Kaida. You're the boss now and you must be ready to show them that leadership comes with responsibility."

"I know, Grandfather, but—"

"No buts Granddaughter. I picked you because you are the most worthy and you're my blood. Honor and duty are just as important as blood. Never forget that. Come let's get this business over with. Then you and I can have dinner. Yes?"

"Yes, Grandfather."

Six men sat on their knees as Luce and her grandfather entered the small office at the warehouse. A low table with an open black lacquer box sat in the center of the table. On the other side were two large pillows for Luce and her grandfather. Tamiko waved off Luce's offer to help him sit. She knew he wanted to appear healthy and vigorous for the men seated before them, but everyone knew she only did it out of respect. Tamiko, though small in stature, was a giant among the men who's heads were bowed before them.

The tension in the room rose as hushed murmurs traveled through out the group of men and the two women present. Luce was proud to say that she had personally made it a point to add the two women to the bosses. Another buck in tradition, and she had heard through the grapevine that the male bosses weren't happy. It didn't happen overnight. No, it had taken a lot of work to find the women and move them up the ranks. The years that it took to cultivate the female bosses had been directly under Luce's own tutelage. As a female, she felt she was the best example of what she wanted the female bosses to model. They hadn't disappointed her either. Their analytical, calm presence had made their businesses take off and Luce was thrilled at the prospect of moving at least one up higher in the ranks. Now she needed to focus on the task at hand, she could pat herself on the back later.

"I've called all of the bosses here to make sure that we have a very clear understanding of what is expected of you, should you choose to continue to work for me." Each boss looked at the other suspiciously and then back at Luce. "It seems we have some things that need to be handled." Luce looked around the room at each man and then continued, "Lately, we have become lax in our business. The Russians sent someone to infiltrate our organization. He was given access because someone stood up for him. How could the Russians come into our city and we not know about it?"

Luce wasn't surprised by the chorus of raised eyebrows and surprised looks she received. It was one thing to call a meeting of the bosses. It was another to insinuate that there might be changes to a boss's position within the organization. She had carefully crafted the last sentence to make each boss wonder about their continued employment. A choice was much different than an assumption of tradition, and tradition is what had kept most of the bosses in their jobs when her grandfather had passed the organization on to her.

"Is there one among you who knows how this has come to pass?"

The silence echoed through the small room, each boss looking down at their folded hands in their lap.

"Who among you has fallen derelict in your duty to the new Oyabun?" Tamiko's voice boomed in the small room. "You have dishonored her and you have dishonored me for your lack of duty to the family."

All sat silent, heads bowed.

"Frank." Tamiko commanded.

"Oyabun." Frank stood and then came forward, kneeling in front of Tamiko.

"You were my Kobun from the beginning and we have been friends for a very long time."

"Yes, Oyabun."

"How is it that the Russian was at the charity ball without you knowing it?"

"I don't know, Oyabun."

"I am disappointed to hear that, Frank. You were my second for over twenty years. Has your age affected your ability to do your job? Has your mind become feeble?"

"No, Oyabun. I trusted someone else to do their job and they overlooked the Russian because he was with—"

"Enough, I don't want to hear excuses." Tamiko grabbed Frank's tie pulling his face closer to his own. "Kaida is my blood and that is thicker than our friendship. I trusted you with her life and you've disappointed me."

Luce knew her grandfather had purposely cut Frank off. If the men knew that JP was with the Russians, they might question her loyalties. It was why the ceremony had taken on a new importance. The rumors had already made their way through the ranks. Now Luce had to prove her own fidelity to the organization by making an example of the man who had let him slip past. Luce blanched at her grandfather's anger. It was rare to see him so upset and she didn't yet quite know what to say.

"Since no one has come forward to admit their mistake, you, Frank, must take their punishment."

Luce looked at her grandfather in surprise. This is not what she had planned, but she couldn't go against her grandfather, it would be disrespectful.

"Frank, you will perform seppuku since no one has come forward to accept responsibility for such egregious actions."

Seppuku, or ritual suicide, was performed as a penance for failure. Luce had never seen it done and hadn't heard of it being done in years. Frozen, she looked from her grandfather, his stern look fixed on his face, to Frank, her grandfather's only kobun. Frank nodded his head, his eyes down cast as he began to take his jacket off.

"Grandfather," Luce whispered placing her hand on his arm.

"Oyabun. It is my fault not Frank's." Sammy stood, his shame evident on his face as he looked down at the floor. "I admit I vouched for the man Luce caught a few days ago and I missed the Russians. Frank didn't know about their arrival in town or at the charity ball. I thought since I saw them with JP," Sammy pointed at Luce. "with the new Oyabun's father, they were okay."

"So this is your excuse for not reporting to your boss?" Tamiko said.

"I wasn't sure, Oyabun. I thought they were okay since they were in our club."

"Clearly, you don't have a firm grasp of those that are a threat to our organization. Frank, what do you have to say about this underling?"

"My apologies, Oyabun. I have no excuse and offer myself to your punishment."

The room vibrated with a hum as bosses, mumbled comments under their breath. None looked at the head table, but the tension in the room rose a discernable level. Luce felt the few gazes directed at her were less than understanding. She would have to act quickly if she were to be seen as the benevolent boss she claimed to be.

"Grandfather," she leaned towards Tamiko's ear whispering loud enough for the two men in front of them to hear. "Perhaps, we can handle this with less bloodshed and no loss of life?"

"I'm listening."

"I think Sammy losing a digit, and a lowering of his standing within the organization, would suffice."

"As you will it, Kaida." Tamiko smiled and patted her hand on his arm.

"Sammy, do you accept yubitsume on behalf of Frank?"

"I do." Sammy bowed and kneeled in front of the low table, his head bowed in respect.

"Oyabun. This is my punishment to take, please allow me this."

Tamiko raised his hand. "Kaida has decided, Frank. She opted to spare your life and in exchange Sammy must accept yubitsume."

Luce looked at Frank and raised an eyebrow. The fact that Frank would question her order to her grandfather in front of the men was a matter of concern.

"My apologies, you're right, my humblest apologies for speaking out. Please Kaida, accept my apologies."

Luce nodded her head at Frank and reached across the table, opening the black lacquer box. Frank placed the stack of cotton wraps next to Sammy's hand then stood behind him ready to assist in case he faltered in making a clean cut.

Luce watched Sammy pull the polished blade from its resting place. He laid the sharp blade against the first knuckle on his pinkie and wait for her acknowledgement. This was the first time she had seen the actual ceremony take place and she hoped she would be able to handle the drastic action without flinching. Taking a slow deep breath, she surveyed the room. Everyone had their gaze riveted on Sammy's hand. She heard Sammy's labored breath, the rustle of her grandfather's sleeve as he set his hands on the table, and Frank's stuttered breath as he stood behind Sammy with his hands gripping the man's shoulders. Time seem to stand still as everyone waited patiently for her order. Sweat dripped down Sammy's brow as he closed his eyes for the briefest of moments before locking eyes with Luce. The fear that had been evident before was replaced by the stoic acceptance of what was to come.

At this moment, Luce wished she could reach over and grasp her grandfather's hand for reassurance.

She wished to hide, tucked in the crook of his arm, protected, but she had to assume the leadership that her grandfather had personally handed to her. The responsibility was now hers. Her years of protection were over and she was almost embarrassed at the thought of hiding behind her grandfather. She hadn't felt like this in a long time and wondered why now? Why, at this moment in time her mind would travel back to her childhood. Pushing the feelings back, Luce held Sammy's eyes and nodded her head. A chop, was followed by a grimace of pain that flickered across Sammy's face. His eyes closed, Frank reached down to place a cotton gauze around the amputated tip. As was protocol, Sammy wrapped the tip in cloth and handed it to Luce, bowing his head. Luce accepted the severed digit, raised it for all to see, and placed it on the table, still wrapped.

"My father is no friend to this organization or to this family. In case anyone is wondering. If he, or anyone else deemed an enemy of our family, is seen again in one of our establishments and you forget to tell your boss, the same punishment will befall you."

"Thank you Kaida for your lenience. I am in your debt." Frank said, picking Sammy up from his seat in front of the table.

"Take him to Mrs. Sakura and see that his wound treated."

"Yes, Kaida."

"This meeting is adjourned."

Luce stood and shook hands with each person as they approached the head table. A few words of respect were exchanged, but the quiet of the room was chilling. She had done something that hadn't been done in years and she was sure what happened to Sammy would spread down amongst the ranks. The die was cast and there was no going back now. She had spared Frank and Sammy had paid his penance, now she would wait to see what the fallout would be amongst the members.

Chapter Sixteen

W hat do you mean you want me to go to a club tonight, Brooke?" John shuffled the stacks of papers sitting on his desk, trying to look busy.

"Don't tell me you have a hot date tonight, John?"

"Nope a T.V. dinner and my DVR."

"Good, call home and let your T.V. dinner know you'll be home later. I need a wingman tonight."

"A wingman."

"Yeah, I'm doing some research and I want to hit up one of Luce Potter's clubs. I want to see what happens at her establishments. I feel like she kinda blew me off at the interview today and I want to check a few things out. Are you up for it?"

"Do I have a choice?"

"No, do I need to remind you about the bait and switch concerning the charity ball?"

She watched John hang his head. He knew he owed her and now she was calling in her debt. Besides, he did owe his top reporter for his little gaffe the other night.

"Right now?"

"Yep, why do you need to go home and freshen up? You look fine, besides we're a couple for the night. I don't want to be hit on at the club and you're the prefect cover."

"Fine, fine, fine." John grabbed his jacket and opened the door for Brooke. "This had better be good. I think I need a tall, cold drink anyway."

"Me too. After today's interview, I'm sure she won't be so willing sit for me again, so I need to build it up without her."

"Yeah, about that, I was given some information I think you should know. It seems that the board's getting ready to make a big change. It shouldn't affect us, but I thought you should be aware of it."

"What kind of change?"

He shrugged. She could see he was uncomfortable with whatever news he had to share. Patting him on the back, she said, "It'll be fine, don't worry."

"Oh, I'm not worried. Seems there's some new money coming into the company, which is a good thing. I hear it might mean pay raises and a few other perks we haven't had since the downturn in the economy. I'm actually looking forward to it, I think."

"So who's the big spender? Do we know yet?"

Brooke watched as John's boyish looks twisted a bit into the worried editor she had seen the most of recently. She figured he wouldn't last if he didn't try and relax. Hopefully, his home life was better than work, otherwise burn-out was around the corner.

"Yep, it seems that—"

"Brooke, Brooke." Stella said, running after the pair.

"Jeez, is the building on fire Stella?"

"Ha, ha, I wanted to let you know I made that appointment with that psychiatrist we talked about, and I put the schedule for the club on your desk, too."

"Oh, right." Hesitating to look at John, Brooke moved her eyes to the right quickly a couple of times hoping Stella took the bait.

Stella gave her a weird look and then the light bulb moment hit. "Can I speak to you for a brief moment, Brooke?"

"Yes. John can you give me a minute?"

"Sure, I'll be in the lobby."

"Thanks."

"Stella!"

"What? I didn't know he doesn't know what you're working on."

"You don't know what I'm working on, really. So what's the schedule look like and who am I meeting?"

"Here," Stella said, shoving the schedule in Brooke's purse. "Check it out and let me know if you need someone to go with you. I wouldn't recommend you going by yourself the first time. It can be a little overwhelming."

"Okay," Brooke looked at Stella's beaming face. "I don't suppose you want to go, do you?"

"I never thought you would ask. Yes, I'll go with you. Let me know what day you want to go. They have theme days, so you might want to think about what you would like to 'see'."

"I'll look at it tonight and let you know tomorrow. What about the shrink?"

"I set up an appointment for tomorrow, mid-morning. That will give you time to talk to her and then go to the club tomorrow night."

"Why tomorrow night?"

"It's ladies night, also know as lesbian heaven. I thought you might want to hang around your people."

"My people?"

"Oh come on. You really don't think I know you like girls. Seriously?"

"I guess I assumed since it was my personal life it would stay personal."

"Oh."

"Yeah."

"I don't think anyone else knows if that's any consolation. Well except, John, maybe."

"John knows, but I'm sure he didn't say anything."

"No, no he didn't say anything. I assumed when I saw the way you looked at the new assistant for the VP. She's cute and you were like putty in her hands."

"I was not."

"You were, too."

"Not."

"Too."

"Okay stop, give me the information."

"It's on a sticky on the schedule for the Dungeon."

Closing her eyes, she took a deep breath. Tomorrow night she would be doing god-knows-what at a place that the very name made her squirm.

"Thanks, I'll see you in the morning."

"You got it. Have a nice evening."

"Thanks."

The music hit Brooke from a block away. The club had a sound system piping music out on the street, and the vibrating beat worked its way right through her body. She figured this was done on purpose. It was a way to get customers amped before they hit the doors of the exclusive club. Being mid-week and still early, she didn't figure there would be a line, but she was wrong.

A few people were already being wanded outside the club by a bouncer who looked like he could toss a car across a football field.

"Hands up." The command was given as if there was no other option. "Open your purse." Clearly, his bedside manner was closer to that of a drill sergeant having a bad day.

"Two, coming in." He said into a mic hidden inside his jacket. With that, Brooke and John were summarily dismissed and the bouncer was on to the next patron.

Brooke grabbed John's hand and squeezed it to pull him closer. "I guess they forgot to send him to Ms. Manners for training."

"Yeah, I think his job description probably says, 'how far can you toss a drunk?' and 'do you have problems giving people new dental plans?' I'd hate to see what he's like when he's pissed."

"Oh, I thought that was his pissed look."

Brooke thought the long walk down the dark hall would be filled with the smell of puke, stale alcohol and a coppery smell of blood, but she was wrong. It had a clean and fresh smell, a startling difference from the other clubs she had frequented. Clearly, they wanted to present a different picture of clubbing and in Brooke's mind she doubted anyone even paid attention, except her. People came here for one purpose—to get laid. At least that's how it always seemed to Brooke when she went to the meat market. At the end of the hallway, bright, bouncing lights flashed, causing her to cover her eyes until they adjusted to all the distraction. Emerging out into the club, she felt like someone who had fallen down the rabbit hole and had entered into a completely different world. The chrome fixtures and high gloss paint reflected the colors bouncing around the room. The music popped off the walls and bounced around her, thumping her body like hands touching her everywhere. The sensation was stimulating in a way she'd find exhilarating if she were dancing with someone.

Brooke looked around and made a mental note of the layout of the club, spotting the most important room in the club, the women's room. It was hidden behind a set of stairs that went up to a dark balcony roped off with the proverbial velvet cord. Another imposing bouncer that stood with his arms crossed, formidable and foreboding. Obviously, with all the muscle Brooke doubted that the club suffered any of the issues most of the others did with drunk kids, drugs and solicitation. But it was only a guess on Brooke's part.

"Nice." John yelled, tossing his head in the direction of an empty booth.

A woman walked over to the booth, waiting for Brooke and John to sit before speaking. "What can I get you?"

"Screwdriver." John spoke first.

"I'll have the same."

"Well okay or are you topshelf?"

"Well's fine for me," Brooke said, as she tried to scope out the room.

"Topshelf," John said.

Brooke shot John a surprised look then watched the waitress talk to the bartender and point them out.

"What? That house shit gives me a headache. Besides, you know they put the house vodka through a few coffee filters and pour it into one of those high priced Swedish vodka bottles."

"What do you think she's telling him?"

"Who him?"

"The bartender. What do you think the waitress told the bartender? She pointed to us when she was talking to him and then next thing I see is him picking up the phone talking to someone."

"Since we're the only ones here, she probably pointed out how early we are and that one of us is a cheap drunk."

"Can't you be serious for one minute, John?"

"I am being serious. You, on the other hand are being paranoid. He probably called for some topshelf stuff since I can't see any on the bar. Besides, Captain Obvious, look around, we're the only people here and our money is green, the only color that matters in a place like this."

"Hmm."

Brooke watched as a man came out of a door behind the bar with a new vodka bottle and placed it on the bar. Maybe she was being too paranoid. Lately, it seemed like the little things were starting to get to her. She jumped to conclusions more and didn't wait for an answer when things looked out of place. She thought about her recent interview with Luce Potter, the whole reason she was here tonight, and how the mere mention of JP Potter's name had physically launched Luce at her. She found herself thinking about the way Luce's body felt on hers, not the danger she could be in, or the smell of Luce's exotic perfume. Not the threat that was whispered in her ear. Brooke never had a thing for bad girls, and Luce Potter had bad girl written all over her. Feeling like she would crawl out of her skin if Luce didn't touch her again was a different sensation for her.

"Excuse me, Earth calling Brooke, come in

Brooke. Are you reading me?"

"Funny, John."

"Where were you just now?"

Brooked looked down at the two drinks in front of them and shook her head. Had she been so out of it that she hadn't seen the waitress deposit them? Clearly, she needed to get her head back in the game and not on Luce Potter, except professionally.

"I was thinking about my interview with Ms. Potter."

"Yeah, how did that go?"

"I'm not sure."

"What do you mean you're not sure? Either you got what you needed or you didn't. She either answered your questions or she bobbed and weaved right out of them."

"Yeah."

"Yeah, what? Brooke, I'm worried about you. You haven't been yourself since the accident. Do you need time off? Remember, I can get someone else to take your story if you like."

She could hear the frustration in John's voice. "No, no, I'm fine. I'm just thinking about a few things she said." Turning towards John, she gave him a puzzled look and continued, "She's a very hard person to read. I've never interviewed someone who said they wanted to be okay and then threw up a wall when I got there."

"Anything I can do to help?"

"Nope, I'll figure it out, but keep your eyes open here. You never know what you'll see at these clubs."

"Oh probably the usual. Women and men dancing, hooking-up, or getting drunk and leaving without a date for the night. You know, the usual bar scene." John raised his empty glass towards the bar and nodded his head.

"Finished already?"

"Yep. It's topshelf, Honey. It goes fast."

"I thought you said they put it through a few coffee filters and put it in—"

"Brooke."

"What?"

"She's coming."

"Who's coming?"

The house lights dimmed and Brooke had a hard time looking around the bar. She could barely see the waitress walking toward their booth.

"Oh right, you don't want them to know, you know, that they know, you know, they pass it through a filter and that it isn't—"

Brooke felt the edge of John's shoe make contact with her shin. The pain shooting through her leg shut her up immediately. Rubbing her leg, she tossed a nasty look at John who was acting as innocent as he could without laughing.

"That wasn't funny."

"No, but I don't want to piss anyone off."

"Then you shouldn't have said that. At least stand behind what you say."

"Remember where we are, Brooke. I don't feel like sitting in timeout while someone tickles my ivories with their fists. I'm kinda partial to my smile. If you know what I mean."

"Oh jeez, John, really."

"Yes, my parents paid a lot of money for my teeth. I'd like to keep them as long as possible. Thank you, Miss. Please keep the change." John passed the waitress a twenty for the two drinks and slid a drink to Brooke.

"Glad you're paying."

"I'll expense it. We are on the clock, remember? I need to talk to you about what happened in the office." The puzzled look Brooke gave him worked, she didn't remember much of their conversation after Stella barged in waving the club card for the dungeon. "The new board changes. Remember?"

"Oh right, so what's going on? You said something about the company getting a money infusion or something."

"It seems the new investor now owns controlling interest in the magazine and wants to sit on the board. Watch over their investment."

"Sounds logical. We see this all the time in business, John. It shouldn't surprise you when it happens at a financial magazine."

"I'm not surprised. It's who the investor is that might be surprising."

Brooke tried to study John's face, but the club had turned the house lights down and a waitress deposited a candle on the table, adding to the allure of the evening. John was sweating now as he downed his second drink in less than ten minutes. Something was definitely bothering him. The music changed from house music to something more danceable as the club started to fill up. John stared across the bar. When Brooke turned to see what John was staring at, he suddenly grabbed her forearm and turned her towards him.

"Speaking of which, don't look now but I think your interview just walked in."

Brooke tried to turn around again, but John stopped her. "No, you don't want her to know you're here do you? She might change how she acts tonight if she knows you're here."

"Oh, good point."

"Come here." John wrapped his arms around Brooke and pulled her close, laying her head on his shoulder. "Don't move. Good thing the booth is dark otherwise…"

"What?"

"Wow, she's even better looking up close."

"Up close?"

"Yeah, she walked right past the booth," he whispered. Lowering his head, she felt him place a light kiss on her lips.

"What the fuck."

"Hey you want to blend in right?"

"Yes, but you didn't have to kiss me. God, John."

"It wasn't as good for me either."

"What? I'm a good kisser."

"Not if the guy you're kissing is gay."

"Still."

"Stop."

Brooke righted herself and sat back in the booth, her gaze following the tall dark figure walking up the stairs to the VIP area.

Chapter Seventeen

L uce took a long deep breath. She felt her soul settle as the aromas of the Korean restaurant soothed her.

"Come on, Grandfather. Auntie won't bite and if she does, I'm sure she has good reason." Luce pulled on Tamiko's hand, dragging him in to the restaurant.

"When you said you were taking me for some home cooking I was thinking Sushi or that diner down the street that serves those big fat French fries we like."

Luce chuckled watching her grandfather search the restaurant. She pulled his hand harder before she stepped behind him and nudged his shoulder.

"No greasy kid stuff tonight. Come on and stop acting like you're going to get a spanking."

"Ugh!"

"Stop already."

"Goddaughter."

Luce felt her grandfather stiffen at the sound of her aunt's voice.

"Stop it," she whispered. "Auntie, how is my favorite aunt?"

"I see you brought the riff-raff with you."

"Don't push it, old woman." Tamiko rolled his eyes at Luce.

"Grandfather."

"Kaida."

"She's my godmother."

"She's a pain in the ass."

"Maybe, but she's as much my blood as any aunt could be, so be respectful."

Luce couldn't believe she was schooling her grandfather on the rules of respect when he had taught her everything she knew about the subject. Tamiko and her aunt had kept a respectable distance ever since her mother's funeral. She wasn't privy to all the details of their falling out, but she knew it had to do with her mother's decision to stay married to her father. She could guess whose side her auntie was on. She also guessed by the guilt her grandfather carried, he had convinced her mother to stay married because it was expected in their culture. Luce's aunt didn't agree with the decision and told him so at the funeral.

"Tamiko."

"Sung."

"How's your hand, Kaida?"

Her aunt scooped Luce up in an embrace that forced the breath out of her and almost lifted her off her feet. The overly demonstrative hug wasn't for her benefit and she knew it. She was starting to feel like a pull-toy as each of her elders tugged her in different directions, trying to show who loved her more.

"Put her down, old woman before you hurt yourself and I have to pay you disability."

"Oh stop barking like an old junk yard dog. You get your money's worth from me. By the way, sixty isn't old."

Luce's gaze bounced from her aunt to her grandfather and back again. Her eyebrows raised in a question and she caught and searched her grandfather's gaze for an answer.

"What's she talking about, Grandfather?" Luce said.

"What's your aunt talking about? What happened to your hand?"

Luce shoved the gloved hand deep into her jacket and rocked back on her heels. She had tossed the bandages a week ago, but the stitches were still in and she hadn't thought to tell her grandfather about her self-inflicted wound. Actually, it hadn't come up and she wasn't in a rush to remember that night and why she'd accidentally cut her hand. She knew she would have to fess up, as soon as her grandfather told his secrets.

"I'll let you two chat. Kaida, you know the way," Sung said, sweeping her hand forward before she continued. "Soju for you both?"

"No."

"Yes," Luce said.

"Well?" Sung said tapping her foot impatiently.

"Do you have any sake?"

"I'm sure I could scare some up for you, old man."

"Hmm."

"Soju for me, Auntie and my usual. Grandfather?"

"Kimichi soup." Tamiko said turning and dismissing the two women.

"Why did you bring him here, Kaida?"

"Auntie."

"What? He's so infuriating."

"What were you talking about a minute ago when you said he gets his money's worth?"

"It's not my business to tell, so you'll have to talk to him."

"Auntie."

"I'll bring your drinks," Sung said over her shoulder, disappearing behind the curtain that separated the restaurant from the kitchen.

Shaking her head Luce walked towards the back and to her booth. She pulled off her gloves and stuffed them into her jacket before she plopped down on the edge of the seat. She had hoped a good dinner would get rid of the tension of the nights events, but the bickering between her aunt and grandfather had only added to her already tense mind. Pushing her shoulders forward she tried to release the knot that had already started to form between her shoulder blades. Using a stretching technique she taught in Tae Kwon Do class, she reached across her body, patted her shoulder blade, and pulled her elbow closer. Switching arms, she took a deep breath rolled and her head from shoulder to shoulder. Finally, she released the breath she was holding.

"Are you all right Kaida?"

"Just tired, Grandfather."

The bench seat bucked Luce up as her grandfather plopped down, practically tossing her on the floor.

"Sorry."

"No apologies necessary. These seats are so old I'm surprised management hasn't remodeled the place and replaced these old things," Luce said slapping the worn vinyl.

Tamiko cupped Luce's hand in his and raised it to his lips. "I'm proud of you."

His behavior puzzled her. He never was shy about showing her affection, but she suspected it had more to do with what happened earlier with her aunt. *Perhaps she didn't need to be so cynical when it came to her family,* she told herself.

"Thank you. It was tougher than I expected." A

tremor ran through her looking down at her pinkie. She wondered about the force it took to dislodge the digit, remembering how the blood coated and dripped from the ceremonial blade. Bile rushed up her throat, making her gag.

"Here, take a sip." Tamiko handed her the cool glass of Soju while he still held on to her other hand. She had been so lost in the memory she didn't hear her aunt deliver their drinks.

"How did you get this?"

His finger ran across the stitches in her palm. As usual, she gulped down the first glass, then blew out a breath through pursed lips. She would never get use to the throat burn, but she needed to prime her mind if she was going to discuss how she had sliced open her palm.

"Kaida?"

"You first, what was Auntie talking about?"

"This isn't a negotiation, Granddaughter." Tamiko's voice held firm.

"Are we keeping secrets about business?"

"No, but I do have a few business dealings of my own that I didn't turn over when I gave you control of the organization."

"I see." Luce wasn't sure if she should be offended that her grandfather didn't trust her to tell her, or if he was a smart business man who always had a reserve for a rainy day. She liked the later idea, so she wouldn't read too much into his words, at least not yet.

"So, you own this restaurant." It was a statement more than a question. "How long have you owned it?"

"Your mother and grandmother loved to eat here so I made a small investment. It's paid off and I still get to have a small piece of what pleased your mother and my wife. Is that so bad?"

Patting her grandfather's hand, she smiled and shook her head. "Not at all."

"So what happened to your hand and don't be evasive again."

"I cut it on a knife," she said shrugging her shoulders. "About a week ago."

"Why?"

"I got an envelope delivered to my office. I recognized the handwriting, and didn't feel like dealing with anything from my father until I had a drink and some time to center myself."

"I see."

"I didn't want it to ruin my day so I figured it could wait. I came here, opened the envelope with my knife and my hand slipped. No biggie."

"What did JP want?"

Luce could hear the nervous tone in Tamiko's voice. She was sure it had been years, if not a decade since she had seen her father and here suddenly he was back in her life. Luce wasn't sure if he was scared for her or for JP.

"Nothing. It was full of pictures of my mother, me, and you and nana." Tossing back another cup of Soju, she whistled and lightly slammed the glass on the table. "No note, no letter, nothing. I think he is poking at me. I don't see or hear from him and suddenly he's here and I get an envelope."

"Try not to read too much into it."

"I'm trying not to, but when I hear he's hanging out with the Russians and a friend of his ends up in our organization, I get concerned."

"Well—"

"What's this I hear your father's in town?" Sung

slid a boiling pot of soup in front of Tamiko. "Careful, it's hot."

Swishing his hand back and forth to clear the steam that was bubbling off the soup, he finally pushed it away and frowned at Sung.

"Really, I didn't notice."

"That's why I warned you. I'm afraid you'll burn your tongue and won't be able to bark."

"Auntie."

His raised hand stopped Luce. "It's fine, Kaida. She's just like her mother."

"Like you knew my mother."

"As a matter of fact, I—"

"Grandfather."

"Don't," Sung said, pointing a pair of scissors she had brought for the rice noodle dish, chap che, she knew Luce liked. "I'll cut your throat and you'll have a new drinking hole, old man."

"Auntie. Geez, you two fight as if you're married. Stop." Luce threw her hands up in retreat. Looking at her auntie, she could only laugh at the angry stare she threw at Tamiko. Nether looked as if they would back down. She missed the interaction between the only family she had left, so she let them continue to go at each other.

"What do you mean JP's back in town? Is that where you got the photos the other night? From him?" Tamiko said.

"They were delivered to my office."

"What are you doing about this Tamiko? She doesn't need to be around that bastard. You need to do something."

"What do you suggest I do, Sung? Track him down like the dog he is and kill him? That's illegal, remember?"

"Hmm, seems he got away with murder." Luce knew Sung instantly regretted her words when she slid into the booth and wrapped her arms around Luce's tightly wound body. "I'm sorry, Kaida. I didn't mean to drag-up old business. I mean, I didn't...I shouldn't have said anything. I'm sorry."

Patting her aunt's arm reassuringly, she leaned her head on Sung's arm and sighed.

"It's fine. Trust me. I hate him as much as everyone at this table, maybe more."

Luce felt the tension ease as the three sat silently trying to rectify their feelings about JP and her mother's death. The pain was gone, but the guilt lingered like fog covering a beautiful meadow. Eventually it would lift and life would resume, but until then Luce realized that there was a day of reckoning was just past the fog bank.

"I need to get the rest of your food before it gets cold."

"Okay."

Luce poked her chopsticks into the glass noodles and vegetable dish and slid some on her plate. Her mind was reeling from the banter, the memories of her mother and now the realization that JP would torment her until she dealt with him.

"She's a little high strung if you ask me," Tamiko said.

"She's definitely opinionated when it comes to JP."

"She's right, I should hunt him down like the dog he is and put him out of our misery."

"No." She patted his hand and smiled reassuringly. "He's my problem and I'll handle him."

"Don't let him push your buttons and think before you act, Honey."

"I know. I'll be careful, I promise."

"I know the Russians are cooking something up. They don't come to town and take some 'friendly advice', Kaida."

"I'm thinking two things, Grandfather, and both are troubling to our organization. The drug industry has become mobile, dangerous, and legal."

"What do you mean?"

"Any kid can start-up a meth lab and make some easy money. I've heard they're putting these labs in vans and cooking it up on the road. It makes it mobile, harder to catch and easy to get rid of when they're done with the van. That makes them dangerous too. Traveling bomb shops, basically. The Russians fund these dirt bags and take the profit. It's all done hush hush, and there aren't any fingers pointing back to the Russians. Everything's done through a third person."

"And the legal?"

"Prescription drugs. Oxy and all the other stuff that only a doctor can prescribe. They hire a few to write prescriptions for them, mostly guys who owe them favors, and they set up an office in a strip mall that dispenses, too. They limit the traffic by limiting the prescriptions, mostly high-end users, those with money. If that runs out, then they open it up to low-end users, soccer moms, kids with habits and the list goes on. It's a smooth operation. If it gets dicey, they close up shop and move to another part of town or a new city."

"How'd you find this out?"

"That mole I found in our organization? We had a long talk that night."

"That must have been some talk. Did he say

anything else?"

"That's the number two part of the problem."

Luce laid her chopsticks down, wiped her mouth, and rested her hands in her lap. She knew what she was about to tell her grandfather would upset him.

"Yeah, it seems that JP told the Russians he could deliver me to them. Alive or dead, probably better dead, actually."

Luce had always been able to gage Tamiko's reactions to news of any kind. He had lost his ruby complexion, courtesy of the sake, and now sat before her almost translucent. She watched him wipe at the sweat that was starting to moisten along his temples and upper lip, then fold his hands and place them on the table. His composure scared her.

"What else and don't sugar coat it, Kaida." The firm tone told her all she needed to know about his feelings.

"That's it."

"Don't lie. You've never lied to me don't start now. It's a dangerous habit to get into, Luce."

She winced at the use of her name. He only did it in public or when he was beyond anger. Her hands started to tremble so she gripped them tighter hoping to still them. Her own face was red, she could feel the blush rising, the tips of her ears felt like they were on fire. Rubbing a hand over one she could feel the heat coming off it. She felt her chest rise as she took a slow deep breath. Fidgeting, she rubbed her chin, itched her nose, and then finally looked at her grandfather.

"He told them I would die a slow painful death and that he would see to it personally."

"That fucking bastard."

Luce bit the inside of her cheek, the pain

grounding her. She knew she had bitten too hard when the coppery taste of blood flooded her mouth. She could handle anything, except her grandfather's disapproval, and right now, she felt as if she had let him down by not telling him everything. Her shoulders sagged at the weight of his stare, his eyes were on fire and anger flowed off him.

"I'm sorry, I should have told you, but I didn't want you to worry or think I couldn't handle this." She bowed her head in shame.

"Why are you sorry, Kaida?" Tamiko said. "You've done nothing wrong. You can't control the action of a man like JP. He got away with murder because I let him. I allowed him to live because he was your father, because I thought he would be a father to you. I am the one who should be apologizing to you. I have put your life in danger because of one bad decision."

"As you've said, you can't control the actions of JP, but I need your permission."

"For what?"

"I need your permission to kill him." She kept her head bowed out of respect, not because he was her grandfather, but because now she was asking the *Oyabun* for his permission to carry out a hit. As a *Yakuza*, it was against their rules to indiscriminately kill someone. She needed permission.

"I am no longer the *Oyabun*, Kaida. You are, and you must do what you must to protect yourself and the organization."

"I don't want to dishonor you without asking first. I may lead, but you are my *Oyabun* as well as my grandfather. As long as you are alive you are my *Oyabun*."

Luce felt tears start to gather and before she could

wipe them, they fell onto her trembling hands.

"Oh, Kaida," Tamiko said moving to her side of the booth. "You are my life now. You have my permission to do what is necessary to protect yourself." He moved to wrap her in a tight embrace and pulled her head to his chest. "I'm only sorry that I have let you down, Granddaughter."

"You haven't. You did what you thought was right. I think we all hoped JP would have a change of heart." The truth sliced right through Luce, her heart clenched as she finally realized that it would be her or JP. One of them would be dead before all of this was over. She only hoped she hadn't pushed her luck letting the Russian live the night of the charity ball. Wiping her eyes, she smiled up at Tamiko and kissed his cheek. "Go back to your side and let's finish eating. I'm starving."

"Kaida, I want to talk to you about Frank especially in light of what you have just told me."

Tamiko blew on the hot soup before sipping it out of the spoon. The kimchi gave the spicy soup its flavor and was an acquired taste for some. Tamiko, speared a chunk of tofu and blew on it before slipping it into his mouth.

"What's on your mind?"

"I'm not sure Frank is a good second for you. I think he's hampered by the old ways and ideas about women. I worry you might be in danger."

"From Frank?"

"Not directly, but perhaps indirectly. He's an old friend and it pains me to say, but I don't like his attitude about business lately. It might be time to retire him or at least have him come and work with me."

"I worry about his judgment sometimes, but I think he's doing his job. I mean, I wouldn't have him around if I wasn't sure he was capable. However, if you think he would be a better fit working with you, I can release him from his obligation to me. I have my eye on a few new bosses that are looking promising." Luce smiled at her grandfather.

"Oh, they wouldn't be those young female bosses I saw sitting in the back of the room, would they?"

"Maybe, they're showing a lot of promise and you know me, I'm all for shaking things up a bit."

"Kaida, there is an order to our operation. It wouldn't look good if a couple of women jumped ahead of the men who've been waiting for a chance to move up. They've earned their chance and shouldn't be overlooked."

"I understand, but I think they can take on my personal security. Things are starting to look dicey now that the Russians are hanging around and I'm thinking I might need some muscle that doesn't look like beefcake, if you know what I mean."

"Hmm." The look of pleasure on Tamiko's face almost made Luce laugh aloud. In fact, she wasn't even sure he had heard her over his humming. Tamiko had always hummed while eating. It was like a man who groaned during sex, it was natural. Scooping a spoonful of rice, Luce watched him dip it into the hot, red liquid then swallow the concoction. Shifting the spoon and chopsticks, Tamiko used his chopsticks to spear another soy bean curd and place it on Luce's plate.

"Eat and stop watching me. It's not polite."

"It worth the entertainment value alone."

"Cute, Kaida, cute."

Focusing on their food, they ate in companionable silence. Alternating between the different small dishes of kimchi, they managed to get a second helping of their favorites as they finished their main courses.

"So, what do you think about my idea?"

"It has merit. Do you think the women can protect you better than one man?"

"Is that a question about their gender or their abilities?"

Tossing a cup of sake back, Tamiko let out a slight burp then excused his action. "Both."

"Why?"

"You're my only granddaughter, it's my job to worry, *especially now.*"

"How about we get a drink at the club after dinner? I don't know about you, but I sure could use one."

Chapter Eighteen

The velvet rope was pulled aside for Luce and her grandfather to go to the upstairs VIP room. The club was starting to fill up as they ascended the chrome gateway. Luce looked around the room downstairs, feeling as though something was off, but she couldn't put her finger on it. Handing her coat to the bouncer, she helped her grandfather with his and handed it over.

"Put these in my office. Make sure the monitors are on in there, too. I might want to check things out later." She told her grandfather, "I like to keep a watch on what's happening in the club. The monitors keep me in the loop without having to work the room."

"You don't like playing host at your own club?"

"I don't like to get swamped by all the wanna-be gangsters down there."

"If they only knew."

"Yeah, they think they do if you ask them."

"Organized crime has taken a back seat to thugs and thug-life hasn't it?"

"Grandfather, you sound like you watch too much T.V."

"You're not the only one who has to stay on top of things. The world is changing, Kaida. There's no honor in the new gangs that are coming into town. Drugs changed everything. Now the drug cartels are ruthless and dangerous to our way of life. The availability of guns and more money than these kids know what to do with will make them disposable. They don't know how disposable. There's no loyalty in the new breed. They call themselves gangsters as if it's a badge they wear, a tattoo they put on to prove they're cool. They've ruined the idea of what a true family is. It's shameful, really."

"The rules are different for families like ours, Grandfather. We must change with the times or deal with the new breed of thugs." Luce felt bad for her grandfather. He had been part of the heyday of the Yakuza life, and now that life was changing right before his eyes.

"I'm glad I've turned it over to new blood," he said clapping her hand that had covered his.

"What would you like to drink, Grandfather?" Luce asked, turning to the waitress who had arrived to take their drink orders.

"Surprise me."

"Bring us a bottle of that Piemonte Moscato I ordered."

"Of course."

Looking down on the dance floor, Luce wondered what her grandfather was thinking. He rarely came to the clubs, and now she had dragged him down to survey her newest acquisition. The remodel had come along nicely, if she did say so herself. The old bar was a hole in the wall so it had been easy to gut and refurbish. The VIP area they were standing in could hold at least a party of fifty people, and the smaller rooms to the right of the staircase offered an intimate affair at a higher price. She had made it a point to paper the city with club cards announcing the new club, so opening night was packed. They ended up turning people away because so many of the city's affluent had suddenly appeared, not that it was a bad thing. The money wasn't in the wealthy, it was in the club hoppers who spent more than they made. The bar was almost a total cash operation and needed watched diligently or she would be robbed blind. She had made a great deal with the alcohol distributors, getting topshelf for almost nothing, in exchange for their access to her clientele.

"Ms. Potter."

The waitress handed Luce a glass of bubbling champagne, then handed one to her grandfather. The lightly sweet champagne was a favorite of Luce's and she hoped her grandfather would appreciate it.

"Cheers, Grandfather."

"Cheers, Kaida. May you enjoy success and a fruitful new business venture."

"Thank you Grandfather. I hope you like it."

"The club or the champagne?"

"Both."

"You've done well, Kaida. Very well. I couldn't be prouder."

His reassuring smile put Luce at ease. She hoped she would always have his approval, but she knew there would come a time when she might have to do something that might push the limits of his own boundaries. If that time came, she hoped he would understand, eventually.

Movement at the bottom of the stairs caught her eye. Focusing in the dim of the club, she recognized the slim figure moving towards the bathrooms.

"I'll be damned," she said loud enough that her grandfather turned toward her with a puzzled look. "That reporter I was telling you about, she's here." Luce pointed to the figure slipping into the bathroom.

"Really."

"Really."

Whistling the bouncer over she whispered something into his ear then turned to her grandfather.

"Want to meet her?"

"Kaida?" His warning tone was lost on Luce.

"What?"

"This isn't time to play cat and mouse with the reporter. I know you're not happy about her asking you about JP, but don't toy with her. I'm sure she was doing her job."

"I thought I would give her the opportunity to meet the original Oyabun, but if you're not up to it...." She whistled for the bouncer again.

"It might be nice to be interviewed." Luce let Tamiko put his hand on her arm stopping her. Waving off the bouncer, she looked at her grandfather. Perhaps she had underestimated her grandfather. She had figured he would balk at her being interviewed, but it was the exact opposite. He had encouraged it. *Change the face of who we are, Luce, he had told her. People think they know things they have idea about. Give the reporter the opportunity to show a different side to our organization. You are me and as such you have become the new face of success.*

"She might want to ask you questions."

"I can always say no, right?"

"True, but I should warn you she is persistent."

"I've dealt with worse, trust me."

"Grandfather, I assure you, she doesn't know what she's gotten herself into." Smiling, Luce watched as her bouncer approached Brooke Erickson. Pointing up to where she was standing Luce watched the woman's expression change instantly. What was a smiling face instantly became expressionless. Luce smiled at the stark gaze sent her way. She was toying with the woman now, and intended to enjoy every minute of it. Luce watched as every step the woman took looked as though she were being led to the gallows. Brooke took slow, methodical steps, one after the other, until she finally reached the top of the stairs and stopped. The bouncer pointed in Luce's direction, but Brooke stood silently for what seemed like an eternity and then looked directly at her. The puzzled look was replaced with a half-hearted smile when she saw Tamiko standing next to Luce. *Aw, now it's worth the walk to the gallows, isn't it,* Luce thought watching the whole thing unfold.

"Ms. Erickson." Luce walked towards Brooke with an outstretched hand. "I see you've made it to one of my clubs. More research, I'm sure."

"Ms. Potter. I didn't think I would see you here."

Luce's brows crinkled together when she remembered passing the booth with the only couple in the club. "Is that your boyfriend I saw you kissing?"

"What? No, no, you must be mistaken. I'm here with a friend."

"I see, friends with benefits. I'm familiar with the concept."

"Ah, nope, wrong again. He's really my boss. Actually he's my editor."

"Ah, now I do see. Employee benefits, interesting you would find my situation...shall we say...deplorable, and yet you have the very same thing going on. Interesting indeed."

"NO. It's not that at all, I mean, John's gay, I mean...oh shit, I just outted my boss, great. How much worse can this evening get?" The last part she whispered under her breath.

"Since I have no idea what the hell is going on, lets

see if I can change that for you. Brooke Erickson, this is my grandfather, Tamiko Yoshida. Grandfather, this is the reporter I was telling you about during dinner."

Luce watched Brooke try to compose herself as quickly as possible as Tamiko extended his hand.

"Nice to meet you, Ms. Erickson. My granddaughter has told me so much about you."

"Nothing good I'm sure, Mr. Yoshida."

"Quite the contrary, actually. Seems, she is impressed with your thoroughness."

"Really."

Luce could feel the glare Brooke lasered on her as she focused on her grandfather. She could slap the lying old man right now, but only chuckled at the patronizing comment her grandfather bestowed on the reporter. If Brooke only knew she was now in the dragon's lair, she might rethink the whole interview.

"Yes, it seems she's quite taken with your persistence."

"Grandfather," Luce said, shaking her head. She knew the comment would be misconstrued but it was out and little could be done to retrieve it.

"Your granddaughter is quite interesting in her own right."

Again, Luce couldn't miss the sickly sweet smile aimed at her. She was sandwiched between two individuals who were well-versed at the game they were playing and she was a not-so-innocent bystander.

"Yes, yes she is, isn't she? Would you like a glass of champagne? Perhaps you would like to join us in one of the private rooms my granddaughter has on the other side of the balcony. I'm sure you have tons of questions for me. Don't you?"

"Grandfather—"

"Kaida, it's fine. Why don't you give me a few minutes alone with this lovely woman and then you can join us. Would that be all right with you, Ms. Erickson?"

Luce watched Brooke squirm at the invitation. She wasn't sure what her grandfather had up his sleeve, but she would have to trust his judgment. Calling the bouncer over again she waited for Brooke's answer.

"My friend is downstairs waiting from me. I'm sure he's concerned."

"Luce, send the bouncer down to tell her friend that Ms. Erickson is up here with friends and she'll be down in a few minutes." Turning towards Brooke, Tamiko continued, "I assure you, you aren't in any danger. I'm pretty harmless now that I've let Luce take over the business."

"I'm sure you're understating your importance."

"Probably, but humor an old man, besides who wouldn't want the company of a beautiful woman such as yourself? I'll have Luce standing outside. If at anytime you feel threatened, yell, and she'll come to save your honor. I promise. Right Luce?"

"I would be honored to be your champion, my lady." Luce performed a sweeping bow, before instructing the bouncer.

Before Luce could say anything else, Tamiko had Brooke by the elbow and off into one of the soundproof rooms. She watched as Tamiko played host to Brooke's guest status, pouring them both a fresh glass of Piemonte Muscato. Minutes etched slowly, as Luce watched Brooke laughing and then silent as her grandfather seemed to be detailing something that had Brooke enthralled. The bouncer arrived by her side with what looked to be Brooke's purse. Upon seeing what

Luce was handed, Brooke jetted to the door, opened it, and took the oversized bag from Luce's grasp.

"Thanks." Brooke whispered before she shut the door.

She watched as Brooke asked her grandfather something, then took out the same pen and pad she had used in their earlier interview. Brooke scribbled furiously, talking intermittently to her grandfather. Tamiko gestured every once in a while, she was sure to emphasize a point, but each time it was followed by raucous laughter, so Luce wasn't quite sure what he was saying. If this was an interview then what had happened earlier between them? Her grandfather looked like he was enjoying what Luce could have only described as something akin to having a root canal earlier in the day. Finally, the door opened and Tamiko strolled out smiling.

"She's all yours, Kaida. It's been a long night. I'm going home, Sweetheart. I'll send the car back for you." He leaned in and whispered, "She is delightful. I don't know what you were worried about, and she's very easy on the eyes, Granddaughter, if you know what I mean."

"Grandfather."

"What? I'm saying, smart women are a turn-on."

"Grandfather."

"You said that already." Tamiko waved over his shoulder. "Good night Ms. Erickson. It was a pleasure meeting you."

"I'm very honored, Mr. Yoshida."

"Please, remember you promised to call me Tamiko."

Luce couldn't believe what she was hearing. Her own grandfather was flirting right in front of her with a reporter who could very well take her, and her family down. At least that's what she wanted to believe. It helped to keep Brooke in a tightly bound package.

"Of course, Tamiko. I look forward to lunch."

"Lunch? Grandfather?"

"Luce, please you'll catch flies if you keep your mouth open like that, relax. Good night Ms. Erickson."

"Good Night."

Luce wanted to pull her hair out. Tamiko was consorting with the enemy and now they were going to have lunch together. She felt her body charge up as her grandfather gave the reporter a hug. *Betrayal*, that was it, she felt betrayed by her own grandfather.

"Relax, Kaida, I softened her up for you." Leaning back from the hug, Tamiko continued as he looked at her. "Jealousy doesn't look good on you. I'll call you tomorrow. We'll talk about Frank then."

"As you wish, Grandfather."

She knew her tone was stilted, but she was shocked by his accusation. *Jealous?* Impossible, she thought as he walked away.

"So Ms. Erickson. I see you've charmed the pants off my grandfather," Luce said, redirecting her anger at Brooke.

"Actually, I think he still has his pants on."

"You know what I meant. So what wild questions did you ask my grandfather?"

"Actually, he did most of the talking. Seems you were an impetuous little girl."

"Really?" Luce knew her tone was mocking, but she couldn't help it. She had to watch the two verbally cavorting for almost an hour and now she could only guess at what her grandfather had said.

"Your grandfather is really a charming man. Now I know where you get it."

"Really?" Luce's new tone was surprise and this time she actually was.

"Is that all you have to say, one word answers? If that's all you've got, then I guess I should go. It's been a long day and John's waiting for me downstairs."

"I took the liberty of telling your friend to leave, since it looked as though you might be a while."

"He wouldn't leave me here alone."

"No you're right. I gently persuaded him that I would be responsible for your return home. After I insisted, he decided I was more than capable of seeing you home."

"I see."

"I promised him I would be a good girl. Scouts honor and all." Luce crossed her heart and held up a three-finger salute. "I promise."

Chapter Nineteen

Brooke didn't know if she should be frightened or thrilled to get another shot at interviewing Luce Potter. Tamiko Yoshida had been engaging, entertaining, and wonderfully talkative. His reminiscing of Luce's childhood had brought a completely different dimension to Luce. He made her more personable, but she doubted the woman would appreciate the candor by which her grandfather had described her.

A knock on the door brought both women back to the conversation at hand.

"Come in." Luce said in a commanding tone.

A waitress brought in a bucket with more Piemonte Muscato in it. Was Luce trying to get her drunk? Brooke watched Luce sit on the back of a chair and then deftly open the bottle without a sound. She poured them each a drink. Wondering aloud she said, "So, John left me here to fend for myself, huh?"

Brooke almost laughed at the expression on Luce's face. She was thinking she should have censored her comment, but now that it was out in the breeze there was little she could do to take it back. For the second time that day, the look Luce gave Brooke made her heart flutter. She would have to slow down on the champagne if she was to take charge of the interview, again.

"You're virtue is quite safe with me, Brooke. I guarantee it."

"That's wasn't what I meant...I mean...what I meant to say was that I can't believe he would leave because you asked him to."

Brooke raised the glass of champagne, wiggling her nose as the bubbles tickled it. A long, slow sip of the cold liquid felt good as it soothed her throat and her ego. Suddenly, she was mesmerized by the way the bubbles seemed to ease off the side of the glass, wondering how champagne effervesced. Another long sip and she could feel her courage coming back in droves.

"So, Ms. Erickson, what else did my grandfather say?" Luce said, topping off Brooke's glass.

"You're grandfather is quite charming. I'm surprised he is still single."

Brooke's gaze followed Luce as she walked over and looked out of the tinted glass. Luce cut a fine figure, if she did say so herself. She was taller than most men, and Brooke was sure Luce came off as an imposing boss because of her height. Now, she could study Luce the woman, in a different environment, as a business woman. One where Brooke could watch her interact with her employees. Everyone was different at home, the comfortable atmosphere usually allowed a reporter to see the casual, laid back side of an individual, but Luce's home environment was something else. Remembering everything from those two days made Brooke's heart tumble in her chest and flamed a heat that stirred every time she thought about Luce.

Brooke admired the crisp lines of the black slacks that hung off Luce's well-defined ass. The tucked white fitted dress shirt with cuff links was enough to make the femmiest of femmes drool. Brooke wanted to release the long black hair that was plaited in a French braid and run her fingers through the shiny silk strands.

The braid cut between her shoulders and led Brooke's gaze to the gun tucked safely in the small of her back. It added an inescapable edge of danger to the tightly wound persona of Luce Potter. Fear gripped Brooke as she focused on the chrome gun. Sliding back into the memory of the night Mike was killed, she shivered. She could almost feel the cold of that night seeping into her bones, the imaginary copper smell of blood assaulted her again. Closing her eyes, she tried to mentally bounce out of the events of that night. She forced the memories into a tight little box, with all the other little secrets of her life she kept hidden, to be pulled out another time. Thinking about all the things she had tucked away for safe keeping, she ping-ponged between events in her life, searching for new memories to replace the events of that night in Europe. One of those recent memories she had yet to put into a box was the first time she went to Luce's house. She felt her body amp up at the thought of Luce tied tight, doing the bidding of the woman whose face she barely remembered now. *Dr. What's-her-name, what was her name?* Brooke thought. Looking back at Luce, standing almost ramrod straight, her hands behind her back, breasts jutting forward.

Taking another sip of champagne to chase the images from her mind, she straightened herself on the sofa, pulling the hem of her dress down, trying to prevent it from traveling up further. Crossing her legs at her ankles, she chastised herself for thinking of Luce Potter in such a provocative way. *I wonder what she has on under all those clothes?* She took another sip. She could feel desire start to replace the anxiety that had taken up residence in her chest, a sure sign the alcohol was having an effect on her. She always became sexually stimulated when she drank, and looking at Luce only added to the sexual tension building inside. Shaking herself, she tried to free her mind from the thoughts of Luce naked on the floor of her bedroom. She set the nearly empty glass on the table and pulled a mint from her purse.

"Yes, he can be rather charming when he wants. As for being single, ever since my grandmother died, he has made it a point to tell me that, 'once you've had the best, it's pretty hard to replace it.'"

"Have you had the best, Luce?" Brooke said without thinking. *Strike two for alcohol,* she thought, slipping the mint in her mouth hoping it would keep her tongue tied long enough for some sanity to reenter the picture.

Her heart sped up when she found Luce watching her, studying her. Diverting her eyes away from Luce's stare, she ran her tongue across her suddenly dry lips and shivered slightly. Her body reacted to the interaction between them, as her nipples tightened and hardened and the hair on her arms stood. Luce cocked an eyebrow as her gaze roamed down Brooke's body with a slow visual caress of her legs and then back up to her face. A smile broke past the placid exterior.

Great!

"I don't think so."

The candid answer surprised Brooke. "A woman such as yourself could have any *woman* she wanted. So it's hard for me to imagine that you haven't met the right woman."

Brooke wanted to slap herself. She had all but called Luce Potter a lesbian without evidence, but then again she had witnessed Luce practically finger fuck her help this afternoon. So it was a given, right? As Luce came closer Brooke felt the energy in the room turn electric. Sucking on the mint she almost choked as it hit the back of her throat then disappeared. A coughing fit ensued.

"Here this will help." Luce offered a refilled glass.

A sip and more coughing made her take another drink until the glass was empty again.

"I'm fine, really, I'm fine." She set the glass back on the table.

The couch next to Brooke dipped as Luce sat on the other end, staring at her.

"I'm curious, what kind of woman do you think I like?"

Brooke looked up to find Luce's green eyes searching hers for an answer. "I don't know. I would imagine that depends on your mood." Brooke wasn't about to say what she thought, that Luce wanted someone who could control her one minute, then someone she could control the next. If she were guessing, Luce was asking about physical characteristics and not emotional ones. "You look like the type who likes a woman who's high maintenance, heels, lacy under things, stockings, the whole nine yards, or maybe you like 'em built like a brick shit house, as my father used to say. Actually," Brooke raised her finger to her pursed lips. "I'm not sure what that means."

"I think your father means, he likes a solid gal. You know, hearty."

"Hmm."

"So you think I like a more feminine woman." Luce leaned forward, her voice dropping as she continued, "The soft, silky kind that comes to bed in almost nothing, ready to be ravished? Or, the kind who likes to take control and be in charge in the bedroom.

A woman who thinks leather's a second skin and the tighter the better. A gal who likes it rough, one who likes to be shown who's boss and does what's she's told. So what kind of woman do you like, Brooke?"

Brooke stared into Luce's eyes. She could feel herself falling into the fathomless depths or maybe it was the alcohol, she couldn't be sure. Her skin was on fire and the only way to douse it would be to...no, she was clearly in over her head now and she was sure Luce knew it. The long form before her slinked closer, making Brooke feel like a trapped animal with no escape. She watched Luce's gaze focus on her lips. Suddenly self-conscious she slipped her tongue out and wetted them. Another mistake as Luce's gaze began to smolder under her now hooded eyes. Instantly, she regretted the invasive question, but there was no going back. The Luce Potter sitting before her was a different animal, predatory, stalking its prey and ready to pounce.

"I'm sorry, I shouldn't have said anything. Uh, would it be possible to get a glass of water?"

Luce picked up a slender black box with buttons on it and pressed one. Within a few seconds, the waitress appeared and left just as quickly.

"So are you going to answer my question? Or is this a one way conversation?" Luce questioned, the taunt saying it all.

"What's that?" Brooke asked pointing to the box on the table hoping for a diversion.

"Oh, this. It's a controller for the room. This button," Luce said pointing to a green one, "sends a call to the waitress. This blue one changes the glass to privacy and this red one is an emergency button. If something happens and you need help fast, the bouncer outside will be here in about two seconds. The one with the musical notes on it, I'm sure you can guess that one."

"Wow, you've thought of everything."

"If you want a top notch club, you have to give your clientele the best. On this floor we have a dedicated bar and waitress, restrooms with an attendant, and close-circuit T.V. so the clients can come in and watch what ever game is on at the time."

"Nice. So are your other clubs like this?"

"Not yet, but I'm working on it. So are you going to answer my question?"

Brooke swore the temperature in the room rose ten degrees and she peeled off the little sweater she had been wearing. Taking another sip of champagne, she swirled it in her mouth before swallowing it. *The question, answer the question,* she heard, but was it in her mind or had Luce asked again? Her body relaxed into the sofa and her mind wandered as she looked into the green eyes of the dragon sitting before her. She'd seen the tattoo on Luce's arm from a distance, but suddenly she wanted to see it again, to touch it.

"You...um...you have a tattoo on you arm. Is there a meaning behind it? I saw the huge carved dragons on your front doors, impressive I might add, and noticed they had green eyes." She shrugged. "I was wondering if it was a family crest or what the symbolism meant."

"How do you know I have a tattoo?"

"Oh, that first day I came over to interview you..." Brooke panicked, how would she explain seeing the tattoo. Her thoughts raced as Luce gave her a puzzled look. "You reached out to shake my hand and I saw the tail of it peak out from under your robe. The sleeve had slipped up enough to give me a good look. I assumed it was the tail of a dragon, I mean the colors and all."

Brooke was babbling now and she knew it. *Fuck, fuck, fuck, no more alcohol.*

"Hmm, I didn't think it could be seen."

"Oh, it was just a little bit." Brooke put her fingers together and then widened them out. "It was only about that much."

Luce took the motorcycle cuff link out of her cuff and laid it on the table. She began rolling up her sleeve. Each inch the sleeve went up, the more of the dragon became exposed, and the more Brooke's body betrayed her. She had thought that she could see the dragon without any problems, but here it sat before her ready to strike out. She could almost feel the power of the animal as it disappeared under Luce's shirt. Its attempts to hide under the shirt and wanting to be concealed, seemed apropos. The fiery red, oranges, and greens of the dragon peeked out, curled around Luce's arm, and disappeared under the top of the sleeve. Brooke felt mesmerized as she studied the artwork. Automatically, she reached out and fingered the tip of the tail, turning Luce's forearm over to follow the blazing red feathers along the sinewy expanse of her bicep. The electric charge she felt at the contact made her suck in a breath, her body reacted viscerally to the not so innocent touch.

Luce felt the soft fingertips trail up her arm following the tattoo. Whatever game Brooke was playing she was in for a pound. The unexpected touch had stoked the already smoldering fire that had been banked in Luce since their last meeting. Now she could feel the tension rise as Brooke continued to stroke her arm.

"I guess you would have to take your shirt off to see the rest huh?" Luce reached for the buttons on her shirt and began to unbutton them, but her progress was stopped when Brooke covered her hands. "I...a...I...."

Luce slipped from Brooke's grasp to pull her on top, and covered Brooke's mouth with her own. Threading her fingers through Brooke's hair, she took command of the encounter pressing Brooke's hips tighter against hers. Their lips wrestled against each other, fighting for domination. Finally, Luce won when her tongue gained entry into Brooke's mouth. What had started as a battle quickly ended when she felt Brooke acquiesce and moan into her mouth. The taste of champagne mingled with Luce's tongue as she probed deeper into the warm invitation. She heard the buttons of her shirt falling to the ground as Brooke ripped it across her chest and pulled it down her shoulders, exposing her tattoo. Looking down, she watched Brooke's tongue follow the tail of the dragon, up her bicep, around her shoulder, and down towards her breast. Every nerve was firing in Luce's body, the work of her hips grinding harder against Brooke's made her pant in Brooke's ear as she broke through the thin grasp she had. Grabbing Brooke's head with both hands, Luce stared into the hazy blue eyes.

"You're playing with a fire you can't put out. Are you ready for that?"

The desire in Brooke's eyes couldn't be denied, but Luce didn't take advantage of someone who wasn't in full control of their faculties. Brooke's head slipped through Luce's hands. She felt her tongue trace the head of the dragon as it moved closer to her breast. The moist path left a trail of desire that coursed through Luce's body, spreading like fingers aching to grab her insides and twist them. Brooke pulled down the strap of her lace bra and slid her tongue across the erect nipple, and Luce felt a gentle pull of the hardened tip. Brooke pulled on the areola in the exact same way the dragon tattoo had been placed. The erotic scene made her wince in pleasure as Brooke tightened her grip on the throbbing nipple. She grabbed Brooke's hips and forced Brooke's knee between her legs, begging for the friction that would release her from the sensual torture. Her other nipple was suddenly experiencing the same torment, but this time she felt it twisted between Brooke's fingers, then gently tugged and squeezed. Ache, that was the only word that came to mind as she ground on Brooke's thigh. An ache that had to be answered, that needed to be taken care of, the need of release. Just as she started to feel her body corkscrew into an orgasm, a phone rang somewhere in the room.

"Fuck."

"Don't answer it, please," Brooke pleaded as she continued her ministrations.

The ring tone wasn't Luce's so she let it fade from her mind. The gentle gyrations against her hips kept her body pulled tight, but the torture her nipples were enduring nearly snapped the taut bow of her body. She was ready to release when the phone went off again, this time it was hers.

"Fuck. I have to get this. It's my private number for emergencies." Luce forced Brooke backwards onto the couch. Her hand slipping up Brooke's skirt as she flipped the phone open. "This better be good, Frank."

Her attention was instantly diverted when she felt the slippery wetness between Brooke's legs. She slid a finger into the cleavage and then another, slowly pumping them in and out as she watched Brooke's eyes close in ecstasy.

"Where are they?"

She kept up her steady pace, then lowered her mouth to Brooke's breast and tongued the tight fabric that stretched across her hard nipple. Biting it, she felt Brooke's stomach lurch and her pussy tighten around the fingers she had buried in the moist, wet confines. Her pussy tightened again when Luce bit a little harder, this time tugging the nipple into submission. Brooke's body pumped on Luce's hand as she stilled her motion.

"Keep an eye on them and I'll be right over." Luce tossed the closed phone onto the table and withdrew her hand from its warm confines. "I'm sorry I have to go," She said licking a wet finger.

The look of disappointment that etched itself across Brooke's face made Luce wonder if the reporter had planned for this all along. Her bedroom eyes nearly pulled Luce back down to finish what she had started, but unfortunately the phone call had come at a bad time for both of them. Luce's own body screamed for release as she shifted her slacks from the contact they were making with her engorged aching clit. Pulling her shirt together, she knew it was a lost cause and stripped it off, tossing it into the trash can.

"I'm sorry about that," Brooke said pushing her skirt back in place. "I mean, everything. I had not intended mixing business and—"

"It was an unfortunate situation, nothing more. Please don't apologize. You're a very, very attractive woman, Brooke. I think that answers your questions about the kind of woman I'm attracted to, doesn't it? Now, I should apologize, the phone call was urgent and needs my attention. I'll be happy to give you a ride home and then I'm afraid our business is concluded."

Raising Brooke's fingers to her mouth, she kissed the back of Brooke's hand. Her own hand still held the scent of the woman and she inhaled deeply. The taste of the woman still fresh on her lips and tongue sent a jolt of energy through Luce's body. *This had better be important, Frank,* she thought before releasing Brooke's hand.

Chapter Twenty

Brooke sat across from Luce in the limo. She recognized this woman, the tightly buttoned-up, all business, successful woman who sat before her looking anywhere but at Brooke. The moment they had shared earlier was partly alcohol induced, but the sexual tension that rolled off Luce wasn't just in her mind. It had happened. She reached up and felt her puffy lips and smiled behind her hand. She had almost had Luce Potter, but why did it matter? She wanted to reach across the expanse between them, pull Luce on top of her, and finish what they'd started. However, Luce was beyond reach. Whatever had transpired on that phone call had been the equivalent to a wet blanket for Luce. Trying to right the ship she felt listing to the side, she reached into her purse and pulled out her pen and reporters pad, and secretly pushed the record button on her digital recorder.

If Luce wanted to be all business and not acknowledge what had happened, she could play that game, too.

"Do you mind if I ask you a few more questions? I'd hate to waste this time since I'm sure it will be the last time we get a chance to talk before the article goes to print."

Luce took a deep breath and rolled her eyes. Clearly, Luce had thought they were done chatting for the night, but Brooke wasn't going to let Luce control every situation that involved her. That included how this evening ended.

"Please. I'm not sure there is too much more I can add, but I'm sure you've thought of something."

"What makes you different than your average street gang?"

"I'll assume you mean the average street thug? Those kids who walk around with their pants hanging around their knees, the wanna-be gangsters? Or are we talking Russian mafia, the drug cartel type thugs?"

Brooke shrugged her shoulders and weaved a bit before answering. "Yeah, those."

"You clearly haven't done your research, Ms. Erickson. I'm not a common street thug. I come from a family that has a long history of tradition. Not that you'll remember this in the morning, but Yakuza have an honor code we live by, respect for rules and for the code."

Brooke felt the scorch of Luce's glare as she continued.

"I honor my word, my family and my culture. I work within the system and I follow the rules you've set down. If I bend them and get away with it, then so be it. I can tell you this, we don't go around killing people, like street thugs. However, let me be clear; try to take what's mine or try to hurt someone I love or my family, and I will do my best to eliminate that threat. If someone doesn't do their job within my organization there are consequences, but it rarely involves someone losing their life."

"So you think you're different than, say the Russians?"

"There is no honor amongst the Russians. They—"
Luce paused as her private line rang again.

"Yes. How long have they been there? Okay, keep an eye on them. Let me know if they go into the warehouse. I'm on my way." She refocused on Brooke. "Where were we? Oh yeah, the Russians. They have no respect or honor. Their word means nothing and they can't be trusted. If you get in their way, they eliminate you." Luce pulled the gloves she wore further down her hands, then flexed them open and shut. Glancing out the window she continued, "I believe we are at your home. Yes?"

Brooke looked out the tinted window and recognized her bungalow, but how had Luce Potter known where she lived? Shaking her head, she realized Luce Potter probably knew as much about her as she didn't know about Luce Potter. Ironic, really, she thought. Tonight she had made a pass at one of the most successful women in business and it seemed she had egg on her face instead. Stepping out of the car behind Luce, she turned to shake her hand but found Luce waiving her forward.

"My grandfather taught me to always walk a lady to her door."

"Your grandfather is a wonderful man. I'm sure he's proud of how you've turned out."

"If he told you as much then I am honored he would share that with you. Now," Luce reached for the keys dangling from Brooke's hand. "Would you like me to walk you in and make sure everything is safe?"

"I'm sure I'll be fine. Thank you once again for an interesting evening. I'll make sure I send you any quotes I might use in the article. Otherwise, you will have to wait until print to see a copy of it. Good night, Ms. Potter."

With that, Brooke slammed the door in Luce

Potters face. Frustration and anger made her put finality to her words and she suspected it was a rare woman that didn't give Luce the last word. She didn't care at this point, the sexual tension that pulled her tight had almost been her undoing. For Luce to not even acknowledge what had happened between them was a slap in the face, at least that was how she felt.

"Jeez," Brooke threw herself into a side chair in front of the fireplace. "I'm acting like a jilted lover. Great. A few kisses, a little second base action from Luce Potter and I'm a sniveling fifth grader with her first kiss. Fuck me."

Resting her head in her hands, she felt as if her world was spinning out of control. "Water and aspirin, lots of aspirin, or I'm gonna be sick tomorrow. How could I have allowed myself to drink so much? What was I thinking?" She said to no one in particular. The flashing light on her answering machine caught her attention on the way to the kitchen. *Why did she even have a landline anymore, and why did she keep that stupid antique of an answering machine. She often thought about throwing it out, but if something ever happened to her cell service she would still be able to make a call in a disaster,* she told herself. Stopping, she noticed two messages flashing. She pressed the button and then continued into the kitchen.

"Brooke, Honey. It's your mother. We were wondering if you were coming for holiday dinner? Also, your father wants you to come out for a visit. I told him you were busy, but he wants you to come anyway. Besides, we're only thirty minutes outside of town. What could it hurt to come out Sunday for the family barbeque? Bring that salad you make with the candied pecans, cheese, and apples. Your father loves that. Okay, Honey I'll talk to you later. Love you. Oh, this is your mother in case I forgot to say it earlier. Bye, bye."

Before her mother hung up, Brooke could already hear her father in the background quizzing her mother on what she had said. She loved her family and wished she had more time to spend with them. Tight deadlines made it tough to go over for a Sunday BBQ when she could write all day Sunday and get her story submitted before the deadline. She would make it a point to call, and go by and see them for the next family BBQ. Erasing that message, she swallowed her pills and drank half the water bottle before pressing play, again.

"Brooke, its John, your editor." Brooke shook her head. Why did everyone think they had to explain who they were on an answering machine? "I tried calling your cell phone but you didn't answer, so now I'm calling your home phone. Thank god, you have one. Most people get rid of their landlines and then regret it later. Anyway, call me tonight when you get in. If I don't hear from you by midnight I'm coming over."

Brooke looked up at the clock and noticed she had about fifteen minutes before John showed up. The last thing she wanted to do was play fifty questions with John in her living room. She wasn't sure she would be able to lie to him if he asked her what happened between her and Luce. Not that anything had happened as far as Luce was concerned, she was sure of it.

Flipping her cell open she speed dialed her editor.

"Brooke? Are you okay?"

"I'm fine, John. I just got home and am getting ready for bed."

"Oh, good. I was so worried. I didn't know what

to do when she came downstairs and told me I could leave and that she would make sure you got home okay. Phew, I'm so relieved you called. Everything went okay, didn't it?"

"Yes, John. In fact, I was able to meet and interview Tamiko Yoshida, her grandfather. He's an interesting man. You would like him, funny, smart, and an all around great guy."

"Wow, you scored then. I hear he doesn't do interviews. Good for you Brooke. Anything else you want to tell me?" The question hung for a moment before Brooke answered him.

"Nope, I think I'm good. I'll talk to you later. Oh, I have an appointment with a doctor so I won't be in until later."

"You okay?"

"Yeah, it's a shrink that I want to interview about another story. So, I'll be in late. See you tomorrow."

Brooke hung up the phone before John could respond. She didn't want him asking any more questions that she might have to lie about. It wasn't a good relationship between editor and reporter if it was built on lies, so avoiding the truth made a lot more sense, at least to Brooke.

Heading for the shower, she thought about the nights events. What a jumbled mess she had made of things, first, asking to see Luce's tattoo and then stretching the truth when Luce asked how she knew about it. Even more disturbing was the fact that she had touched the ink. She'd run her fingers along the lines that made up the artwork and then without thinking she got caught-up in the sexual frenzy and ripped off Luce's shirt, exposing the full length of her desire. The warmth ran under her tongue as she trailed it along the lines. Every voice in her head screamed "don't" but every other voice in her body egged her on, daring her tongue to swath a path down to what the dragon's jaws held, Luce's nipple. The first taste of the puckered circle made her tingle inside, then she gently bit the hard nipple and tugged on it. Hearing Luce release a groan only spurred her further into the torment she felt when Luce grabbed her hips and pulled her along the strong thigh. Her body didn't revolt as she thought it should, instead it followed willingly as Luce pushed Brooke's hips harder on the sinewy muscle.

Brooke jumped into the warm spray, hoping for a reprieve from her over-stimulated mind. If it hadn't been for the cell phones ringing almost in tandem they would have consummated the act and Brooke would know what she was sure many women knew, what it felt like to be fucked by Luce Potter. Now, she would only have to wonder, since she knew she would never put herself in that position again. It was unprofessional and highly unethical to have sex with someone you were doing a story on. If others found out, the article wouldn't be seen as unbiased, in fact the opposite. So ultimately, Luce Potter had done her a favor and saved her reputation, but if the truth were to be told, she wasn't so sure she wanted Luce Potter to save her reputation, did she?

Chapter Twenty-one

The long black sedan with blacked out windows pulled up to the curb. The door opened to allow the tall man waiting to step inside. Luce let out a long deep breath of disappointment as she watched Frank sit down. He reached forward and extended his hand to shake hers. Hesitating for a brief moment, she decided to leave her gloves on since she hadn't had time to wash her hands after her evening with Brooke. Smiling at the memory, she shook the offered hand and mumbled an excuse of being cold.

"Are you all right, Kaida?"

"Yes, why?"

"You look a little pale and you have something on your neck?"

Luce slapped her hand up to her neck. *Shit, did Brooke give me a love bite? Fuck.* She dropped her hand back into her lap, trying to act normal.

"Oh, it's probably from earlier." She shrugged. "Curling Iron accident." She nodded and stared out the window. She knew how stupid that sounded, and then realized her hair was still in its braid when Frank looked at her hair and raised his brows.

"You should probably get that looked at before it gets infected. I hear burns are the worst."

"Thanks, I'll do that in the morning."

When he sat back his jacket swung wide and she could see his semi auto tucked under his armpit. Her own gun sat securely in the small of her back, so she reached around and took it out for comfort and laid it on the leather seat next to her. She watched Frank's eyes widen at the movement then focused his gaze on her.

"Don't worry Frank this isn't for you."

"I never got a chance to thank you for saving my life at the meeting, Kaida. I don't know what I would have done if you hadn't stepped in and persuaded the Oyabun. I owe you my life."

"No thanks necessary, Frank. We're faced with a younger generation that has a short attention span and has problems with authority. I'm surprised it was Sammy, but he did the right thing and we can put all of this behind us and get back to business. By the way how is he?"

"He's thankful too, Kaida. He knows this could have been much worse for him, too." Frank looked out of the window deep in thought. He was troubled and it showed, but Luce wasn't sure that she could do anything for him at the moment. A change was coming and he knew it. In her mind, whether he was part of that change or not was up to him.

"Where are they?"

Frank tossed his chin in the direction of the massage parlor. "Over there."

"Slimy bastards."

Luce knew the massage parlor's owners and while they weren't under her tutelage, they did skate past her business footprint. The territory was almost in what was considered no man's land, a neutral space that the Yakuza had allowed to flourish without interruption. However, it was clear now that the Russians were trying to take advantage of that agreement and move themselves into the slim slice of property.

"Who else is in there?"

"JP."

"Figures. Do we have anyone inside?"

Luce knew the answer, but asked anyway, in case they were fortunate to have an informant working in the small parlor.

"Afraid not."

"Okay, I want two people on the Russians and JP. I especially want to know where JP goes, where he spends his time and money, and who he spends it on."

"You got it," Frank said reaching for the door handle.

"Hold on Frank. I need to make some reassignments for a while."

She overlooked Frank's furrowed brows, a clear sign he wasn't happy with what she had said. Sitting back down, Frank pulled his jacket closed and stared down at his hands.

"I need you to stay with my grandfather. If JP wants me dead, I'm sure that if he can't get to me, my grandfather will be the next logical target."

"Are you sure?"

"You and the Oyabun are close friends, so I figure you're the only one I can trust to keep him safe. Am I right?"

"Of course, I would lay down my life for Tamiko. I mean the *Oyabun*."

"Let's hope that's not an option."

"Who replaces me, Kaida?"

"I want Lyn and Sasha brought in so I can talk to them. They'll share the role as my seconds and they'll keep their positions as bosses."

"But Kaida, there—"

"Stop, my grandfather has already voiced his displeasure, but I assured him and now I'll assure you, the women can get into places even you can't get into. They don't look like muscle and they can switch out duties making it easier to keep me protected. This isn't forever Frank, just until we get a handle on the Russians and JP."

"Frank, we have to change with the times. It was only a matter of time until women made it up through the ranks. Lyn and Sasha have been with us for years and I think it's time we allow them to prove themselves. If it doesn't work out, I'll send them back down and pick someone else. If the men give you any problems, let me know and I'll call another meeting."

She observed Frank as he rubbed his pinkie at the suggestion of another meeting. She knew he had missed forfeiting his own life, so she didn't expect there to be any blow back. If there was she would handle it.

"I understand, Kaida. You can count on me."

"I hope so Frank, I hope so. Now, I have a plan for JP and don't expect that he'll be a problem too much longer."

Luce discussed her plans for her father and detailed exactly what she wanted to happen in the next week. She wouldn't allow the issue to linger too much longer, otherwise she would be viewed as weak and a target for take over from her own men. The decision to move up the two women would infuriate a few bosses and she needed to keep that type of discussion squashed permanently. So, eliminating the Russians and JP in one blow was the only way to keep the organization firm and intact, without internal damage she was sure would come if they stayed around much longer. She knew money was a great motivator and, given enough cash and promises, even she wasn't safe from her own bosses. She rubbed her forehead trying to smooth the stress lines that were developing there again. Frank's firm hand covered hers as he tried to reassure her.

"It's a good plan, Kaida. I don't envy you, but you can do what has to be done. The bosses will see this and know that you will stand-up for them no matter who or what comes between the family and you."

"Thanks, Frank. You can go. Keep me in the loop with my grandfather. You know how he doesn't want me to worry. Oh, and watch his drinking. If he gives you any guff let me know and I'll come over and straighten him out," she said chuckling.

Frank knew who ran whom, and she wasn't fooling him. Waving at his departing back she buzzed the intercom and instructed the driver it was time to go home. The day had been long and the night even longer. She couldn't wait to get home and relax, finally.

Chapter Twenty-two

S tella, I'm not sure about this." Brooke slipped from the passenger seat, struggling with the remnants of her hangover, along with her anxiety which was starting to kick in. She had barely made it through her morning appointment with the shrink, who gave her the ins and outs of bondage, submissions, tops and bottoms, and a host of other terms she had never heard of. The doctor had recommended two books, one called The Handbook for Tops, and another The Handbook for Bottoms. Both, she promised, would answer most of the questions Brooke would have about the dynamics that came into play in a true dominate and submissive relationship. They had talked about so much. Brooke was thankful she had her digital recorder, since there was no way she was going to be able to focus and remember anything through her migraine/hangover.

She had let Stella talk her into going to "Newbie" night at the Dungeon and now was regretting every short minute of it. The door loomed large as the red neon sign that hung outside flickered. "This looks like it is right out of some Hollywood movie set."

"Oh come on. You'll be fine. Remember, rule number one: look, but no touchy. Rule number two: if you recognize someone keep it to yourself. Rule number three: spank me when we get inside."

"What?"

"Just checking to see if you were paying attention.

By the way, what happened to your neck?"

Slapping her hand to her neck, she looked everywhere but at Stella. Shit. "Curling iron accident."

Stella stepped closer narrowing her eyes at the reddish mark on Brooke's neck. "Really, 'cause it looks like a hickey. Who'd you get lucky with last night?"

"No one. It's a burn, trust me."

"Okay, if you say so."

"I say so. Let's get going."

"You got it. Stay close to me and everyone will think you're with me."

Shaking her hands out, Brooke examined her outfit, and suddenly felt over dressed watching other patrons entering the club. The little black dress was great for most outings, but latex, leather, dog collars, and leashes seemed to be more in line with club attire for the Dungeon. A few patrons wore replicas of actual police, nurses, and military uniforms made out of something that looked like rubber and leather.

"Is that a rubber nun's habit?"

"Latex."

"Huh?"

"Latex, it's a bit cheaper than rubber so they have outfits made out of it. You'll probably see some plastic in there, too. It's even cheaper, and if it tears, no biggie. They can toss it and get another. Some of these latex outfits are in the hundreds of dollars and need special attention, so if you're not sure and want to dabble, go plastic. Personally, I like the leather daddies. The smell of leather is a huge turn on. Wait until you get inside, it will blow your mind."

"I like my mind just the way it is, thank you very much. I'm not sure this is a good idea. I mean...."
Brooke couldn't help but stare at a tall, striking woman

making her way into the Dungeon wearing a leather cat suit. Clearly, she wasn't wearing underwear, there wasn't a panty line or a bra to be seen through the tight outfit. "It does have possibilities. Let's go before I lose my nerve."

Brooke grabbed Stella's hand and pulled her through the huge doors. The first thing that hit her was the freezing cold temperature, her nipples hardened instantly. The second thing she noticed was how dark it was in the club, with the exception of the blue and red lights around the bar. People stood three deep at the bar, some with drinks others tethered on the end of leashes being ignored by their "owners". Brooke couldn't believe she equated people with dogs, at least she thought that's what they looked like. Their submissive posture couldn't be read any other way. A movement on the floor caught her attention and she wished it hadn't. A man was on all fours licking the leather-clad calf of a woman who was chatting with an over-built, muscular man wrapped in military-style latex jodhpurs with suspenders, tall boots and no shirt. Brooke could see the telltale signs of razor burn as sweat glistened off his shaved chest.

"Holy shit. I'm in a twisted version of reality." She said to no one in particular.

"What?"

She felt Stella lean in closer as spurts of hot breath caressed her ear. She leaned back to look at Stella who looked more like a kid in a candy store, than an adult who was here to show her around.

Tossing her head in the direction of the man on all fours, Brooke cocked an eyebrow. "That."

"Oh, Oliver. He'll be anyone's pet. Guess Mistress Eva is trying him out to see if he'll be a good submissive."

Brooke watched the taller woman as she walked away, yanking on Oliver's chain. Now, she wished she hadn't continued to watch. Upon closer observation, the skirt the woman was wearing was plain in the front, but had only buckles across the back, very few of them actually. Her shapely naked ass was on view for all to see, but Brooke suspected that no one in the room, except her, even noticed. Trying to calm herself, she took a deep breath. *Research, research, remember you're here for research,* she chanted in her mind.

"Come on, let's see what's going on in the rooms." Stella yanked Brooke's arm, almost squealing in delight. "Some of the rooms are set-up for different things. You can participate or you can be a voyeur."

"We're playing voyeur tonight, right?"

"Of course."

Venturing further into the bowels of the club, Brooke felt her anxiety kicking into high gear. If she were claustrophobic the dark tight spaces would freak her out, but they enveloped her like a warm cocoon, bodies pressing against her. Stella pulled her hand and they weaved their way through the crowded hallway. Holding on for dear life, she chastised herself for feeling as if she needed the woman as her compass. They popped into a room in time to hear the crack of a whip as it snapped briskly across the exposed back of a woman strapped to a structure shaped like an X. A soft, red welt joined a few others that crisscrossed the woman's flesh. She made a low moan as another was surgically placed in an area that lacked a mark. The precision with which the woman placed her whip was almost admirable, *if you were into that sort of thing,* reasoned Brooke.

"Wow." Stella mouthed to Brooke.

For some reason Brooke couldn't share Stella's enthusiasm at the display playing out before her. She wasn't built like that, pain wasn't a turn on for her. Nevertheless, after talking to the shrink earlier she could understand how some people needed it to feel normal, to let go of their burdens of the real world, and live in some temporary world that allowed them to be subservient to a host that handled everything. The sound of the whip brought more people into the small room as the scene continued to play out. Brooke felt herself being pushed forward, so close in fact, she swore she could feel the air split as the whip moved in front of her to land another blow.

"You know what? This really isn't my kind of thing. I was hoping to see more of the..." Brooke whispered raising her fingers close to her body to type air quotes. "Tying up kind of stuff."

"Oh, right you want the rope tying. Gotcha, down the hall," Stella said pulling Brooke's hand.

Moving deeper into the club, the silence surprised Brooke as the music seemed to be turned lower in the room they entered. Everyone in the room was quiet as a man wrestled with a long red length of rope. A woman hung suspended from the ceiling with one leg pulled up close to her ass. Her hands were bound behind her back, similar to how Brooke remembered Luce being tied. Faint whispers echoed in the room as those in attendance murmured their approval or concern over the woman's suspension.

Watching the scene brought to mind words the doctor had said that morning.

"Look, this isn't rape. There may not even be sex involved and it's completely consensual. It's an act between two consenting adults who want what the other

is offering. It's a contract of sorts. One expects to be submissive and treated that way, while the other expects to be obeyed."

"Yeah, but the power one person has over the other is…it's demeaning."

"Are you sure? What are you basing those opinions on?"

"I wouldn't be able to submit to that type of treatment."

"Would you be surprised at who has all the power? What would you say if I told you that the submissive is really the one in control?"

"I would be shocked."

"Look, this isn't some bad porn movie where men degrade women before they fuck them. Most clubs have rules and standards of play. If you break the rules, you're kicked out. Most of these situations don't involve sex, unless both parties agree. So no agreement, no sexual contact."

"But what about that man you told me about who liked to get his testicles twisted and smashed?" Brooke asked, thinking about the pain involved in the act itself.

"Also, remember he said that if he didn't do this, be a submissive that was mistreated, chances were pretty good he would be a serial killer. The same exhilaration he experienced being a sub was similar to the charge he had every once in a while when he felt the urge to kill."

"Why didn't you contact the police?"

"I did sort of, but until he committed a crime—and he hadn't, there wasn't much that could be done about his 'urges', so I watch him. We meet regularly and so far he's able to control his feelings."

"I don't know, it's pretty far out there for me to be able to understand."

"You're doing research right? Why don't you try it before you pass judgment? At least you can write your article from an informed perspective. Right?"

"No, you're right. I wouldn't be doing my job if I watched from the bench and didn't go in and see what it is like."

"That a girl. Just be safe, pick a safe club and you never know, you might find out it intrigues you."

"I doubt it, but thanks for your time doctor."

"Wow, check that out."

Stella tossed her head in the direction of the woman who, last time Brooke had seen her, was half in and half out, so to speak. Now she was completely suspended from the ceiling her feet pulled up behind her butt, her arms tied behind her back and the crisscross pattern weaved around her body. Brooke strained her head towards the man who tied the woman. He was taking questions from the crowd and she could barely hear them, since those asking seemed to be as embarrassed as she felt.

"Ah, doesn't hurt," he said, pointing to the blushing woman who asked the question. "It can be uncomfortable, yes, but why don't we ask my willing participant. Does it hurt?"

"A little."

"What's the most painful part?"

"My legs, I didn't think they would be pulled back as far as they were."

"Don't worry my dear," he said as he patted her ass. "You'll be down in a minute. Would you like to see my handy work? Please come in and inspect the rope work. The knots and tying are an art. In fact, there is a special name for it in Japan called Kinbaku, and you have to be trained and become a master to tie these particular patterns. The ropes are much smaller in the Japanese style and the knots are much more intricate. For me, I like the thicker red rope, it gives beautiful markings when they are taken off and don't hurt the subject, but I try to use the same style as Kinbaku."

His smug smile made Brooke's skin crawl. He seemed sleazy, creepy actually but she had to admit, his patterns were intricate, symmetrical, and in an odd sense, beautiful. She wondered what it felt like to be tied-up and....*There is rarely sex involved, unless both parties agree.* The words from earlier come floating back into her mind. Brooke shivered as she followed the rope cleaving the delicate skin of the woman's ass and outer labia, and continuing its intricate pattern to her front. The woman's legs were almost spread open from the way the man had tied her and then trussed her up for all to admire. However, the woman didn't seem to mind, perhaps the blindfold helped her to feel removed from the event.

"Wow, what do you think?" Stella nudged Brooke.

"I don't know what to think actually. It wasn't what I was expecting, that's for sure."

"Are you going to try it?"

"Are you crazy?"

"I thought you were doing research for a freelance story?"

"I am, but this is...its so degrading."

"How do you know? I mean I think you should try it. Besides, I already signed you up."

"You what?"

"Don't worry, I knew you would be too scared, so I asked Mistress Eva to put you in a private room." Stella grabbed Brooke's hand and pulled her into the hallway. "Remember rule number one? No touchy. What's rule number two?"

"If you recognize someone you don't tell."

"Right. This is a club which has an exclusive clientele that the public doesn't see. All these people have no idea that down that corridor there is a completely different world. They see what the owners want them to see."

"And you know this how?"

"Because, I'm one of those who get to…let's just say there's a whole side to me you've never seen."

"Oh great."

"Not to worry. I've got ya covered."

Chapter Twenty-three

The sound of the Jacuzzi jets almost drowned out the low methodical voice of the jazz singer playing on the stereo. The steam rolling through the bathroom made everything in it glisten, including Luce. She sank further into the warm bubbles, groaning as her body relaxed from the soothing massage generously provided by the sunken tub. The temperature in the water was so hot that her skin took on a rosy glow making her sweat in the hot water. Dabbing at the beads of perspiration that rolled down her face she wished she had remembered to bring in a pitcher of ice water. She knew she could call for one, but by the time it arrived she would be out and drying off.

She needed this reprieve from the world right now. The week had been hell and it didn't look as if events would improve anytime soon. The Russians were seen all over town. Then there were the stories of her father shooting his mouth off. Each tale was a little more outrageous, a little more over the top than the last. Luce hoped he would've taken the hint she'd left for him by beating the shit out of his friend. Clearly, the note scrawled on the man's chest hadn't been a deterrent. JP wasn't as smart as he thought he was, or he would have realized she knew his every move almost before he did.

Resting her head against the lip of the tub, she tried to think of something more relaxing. Perhaps visions of Audrey in the throws of an orgasm. Moving her lips over the firm body, biting the taut nipple that was willingly offered, made her pulse race. Her tongue flattened against the light smattering of hair above her clit, moving lower she traced the firm ridge with her tongue and sucked lightly, then flicked the tip. She could feel the blood pulsing under the skin as she slipped a finger into the wet cunt below. A second joined in the gentle rocking back and forth and then another until she had all four fingers working the tight space. Luce moved her hand down her own body and worked the hard ridge between her legs. Placing a finger on each side of her clit, she worked back and forth until she felt the corkscrew of an orgasm start. Squeezing her nipple, she focused on the imaginary body under her, the sweat-slicked tight stomach, and flinched with each pump of her hand, the low moan in her ear as she licked the protruding clit. Just as she was peaking, she envisioned watching Audrey's orgasm, but it wasn't Audrey's face, it was Brooke. Luce's body rocked harder on her hand, as she shuddered into her orgasm. Squeezing her nipple tighter, she slipped her fingers into her wet pussy and milked another orgasm as she thought about Brooke, leaning over her body, taunting her with her tongue.

"Fuck," she whispered as she slipped down into the water, covering her head.

She sat up, sputtering, and wiped the hair out of her eyes. Why Brooke? She had lots of women she could fantasize about, so why the reporter? Laying a wash cloth over her eyes she tried to strike the image out of her mind, to release her demons surrounding Brooke Erickson. She had made amends hadn't she? She had given Brooke an interview, allowed her access to her home, and to see a side that no one ever saw.

Wasn't it enough for the karma gods? But the night at the club had been Luce's undoing, and she knew it. No one touched her without her consent. She didn't allow women to initiate intimacy with her, she always initiated contact. Whether through a phone call for services, as with Dr, Williams, or through contact at the club, she always called the shots, but the night at the club had thrown Luce for a loop. The gentle way in which Brooke touched her tattoo, slid her fingers softly across her body, and then followed the touch with her tongue had almost made Luce lose control. She had taken back control, but the phone call from Frank ended what had promised to be an interesting evening.

A soft knock on the door pulled Luce from her haze.

"Come in."

"It's Dr. Williams. Would you like me to take a message?"

"No, thank you, Audrey." Luce said reaching for the phone. "Maggie, I didn't expect to hear from you for a while."

"Luce, I'm not calling for business. I am calling about business, but not that business. That reporter who was at your house the other day...what was her name?"

"Brooke Erickson, what about her?"

"I thought you might want to know she's here at the club. I wouldn't have thought anything about it, but another doctor in my practice told me about a reporter who had come by asking questions about bondage, being tied up and stuff like that. She's here tonight and it doesn't take a rocket scientist to figure out who she might be asking about...you know, you."

"Interesting. Do you know why she's there?"

"According to my pet, Stella, she doing a freelance piece on someone who's into BDSM and wanted to get an inside perspective. Stella reserved her one of the private rooms and convinced her to try it. Something about not being able to write the article accurately if she didn't try it, blah, blah, blah."

"Interesting. Has she started her session?"

"No, they walked in and Stella took her to Maurice's rope tying demonstration. Stella booked a session with Maurice, but I thought you should know."

Luce's mind was working a warp speed. She was worried about what Brooke knew or might have seen. She hadn't thought to check the video tapes of that day, and now her lack of focus might be her undoing, assuming the reporter saw anything.

"She might have seen something she shouldn't have that day she was here, Maggie. I haven't checked the tape, but I'll bet my last dollar she saw something. That would explain her sudden illness and her behavior the other day. Shit."

"What do you want me to do? Pictures in compromising positions, maybe?"

"No, no, that's not...I'm on my way. Why don't you send in a bottle of your best champagne. Tell her it's on the house. I'll figure out what to do when I get there, but don't start her session without me. Okay? Put her in the room with the two way mirror. Can you keep Stella busy while Brooke's in her session?"

"Of course. I'm sure I can think of tons of things for her to do."

"Good. I'll see you in a few."

"Okay, in a few then."

Coincidence, it had to be, Luce told herself. Wrapping a towel around herself, she walked into her closet, searching for the perfect outfit. What if Brooke was into bondage and used the whole doctor's thing as an excuse, so she didn't look like a freak? What if Brooke did see something, would it really be that bad? Panic started to set in as she played through every possible scenario and then as quickly as it rose, it stopped. What was she worried about? There was no way Brooke would write that as part of her story. She smiled and shook her head. She had Brooke over a barrel, she just didn't know it yet.

Tonight would be a game of cat and mouse. She would be the cat to Brooke's mouse and that called for something sexy. Pushing through the clothes, she finally found something perfect for the evening. Calling Audrey, she set the outfit on the bench and searched in her vast collection of shoes. They had to be perfect if she were going to leave a lasting impression on Brooke.

Luce traded Audrey the crystal tumbler of whiskey for the outfit she held in her hand. The warm liquid was already having the desired affect and Luce felt downright giddy as she thought about the night ahead. Brooke had played with fire that night in her club, now it was her turn to find out how the Brooke liked it when the tables were turned. Luce wiggled into the tight black leather dress, presenting her back to Audrey to thread the corset ties down the back. The bright red ties stood out and accentuated the black leather dress perfectly. The second skin felt warm and inviting as it hugged her curves. She hadn't worn the hot little number in a while, often opting for something more reserved, but tonight she felt...demonic. Handing her drink back to Audrey, she slipped into the black stilettos and stood up from her dressing bench. The extra six inches made her even more intimidating. Her attitude changed the minute she slipped into them. Her reflection in the mirror spoke volumes, sexy and dangerous described how she was feeling. She left her hair hanging in waves down her back, the constant braid and the finger curls from blow-drying giving it enough body. A pass through her jewelry box and she was ready to go.

"You look wonderful, Ms. Potter."

"Thanks, Audrey. Maybe I'll get lucky tonight."

"I hope not."

"Shame, shame, bad girl." Audrey giggled as Luce pinched her. "Be a good girl and tell me which of these smells better."

Luce held up two crystal decanters of perfume.

"I like this one. It smells like sin."

"Perfect, not sure what sin smells like, but sin it is."

Luce dabbed perfume in all the right places. Another quick glance at her reflection and she spotted the reddish mark on her neck. *If she could give as good as she gets, Brooke is in for an interesting night,* Luce thought, rubbing the mark with her fingertip. It was barely noticeable, but knowing the mark was there thrilled her in an odd sort of way. Dabbing a bit of makeup on the bite, she powdered it and checked again to see if it stood out. Barely visible, she smiled wondering if she had ever had a "love tattoo". Nope, not that she could remember.

"Set the alarm and if there's any trouble call Frank. He'll know how to find me." Luce said, grabbing her jacket and purse. It was rare that she went anywhere without someone to have her back, but tonight was a rare night and she didn't want a witness for the events ahead.

###

Luce parked behind the Dungeon. She didn't want to be seen at the trendy BDSM club with its affluent cast of regulars, even though the possibility of being recognized inside was pretty good. Buzzing the intercom, she heard Maggie's voice.

"Yeeesss."

"It's me, Luce."

"Hey," Maggie said over the buzz of the door. "I'm in my office. Come on back."

"Will do."

Threading her way through the darkened corridor, she slipped into the unlocked office door marked, Private.

"Dr. Williams. I see you've changed decorators."

Luce admired the newly styled office space. Antique bondage gadgets hung behind the stately mahogany desk, while newer leather accessories dotted the walls.

"Is that new?" Luce said pointing to a huge painting hanging near another door.

"Like it?"

"Hmm, not something for the house, but it is interesting." Luce moved closer to study the subjects engaged in a spanking scene that looked like it was right out of a porn movie. Luce bent over and studied the woman, her ass red with handprints was bent over a chair, and grabbing the arms. "Is that you, Maggie?"

Maggie blushed at the reference to the resemblance between her and the woman. The artist had done a wonderful job capturing the ecstasy or the pain of the moment, but Luce couldn't quite decide which emotion had been saved for posterity. Looking back at Maggie, she smiled at the mischievous grin she was flashing.

"It was done by that up and coming artist everyone is trying to collect, Jean-Luc. He's wonderful, isn't he?"

"It seems he's captured your essence, that's for sure."

"He was guessing. A fantasy he has about how it would be if he were in charge."

"Did you break the news to him that it would never happen?"

"Why spoil a handsome man's dreams. I mean..." Maggie stroked the flogger she had in her hand as if it were a lover. "It could happen."

"Hmm, yeah and I could start to like men." Luce set her purse down, peeled off her jacket and sat in the brocade wingback chair.

"Wow, don't you look hot. I haven't seen you in a dress in a while, Baby."

"I decided I needed a change tonight."

Punching a button on the phone, Maggie called for drinks and then sat in the big chair opposite of Luce.

"So, tell me what's going on with this reporter in my club?"

"Honestly, I don't know, but I'm going to find out. Are the rooms still wired?"

"Of course. Security is always watching."

"Can we see?"

Pulling a controller from her desk, Maggie hit a button that slid a panel sideways, exposing a bank of monitors, with a forty-two inch screen in the center. Pressing another button, she brought up to the full screen, the room Brooke was in. Both women watched as Brooke and another woman sat on a couch drinking the champagne Luce had ordered.

"Who's the other woman with Brooke?"

"That's Stella, she's mine." Maggie smiled.

"I see. Bad, bad, Maggie."

"Not bad, I'm hungry for all types."

"Hmm."

Luce focused on Brooke. She instantly recognized Brooke's telltale signs of being nervous: the twisting of a strand of hair, the way she bit the right side of her lip, and how she fidgeted with her ring on her pinkie. Luce had picked up on all of those clues when Brooke had come to interview her the second time, and now it all made sense.

"When does her session start?"

"Whenever you're ready. She's signed all the paperwork, the confidentiality clause, the insurance liability, you know the usual stuff, but she did make one request."

"Really? What was that?"

"She requested to be blindfolded. She said she doesn't want to see the person performing the tying. Afraid she might connect in some way to the person, either physically or mentally, and she doesn't want that. She wants to experience it raw."

"Interesting."

"If she is doing it for research she's going about it in all the right ways."

Luce watched Brooke gulp down the glass of alcohol and put the empty bottle upside down in the bucket. Clearly, she was feeling a little more at ease as she giggled with Stella.

"Send in another bottle, Maggie."

"Sure, anything special?"

"Yeah, send in a Piemonte Muscato." Luce let

a grin slowly etch her stoic features. She wondered if Brooke would recognize the wine from their last time at the club.

"You got it."

Within minutes a fresh bottle had been delivered, opened, and poured. Studying Brooke, Luce wondered what the reporter had up her sleeve. Had she seen Luce that first day at her house? She chastised herself for letting her security lapse. She needed to step up her game and not be so comfortable at home. Then again, her home was her refuge, some place where she didn't need to worry about the outside world. Not anymore, it seemed.

"It's five minutes to ten. Her session starts at ten o'clock."

"Naked or clothed?"

"Clothed."

"In that dress?" Luce leered at the short mini Brooke was wearing. If she was trying to be modest keeping her clothes on it wouldn't work in that outfit. It would be up around her waist in a few ties.

"I know, but it's her choice. This is newbie night and most of our clients opt for clothing. Now, if they get a pinch or cloth burn, that's on them."

"How about I take over the binding?"

"What? You? Are you sure you want to do that? She might recognize your voice?"

"She'll be so amped she won't even be paying attention. Remember your first time? What did he sound like?"

"Oh, god. All I remember was being ordered to take off my clothes. God it was heaven."

Luce watched Maggie's eyes glaze over as she fell into the memory. Luce laughed as Maggie leaned back against the solid desk and moaned. Her own first time had been…release. It was the only word she could think of as she let go of the world's problems, school problems, family problems, and immerse herself into letting someone else take command for a few precious moments of her life. She could abandon the constraints of her life at the door, a feeling that liberated her for a few hours, before she had to pick up the mantel of leadership once more. The visits were starting to be fewer and farther between as she adjusted to her leadership role, but every once in awhile she needed to feel powerless, like no one depended on her for anything.

How would Brooke feel being confined? Dominated? Would she accept the role of submissive or would she feel degraded and demeaned? This wasn't something most people did on a whim. Most, especially women, seemed to have a romanticized idea of domination from romance books. Old bodice rippers where the man kidnapped them, raped them, and then fell madly in love with them. This wasn't that story. Luce knew she was tame compared to some in the community who liked to be hurt, cut, electrocuted, or worse. She didn't want any part of that world, but she assumed that even what she did would be viewed as deviant. Hell! Thinking about her life, there wasn't anything that someone couldn't point to being outside the norm.

"I'll take her session, Maggie."

"If you're sure, but no funny stuff. Promise me. I don't want some article on the deviant side of the Dungeon." She touched a finger to her lips. "On second thought, maybe that wouldn't be so bad."

"I promise, but I want the camera off. I don't want a video of her visit here. She doesn't need that kind of press, in case it was leaked. Promise me, Maggie."

"Who are you protecting, her or you?"

"Really? I'm sure there's enough video of me you could make a feature film out of it."

"Actually, Hon, I erase your stuff."

"Oh, good to know. Thanks, Mags."

Maggie kissed Luce's cheek and shooed her out the door. "Go, she's in the velvet room. Have fun."

Luce's pulse sped up with each step she took toward the velvet room. She wasn't sure what was going happen since she was playing this one by ear. What was it about Brooke Erickson that made her play outside her own rulebook? She barely knew the woman and yet here she was acting impetuously. The kiss and fondling at the club had been just that, a momentary lapse in judgment. She didn't have lapses in judgment, she made cold calculating decisions. Ever since Brooke practically ran her over with her car, she had been hopelessly connected to this woman. From the charity event, to the first invitation to her home, to the offer of a second interview, and then the evening at the club and her interview of Tamiko, it had all led to their brief encounter that night.

She hesitated briefly, standing in front of the door of the velvet room. It was now or never, turn back and let everything play out or...or what? She wasn't sure. She could feel the cool air pushed out of the doorway and into the hall. The cooler temps made it easier to work in the cramped environment, since the room was really only built to hold several people at the most. Readying herself, she stepped into the room. Brooke sat blindfolded in a chair. A pang of anxiety hit Luce full force as she studied Brooke. The innocence that sat in the chair shook her for a moment. Luce retreated into the hallway, empty. It was now her choice. Who would she be in that room tonight? The rough Yakuza leader, the erratic, aggressive woman Brooke had met on the road, or the woman from the club who had practically melted in Brooke's hands?

Slipping back into the room, Luce first tried to control her erratic breathing, then she clasped her hands together trying to stop the shaking. *What kind of Yakuza are you that you let this woman get to you?* she chastised in her most aggressive mind's voice. Contemplating a blindfolded Brooke, she began to walk around her looking for the best starting point. *Fold, wrap, turn and cinch,* Luce chanted in her head. The roots of Japanese bondage heavily influenced her own binding style, and the fact that Dr. Williams was an expert had made them fast partners. The thick, soft, red nylon rope lay out in three sections. The first two were ten-foot sections for the ankles and wrists and the last was a thirty-foot length for the body binding. Picking up the one of the shorter lengths, Luce folded the rope in half and held the folded end called a Lark's Head. Luce couldn't resist caressing the soft rope between her fingers, and the calming affect put a smile on her face.

"Who's there? I can hear you breathing. Are you the one who's going to tie me up?"

"We call it binding," Luce said in a whisper so soft, she would be surprised if Brooke had heard her. "There's no talking during the process, unless you're uncomfortable or it hurts. Understand?"

Brooke nodded her head and then let it barely drop without realizing she was offering her subservience.

"Please place your arms over the back of the chair and cross your wrists. This won't hurt, but if it does please let me know."

As instructed, Brooke placed her arms over the chair ready for the binding. If the alcohol had an affect on Brooke, her body had probably burned off its sedating affects the minute Luce walked into the room. The exhilaration, the pump one got from a binding, especially someone who was new to the art would burn through calories and alcohol quickly. She would need to make sure Brooke stayed hydrated too, since she would be sweating like crazy once the process started. Her visceral reactions would be so off the hook, Luce could almost feed off the energy.

Luce began the binding process by placing the folded end in the center of Brooke's forearms. She wound the rope around and pulled it through the Lark's Head. Tugging it slightly, she made sure the first wrap was snug, then held the two braided lengths together and wound them around the forearms, moving down towards her wrists. Reaching Brooke's wrists, she had enough length for one more wrap, but instead she turned the end perpendicular and slipped them through the Lark's Head. Separating the ends, she slipped one end under the wound rope and pulled it down, then slipped the other end on the opposite side and pulled it up, cinching the rope, and tied it off with a square knot. When done in this fashion, the arms had an elegant look to them, pulled back and forcing the chest up.

Luce couldn't resist caressing the soft skin at the top of Brooke's arms. Her biceps flexed at the contact and goose bumps rose up, the soft hair tickling Luce's palms. She moved her hands up on the slender shoulders and gently massaged the taut muscles, hoping to alleviate any pressure that might already be deposited there. Sliding her hands back down towards the silken ropes, she bent and whispered into Brooke's ear.

"Are you okay?"

A nod was the only answer to her question.

"Try and relax. If you tense, the bindings will be more uncomfortable. I'm going to start on your legs next. Open or closed?"

"Open or closed?"

"Would you be more comfortable with your ankles together or tied to each leg of the chair? It's up to you."

"Together."

Squatting next to Brooke, she let her hand slide down one of the shapely legs and then back up to her thigh. Her hand was so warm she knew her palms were sweating. She let them glide down, stopping at Brooke's ankles to caress the slender joints. The delicate calves above the bindings were tight as the stiletto heels she wore kept them arched. Trying to focus on the task at hand was more difficult now that she was directly across from the silk panties peaking out from under the hem of Brooke's dress. She swore she could smell Brooke's excitement or maybe that was her own excitement. Either way, she knew they were both ready to combust, Brooke wouldn't be human if she wasn't. Catching a glance at her face, Luce saw her worry her lip, biting the corner of her mouth.

Doubling the rope, Luce placed the Lark's Head in the middle of the Brooke's legs, above her ankles, and began the binding processes again, and ending it with the same square knot she used on Brooke's wrists. Luce marveled at how delicate Brooke looked, her legs tilted to the side in a feminine pose. She couldn't drag herself from where she knelt without caressing Brooke's thighs one more time. Goose bumps tickled her palms again as a charge surged between their touch. How much more intimacy or trust could they share without Brooke knowing who her captor was?

"You look...distressed?" she whispered into her ear. "Are you scared?"

A single nod would be the only movement from Brooke.

"Of me?"

A slight nod and then Brooke cocked her head towards the sound of Luce's voice.

Luce moved around Brooke, letting her fingers trail up one arm, along her shoulders and down the other arm to her binding. "Don't be afraid. This is all about trust. Trust me, I won't hurt you. We don't have that kind of relationship."

Brooke's head followed Luce's voice as she continued to walk around her. The power that coursed through Luce felt like a drug she had mainlined into her veins. Standing in front of Brooke, Luce hiked her dress allowing her to squat in front of Brooke, their knees almost touching. As she ran her fingertips along Brooke's thighs, she closed her eyes and thought about all the things she could do to this woman if she were hers, but she wasn't so Luce stopped at the hem of the black dress following it down to the chair. Placing her hands on the chair seat she stood and hovered over Brooke, her nose barely an inch away.

"You have beautiful lips, the kind that need to be kissed, and kissed often." She brushed her face against Brooke's soft cheek sending a tingle through her body at the simple contact. "Do you trust me?"

There was no reaction. Moving to the other side of Brooke's face she repeated the action and asked the same question, but still no reaction. She liked being in control. She rarely gave up her power and when she did it was always on her terms, but seeing Brooke scared wasn't giving her the jolt she always got when she took the reigns with women. The power left her feeling vacant and powerless. Watching Brooke now reminded her of the night at the charity ball, how Brooke had practically crumbled in her arms when she heard Petrov's voice. The strong, self-assured, no-nonsense reporter trembled in her arms that night, and part of her wanted to protect Brooke.

"Take my blindfold off."

Luce's heart jumped into her throat. She hadn't planned on exposing herself, playing cat and mouse, yes, exposure, no. She chastised herself for not thinking things through, for letting her body overrule her head. She stood there frozen.

"Are you still there?"

"Yes."

"Take my blindfold off. I want to see you."

Chapter Twenty-four

Sitting in the chair blindfolded didn't scare Brooke. Being in the dark did and it was what happened when it was dark that gave her pause. She could feel the cold air chilling her skin. The dress she wore felt coarse and tight now that she was sitting, the hem hiked up her thigh and she wished had wore something more appropriate. Resting her hands in her lap, she fiddled with the signet ring she wore on her pinkie, a gift from her father that she never took off. Her anxiety peaked, and she wished they would hurry up and get the session started so she could get it over with. She had seen the ropes placed in an orderly fashion on the floor to her right. Seeing them laid out had almost made her reconsider her decision, but she was damned if she was going to let her fear get the better of her. Rocking her foot around the slender high-heel on her shoe, she noticed that the edge of the hard wooden chair didn't bite into the back of her thighs. *Interesting what you notice when you can't see,* she thought.

The cold air around her shifted, carrying the smell of perfume into the room. The scent of jasmine and lemons stimulated her senses, somehow familiar, but she couldn't put her finger on it. An electricity charged the air. Someone walked silently around her.

"Who's there? I can hear you breathing. Are you the one who's going to tie me up?"

"We call it binding," a voice said, in a whisper so
soft she could barely hear. "There's no talking during
the process, unless you're uncomfortable or it hurts.
Understand?"

Her heart raced so fast she thought she might
pass out. She bowed her head and tried to relax. As
instructions were given, she obeyed and said nothing.
Warm, firm hands guided her arms behind the chair and
began wrapping a length of rope around her forearms.
Every time a loop encircled her forearms, she felt her
pulse speed up that much faster. A whisper of a voice
said something to her but she couldn't hear it over the
blood throbbing in her ears. Suddenly, she felt strong
fingers glide up her arms and to her shoulders, goose
bumps rising in response to the touch. Her shoulders
were gently massaged and then another passing touch
drew down her arms, followed by another question.

All she could remember saying was "closed" in
response to the whisper. Her mind was slipping past a
point of consciousness as she felt the rope start to wrap
around her legs. Her focus waned with each passing
touch, with each wrap of the fibrous length, until finally
she bit her lip the pain pulling her back to reality. Too
late to run and too late to stop what was going on, she
thought about what was happening around her. The
sound the rope made as it dragged along the floor, the
smell of perfume that lingered around her, and the
sudden pain as the rope was cinched tight. The activity
around her stopped for a brief second and she wondered
why. Hands caressed her thighs and she vaguely heard
words whispered in her ear. Something about being
afraid made Brooke nod her head in agreement, and
then the words trust and relationship snapped her to
the present.

The soft hands and the perfume made Brooke suddenly realize that it wasn't a man binding her, it was a woman. Her body reacted viscerally to the touching as the woman's smooth face skimmed across hers.

"Do you trust me?" She heard whispered in her ear. *Luce!*

"Take my blindfold off." The room froze, nothing moved. "Are you still there?"

"Yes."

"Take my blindfold off. I want to see you."

Brooke felt the world close in on her. The idea that Luce was here confused her. Her body's own betrayal at having reacted to the touching, the binding, and the constraints, only added to her confusion. Was she responding because she liked being tied up or did she respond to being touched by Luce? She wondered if she had subconsciously known that Luce was her captor. A fine sheen of sweat broke across her body as she arched against the ropes holding her legs and arms. The firm bonds kept her controlled as she continued to struggle.

Hands cupped her face and she could feel thumbs run over her lips.

"Before I take the blindfold off, I want you to tell me how you feel. Think about the ropes that are holding you tight. Are you scared, frightened or maybe..."

The sentence fell off and then the hands that held her face released her. She tried to follow the footsteps that moved around the room. What was the woman doing? Brooke wondered as she heard a chair scrape the floor. She wrestled with the ropes on her arms, trying to pull her elbows apart to loosen the bindings, but it was no use, the knots were firm and tight. She was at Luce's mercy. She hoped it was mercy and not anger that she'd come face to face with.

"What did you expect to find here, Brooke?"

When the blindfold was pulled from her face, she tried to open her eyes, but the lights made Brooke squint. Her head down, trying to avoid the bright lights of the room, she looked at a pair of long legs ending in a pair of stiletto heels. *Nope, not Luce that's for sure,* she thought as her gaze followed the shapely legs up to a black dress and the face framed by long black hair and piercing green eyes.

"Luce."

"What are you doing here, Brooke? And don't tell me you're into the BDSM scene."

"I'm…doing research."

"How do you like your research so far?"

A smile pulled at the corners of Luce's mouth making Brooke wonder what she was thinking. *Did she know what effect Luce's touch had on her? Did she see her body responding to the caresses, or was Luce playing with her?*

"You have me at a slight disadvantage, Luce," Brooke said, raising her shoulders. "It seems you have all the power."

"Isn't that what you wanted to find out? How I feel being tied up? I mean that is why you're here isn't it?"

"I'm not sure I'm following."

Brooke didn't lie very well and her body language would alert, even those mildly observant, that she was lying. Her throat felt like it was closing up so she swallowed again and then coughed.

"Water?"

"Please."

Brooke couldn't help but stare at Luce as she stood, towering over her. The little black dress she wore fit like a well-worn glove. The way Luce walked in the dress made Brooke swoon. The confident swagger of her hips and the way she held herself made it known, to anyone looking, that Luce was all woman. Brooke wrestled with the image of the sexy woman who sat down in front of her offering her a drink from the bottle, the image of Luce tied up in her bedroom, and the woman in a tux at the charity ball. How could such diametrically opposed images be the same woman? If she was confused before, she was sure she was even more confused now. She had pigeonholed Luce into a nice, tight little box that had four sides, a top and a bottom. Now all she had was the top, Luce as the in control business woman, and the bottom, Luce tied up and spanked. Anything in the middle was a muddled mess in her mind.

"You look confused."

"I am."

"Don't be. I'm not that easy to put in a nice, tightly wrapped package."

Brooke shook her head at the analogy. Was she a mind reader too?

"What?"

"Funny you should say that, because I was thinking when I have you in a nice little box, you show up looking like that?" Brooke jutted her chin in Luce's direction.

"Ah, you mean looking like a girl and not a thug?"

"Sorta."

"You know the old adage you shouldn't judge a book by its cover and I'm not your—"

A knock at the door stopped the conversation. Sheepishly, a man in a dog collar and shorts peeked in.

"Excuse me, Ms. Potter I have a call for you. They

say it's urgent."

Passing the phone to Luce the man backed out the door and shut it quietly.

"I see your reputation is quite firmly in place, even here," Brooke said, cocking an eyebrow at the closed door.

"You could say that." Luce turned her attention to the cell phone in her hand. "Hello?"

"Frank."

Brooke tried to look away, pretending to find something interesting on the other wall, but if Luce wasn't going to take the call out of the room, then why should she have to ignore it?

"When? When you have it drop it off at the warehouse? All right, I have some business I need to finish up. Why don't you soften it up and we'll see where it gets us."

Brooke knew they were probably talking about someone and not an 'it'. If she could only get out of her restraints. She heard the cell phone close with a resounding clap and then felt Luce's hand on her shoulder.

"It seems it's your lucky night. I've got some business I need to take care of."

Walking to the intercom on the wall, Luce buzzed it, "Can you send someone in to take care of Ms. Erickson. She's done with her session. Thank you."

Sitting down in front of Brooke again, Luce ran her hand down Brooke's thigh smiling. A tingle snapped through Brooke's body at the contact making her blush. Being smitten was one thing, being bitten was another, and Brooke felt as if she was just shy of being bitten.

"Tonight's your lucky night. I have to cut our little session off. It's a shame really." Luce ran her hand over the ropes that tied Brookes legs together. "I was looking forward to showing you the ropes, so to speak."

"Hmm." Was all Brooke could eek out, watching the hand travel up her leg and to the hem of her skirt.

"By the way, I owe you one." Luce pointed to the mark on her neck. "I don't usually let someone tag me like this, so next time it's my turn."

The mark reminded Brooke of the other night at the club. It had shown her a different side of Luce, but the indifference Luce had shown her, while taking the phone call while practically fucking her had left her, shaken and full of doubt. She questioned everything about that night. She'd had too much to drink, that she knew. She had overstepped asking to see the tattoo, but she had lost all objectivity when she became physical with Luce. Brooke looked at her lips thinking about the searing kiss, the way Luce controlled her, and the scorching touch that almost made her orgasm. She had definitely lost her objectivity and crossed the line. Now, she needed to get back to the center, do her job, and be done with Luce Potter before she did something she would regret.

Before Brooke could say anything the door opened and Stella bounded through. "So, Brooke how'd ya like your…oh sorry, I thought she was alone."

"She's all yours."

"Oh, okay. Are you sure? I mean I can come back later."

"That won't be necessary. Our session is over. Good night, Brooke. I'm sure I'll be seeing you soon."

With that Luce was gone, leaving both women staring at the empty doorway.

"Fuck me. Holy shit, she's hot. Was she the person who did these? Oh god these look good. Wow, you lucky—"

"Stella."

"Oh sorry."

"Untie me, now."

"Oh, right. Oh, my god, do you know that woman?"

"You mean you don't?"

"No, I've never seen her before."

"She's never been here before?"

"Not that I know, but I don't usually come to these back rooms."

"Huh!"

"Who is she? God, I would switch sides for a piece of that rock candy. Hell, I'd pay her to tie me up and spank me."

"T.M.I."

"Okay, okay. Who is she?"

"Luce Potter."

"*The* Luce Potter?"

"Is there another?"

"Fuck me."

"I'd rather not." Brooke said rubbing her wrists. "Do you have my stuff? I need to make a phone call."

"Yeah, I dropped it on the couch when I came in. Wow, that's Luce Potter. Wait, isn't she the story you're working on? Oh shit, no way?"

"Nothing, I'd advise you to say nothing to anyone. She's a powerful woman and she could squish you like a bug, trust me."

"I wish. Oh, I would so love to be under her shoe. Did you see those shoes and those legs? Oh man."

"Stop already. Jeez." Brooke hit speed dial and waited. "Hey, can you get me an address for a warehouse? I think it belongs to Kaida Enterprises. Yeah. Okay call me if you find it. Thanks."

"Trouble?"

Shrugging her shoulders Brooke hoped it wasn't trouble, but the idea of Luce softening something up didn't give her a good feeling. Besides, she would only be guessing at the conversation she heard.

"I hope not."

"Okay, there you go. All done."

Brooke stretched her legs out and checked out the marks left behind by the ropes. The pattern of the braided nylon was red and branded on her leg. Reaching down she roughly rubbed the marks trying to rub them out. She wasn't sure if her research had been a success, but it had definitely left an impression.

Chapter Twenty-five

"Good morning can I help you?"
"Good morning, I have a breakfast appointment with Mr. Chambers."

"And you are?"

A smile barely broke Luce's stoic features. Things would be changing fast enough at the newspaper so she would humor the editor's assistant, this time.

"I'm assuming you have Mr. Chambers' appointment calendar in front of you, but if not, I'm the new CEO of the magazine, Luce Potter."

"Oh, my apologies, Ms. Potter. I have, Potter here," She said, looking down at the organizer in front of her. "I guess they didn't give us the particulars of who you are, I'm sorry."

"No problem. I'm sure that won't happen again."

"No, absolutely not. I'll make sure you get put on the security roster and I'll personally make sure to get you an ID card."

"Wonderful, now is Mr. Chambers in?"

"Yes, he's expecting you. Please follow me."

Luce was sure she could find the office herself, especially since it was three doors down the hall, but she would humor the woman who was obviously trying to make up for her mistake. As the door swung wide, she could see the editor racing around the office rearranging a few things. The meeting was a courtesy as far as she was concerned. She could have made changes without getting the editors input, but she had another agenda and being at the office would put her in a position to take care of it.

"Good morning, Mr. Chambers. How are you?"

Luce extended her hand, waiting for him to stop his prepping.

"Ah, Ms. Potter, how are you? Please call me John."

"Thank you, John. It's a pleasure to meet you. We didn't have a whole lot of time to talk at the club last week, so I'm glad you made time to meet with me."

"I couldn't very well say no to the new CEO, now could I?"

"You could, but I wouldn't recommend it."

"Of course. Please sit down. I've had some things prepared for our breakfast meeting."

"Great, why don't you tell me a little about yourself?"

Luce knew the meeting was going to take a while when John started down the long road on how he came to be the editor of the Financial Times. As his voice droned on and on, Luce caught a peek at her watch, noticing the second hand ticking ever so slowly. It was truly going to be a while, so she settled in with a cup of tea and her mind wandering through the magazine's corporate structure. She jotted a few notes, watching John stand up and walk to the window. He gestured wide, saying something about the changing scope of the financial world, and how the magazine had a duty to stay current and relevant. Tapping the eraser end of her pencil on her pad, she focused on the few notes she had taken and wondered how much longer before John took a breath.

"So," he said finally taking a breath. "I think that gives you a pretty good idea about those who work for us. Perhaps you can tell me what you're thinking."

Trust me you don't want to know what I'm thinking. Smiling, she motioned for John to take a seat. How had she missed his briefing on the employees? A mind fade, she knew she had checked out early in the conversation, but couldn't focus on his mundane explanations of the workings of the magazine.

"Could you tell me a little more about Brooke Erickson? And not the details on her resume. I've read that already."

"Oh, ah, Brooke, right." John fidgeted briefly then continued, "Yes, we're lucky to have her. She's a top notch investigative reporter."

"John." She held up her hand to stop him from continuing. "I know all that, I've read her stories, but what I want to know is, why? Why is she here when she could be globe trotting chasing the next big event in the world?"

John's sudden discomfort intrigued her. The wall he sent up was a red flag if she'd ever seen one. She tapped her pencil, still waiting for a response from the wary editor. Focusing on his face she could see he was in conflict. On the one hand, she was his new boss and she was sure he wanted to establish a good working relationship. On the other, he was obviously a friend of Brooke's, and probably worried about disclosing too much information. Clearing her throat made him look up at her and she took advantage by raising her eyebrows and shrugging her shoulders.

"This wouldn't have anything to do with the article she's writing about you, would it?"

"As they say, if you want to control the message,

you must control the messenger, but no. I might be able to stop Ms. Erickson, but another would pop up in her place and do the story. I'm wondering how the Financial Times was able to land a reporter of her caliber to write stories about money."

John visibly stiffened in his chair and then pursed his lips before responding. Luce was starting to wonder if she had opened a can of worms she might not want to know about. Maybe John was worried about betraying a confidence, but surely, he could understand her interest in all the employees of the magazine. It was her job to know about all employees in her employ and assess whether they were a potential risk to her success.

"Look, John. I'm sure you can understand my concern."

"No, no, I understand. I'm…look let me be honest, Brooke's a friend and I would hate to disclose something that might hurt her."

Now John had her full attention. What could have possibly happened that would cost Brooke her job?

"Are you saying you know something that could get her fired?"

"Oh no, it's not that at all. I mean, it's not like that at all. I mean…."

"John, relax, I'm not here to fire anyone, squash a story, or restructure the organization. At least not yet, but now you do have my full attention, so you can either tell me or I'll find out in other ways."

Luce knew she hadn't made it any easier for John to tell her about Brooke's background, but she wasn't the kind of boss that made people feel warm and fuzzy. It wasn't her style, so he would have to deal with it. If she was curious before, she was even more now that John was being so dramatic about Brooke's past.

"Look, I'm not a priest, a doctor or a lawyer, but I can assure you that what's said in this office stays in this office. I haven't gotten this far by compromising my ethics, regardless of what you've heard, John."

She caught John as he bit a nail then pulled at the jagged edge. He started to speak, making Luce lean in to hear his soft, almost boyish voice. "Brooke was working a story in Europe and her camera man was killed in front of her. She's been dealing with the trauma ever since. She had already quit that job when I heard about what happened. I called her up and offered her a job here and she took it."

Luce knew he was glossing over the experience and figured he knew more than he was telling. "So, what was the story?"

"The story?"

"Yeah, what was the story she was working on? What kind of story gets a cameraman killed?"

"Oh, um…she…she was working on a story on the Russian mafia. She was reporting on what they were doing abroad and in the U.S.. I think she was getting too close and they wanted her dead and got Mike instead."

The muscles in Luce's neck tensed and her gut suddenly felt like someone punched her. Petrov. Brooke's reaction to Petrov's voice at the charity ball made sense to Luce now. He had been her story, the reason she looked like she had seen a ghost and fell into Luce's arms that night. She hated the bastard and now she had another reason to want him out of her city.

"It all makes sense now."

"What you mean? What makes sense?"

"The charity ball. Petrov was there and Ms. Erickson looked like she'd seen a ghost."

"What? What're you talking about?"

"You didn't know? Weren't you at the charity ball with her?"

"Yeah, but she didn't say anything to me. Oh shit!" John slapped his forehead remembering Brooke's sudden exit from the ballroom. "She told me she needed to get some air. I figured it was all the people making her anxious, shit."

"Oh yeah, she was anxious all right, but it was Petrov that made her freak out."

"How do you know all this?"

"I was outside with her when he showed up, but I had no idea what was going on. Now it all makes sense."

"Oh god, I had no idea he was in town. She's not safe if he's here. She's got a lot of dirt on this guy. He's not a nice man."

John bit another nail and then dropped his hand when he saw her watching him. She felt sorry for the man, who had no clue what kind of danger Brooke might be in.

"No kidding. I've been trying to run him out of town for a while now."

"He's still in town?"

"He hasn't taken my warnings about leaving, so I'm going to assume he's still here."

"Shit. Does she know?"

"I'm assuming she does." Luce suddenly felt sorry for John, his star reporter was in jeopardy and he had no clue. "Is she in the office today?"

"She usually does paperwork, research, and stuff like that on Mondays, so I'm assuming she's in her office."

"Good. I wanted to have a word with her about the story. This is as good a time as any to have that discussion."

John rubbed his forehead and nervously ran his fingers through his hair. Luce wished she could say something to calm him, but she suspected that he was a worrier by nature. Knowing what she now knew about Brooke's former assignment, Luce knew she needed to make a decision about Brooke's current assignment. It wouldn't look good if she squashed the article so that wasn't an option. Chances were good that Brooke would write it if she worked for the Financial Times or not, so better to have her under Luce's thumb than pissed off and writing a revenge piece.

"I'll walk with you to her office."

"John, I don't want her knowing that I'm the CEO yet. In fact, other than you and your assistant, no one else knows about the change in CEO's. I'm sure you'll brief your assistant on my need for discretion." Luce stood, stretched and slipped her jacket on. "I don't want Ms. Erickson thinking she has to change the story she's writing. It wouldn't look right."

"I understand. You don't have to worry about my assistant. She's quite familiar with the need for confidentiality in the magazine world."

"Good, I'll be happy to make that announcement when it's time, but right now isn't the time. Besides, I'm hoping I can work out a solution to get rid of Petrov for good. That will solve all our problems, including Ms. Erickson's."

"I understand."

"Okay, lead the way."

The maze of cubicles was awash in activity. Phones ringing, people talking, and the click of keyboards echoed throughout the cavernous room. Luce was surprised anyone could focus with all the noise floating above them, but they did, and no one noticed her presence as she walked past them.

Stopping at a non-descript door without a nametag to identify its owner, John tapped on the outer wall before entering. Luce noticed the woman from the Dungeon sitting at the desk across from the office and raised her eyebrows in the woman's direction, as the assistant clearly mouthed the words, *oh shit.* Luce shook her head as the woman started to pick-up the phone. Obviously, she wanted to alert Brooke to Luce's presence, but it was too late as she stepped into the office behind John.

He cleared his throat and said, "Brooke, you have a visitor."

"John, I'm pretty busy, can you take a message?"

Brooke had her back to the duo and didn't look up from her computer. Looking around the room, Luce noticed the disarray and smiled. A mess was exactly as she imagined it would be for the fiery reporter. Nothing hung on the walls and the space lacked a warmth Luce expected to see. In fact, a few boxes sat partly open with the contents exposed. It was almost as if Brooke didn't expect to stay, so she hadn't unpacked or made the office her home.

"It's not a message Brooke, it's a person."

"What?" Turning Brooke started to stand then dropped back in her chair. "Oh, it's you."

"Nice to see you too, Ms. Erickson."

"Brooke?"

Turning towards John, she whispered, "What?"

"Don't worry, Mr. Chambers, I can take it from here. Thanks for meeting with me. I'll be in contact."

"It was a pleasure meeting you, Ms. Potter. Brooke."

"John."

The dueling names bantering back and forth made Luce feel as if she had witnessed a fight between siblings, rather than boss and employee. Both women watched John leave, softly closing the door behind him. The uncomfortable silence dragged on for a moment longer before they both spoke at the same time.

"So—"

"Well—"

"Go ahead."

"No, I'm sorry. You go first."

"May I?" Luce motioned to the chair in front of the desk.

"Of course, please sit."

"Thank you."

Brooke's stare made her feel as if she had something on her face. Instinctively Luce wiped her cheek above her neck, since that was where Brooke was focused. What had started as an innocent gesture to check on Brooke was soon becoming an exercise in restraint. The relaxed office instantly sizzled with energy as both women sized the other up. They hadn't seen each other since the night at the Dungeon almost a week before, and she hadn't stopped thinking about Brooke since. If she had been a different person, Brooke would have found herself, undressed, bound, and Luce knew the circumstances would have been much, much different. That's what puzzled her. Why was Brooke different from all the other women she had at her disposal?

Luce's indifference when it came to women was what kept her single, happy, and agitated most of the time. College had been a fun excuse to experiment. Watching the hot, sexy co-ed's was like sitting in a candy shop, trying to figure out what new delight she wanted to taste that night. Her ability to flip from butch to femme made it easy to find dates most of the time. Her swagger and being a "top" made her attractive to the girls wanting to experiment with women, and when she was in the mood, she dressed the part and had a fling or two with the women who liked something a little more femme. She hated the labels. She could be anything she wanted to be. Luce liked the subterfuge it created for those who thought they could pigeonhole her into a type. It was the same today, when someone thought they had her pegged, she came at them in a different manner and style, sending them off-kilter to reassess who and what she could be.

"You look different today."

"Really? In what way?"

The business suit wasn't any different than her normal attire, with the exception of the skirt. She had opted for it rather than the slacks. She knew that men would be looking at her legs and not listening to what she had to say. Calculated moves on her part to emphasis her assets, and make a surgical strike while their minds were still in their pants. The high heels were the icing on the cake. It made men look up at her, but also added to the overall package, and she played it up. She had gone in for the kill earlier, when she had met with a slobbering banker, before her meeting with John. A critical piece of her puzzle of divestitures was to add a financial institution was big enough to get into the global market of finance. Her newest acquisition today would allow her to do just that.

"I don't think I've ever seen you wear a skirt."

"Really, you don't remember the night at the Dungeon?"

Luce thought the pink hue Brooke's skin took on was flattering on the pale, porcelain skin, or perhaps she enjoyed embarrassing Brooke. Either way, she was being coy with the reporter, and she knew it.

"So, I suppose you've come to try and convince me to squash the story on you after the other night at the Dungeon."

Luce threw up her hands in feigned surrender. "Ah, you've caught me. I did come to douse your story in gas and set it aflame." She smiled at the joke, but continued when a skeptical look flickered across Brooke's face. "I've spoken with your editor, John, and it seems he sees the logic in my argument."

"Really?"

"Perhaps you would like to discuss it over lunch? I know a great restaurant nearby and we can discuss the merits of you continuing the story or other things?"

Her eyes roamed across Brooke's body and Luce was rewarded by the desired response. She smiled when Brooke's nipples hardened instantly with the innuendo. She knew Brooke's questioning and cynical mind would be hard at work dissecting her words. She was sure it was the same quizzical mind that had convinced Brooke that she needed to be tied up to figure out why Luce would subject herself to such torture. She had gone back through her recordings of Brooke's first time in her home and confirmed her suspicions. Brooke had indeed seen her session with Dr. Williams. It was hard to tell what her reaction was to the scene that played out before her. The darkness concealed her facial expressions, but each time Brooke turned to leave, she was drawn back to the door. If Luce had to guess, she would assume Brooke was a little more than intrigued by what she saw.

"I'm sure you have a few more questions for me. I know I have a few for you. But hey, if you aren't up to it, I understand."

If Brooke was surprised before, Luce was sure the reporter's mind was working overtime, if the staccato cadence she was tapping out with her pen was any indication.

"Um...."

Curiosity had driven Brooke to take a second interview with her, even after seeing Luce tied up, and even more, curiosity had pushed her to the Dungeon last week. She was almost certain Brooke wouldn't let this chance slip by either. She was counting on it. She didn't know if the topic of conversation would be about the article or about something else. Luce was voting for the something else.

"You know I'm slammed with deadlines right now. I'm not sure if I can afford to lose an hour or two. Perhaps the end of the week will be better for me."

She buzzed Stella in. Luce stood as the office assistant walked to the desk and waited for Brooke to say something.

"Hello Ms...?"

"Stella, please call me Stella," she said, blushing.

Extending her hand, Luce gently cradled Stella's hand in hers and spoke softly. "It's my pleasure, Stella to finally get to meet you. Dr. Williams speaks highly of you."

"I...um...it's my pleasure, I assure you."

Chapter Twenty-six

Brooke couldn't believe what was happening right before her eyes. Luce was sinfully sensual as she practically came on to her office assistant in front of her. The audacity of the woman who swaggered into her office on the arm of her editor and now flirted with Stella. How much more infuriating could the woman be?

"Stella?" she said, her voice tense. "Excuse me, earth to Stella."

"Oh, yes I'm sorry Ms. Erickson. Did you need something?"

Obviously not as much as you do, thought Brooke as she watched the two women smile at each other.

"I'm sorry I don't mean to intrude on your work day, Ms. Erickson, as you've said you're 'slammed' with work." Turning towards Stella she said, "You have a very dedicated boss. I offered to take her to lunch and she's politely declined."

"Oh, I'm—"

"That will be all, Stella."

"I was going to say, that if you can't have lunch, I'm free."

"Stella." The terse response made both women look at Brooke in surprise. "I mean, it seems that I've found an opening," She looked down at her calendar. "I'm more than happy to have lunch with Ms. Potter."

"Excellent. My apologies, Stella. Perhaps another

time." Luce winked at Stella and released her hand.

"I look forward to it."

"As do, I, I'm sure."

"Shall we?" Brooke walked towards the door without stopping. "See you in a few, Stella."

"Yes, Ms. Erickson. Very well played, Ms. Potter."

"Yes, there are many ways to skin a pussy...cat."

"So they say. I'll give your regards to my Mistress."

"Please do, and tell Dr. Williams she should expect a call if things don't go well."

"I will. Again, it was a pleasure to meet you, Ms Potter."

"Good afternoon, Stella."

Brooke practically sprinted to the elevator trying to get away from the flirtatious chemistry that was playing out in her office. Her own reaction to the two women touching sent fingers of jealousy throughout her body. Luce was practically mind-fucking Stella right in front of her. *How dare she,* she fumed, waiting for the ding of the elevator as it reached her floor. She didn't turn to see who the warm presence beside her was. She knew.

"I'm surprised you can run that fast in those."

Brooke looked down at her own choice of footwear and noticed the tall heels Luce had on, her short skirt and nicely-defined legs practically made her drool as her gaze followed up the taut body next to hers. She knew it was tight, having seen it naked. Oh, this wasn't working out. She had let Luce bait her into having lunch and now she knew it by the smug smile Luce wore. Refusing to justify the statement, Brooke looked back at the elevator and wished it would crash before reaching them, anything to stop what she knew was about to happen.

"You can always bail on lunch. I'm sure Stella would love to go in your place and report back, confirming what a lecherous lunch companion I am," Luce said, smiling.

"Oh, I'm sure you would like that, wouldn't you? A little dessert before lunch."

"Would it matter if I said Stella isn't my type? But then you probably think every woman is my type, don't you?"

"Not every woman, but I've seen enough to know—"

The ding of the elevator broke into Brooke's admonition of Luce's sexual proclivities. Stepping into the empty car, Brooke wished it had at least one other occupant, so she wasn't alone with the sexually explosive cargo she was riding with. Brooke stepped to the back of the car. When she turned she found herself face-to face with Luce, her hands on either side of her shoulders trapping her against the wall. Warm moist breath caressed her ear as she heard Luce inhale deeply before she spoke.

"For the record, I don't fuck everything I see, but I do go after what I want and I'm usually successful at getting it. Just look at my portfolio."

Luce stepped back, reached down for her briefcase and faced the door. The sudden emptiness made Brooke's body ache for the promise of a touch. She couldn't deny the attraction she felt for Luce The power, the swagger, and the self-confidence were all a turn-on. She had to turn this situation around quickly or it had the potential to spiral out of control.

"Are we talking about business now?"

"Aren't we always?"

The look Luce tossed over her shoulder at Brooke almost sent her to her knees. She felt the same erratic pulse beating in her chest, throbbing down her body to her wet underwear. Her sweaty palms made it difficult to hold her purse, so she slung it on her shoulder and rubbed her palms together hard enough that she thought they might catch fire. The warm air in the elevator seemed to crackle with energy as Brooke focused on Luce's back. Looking up, she could see Luce was studying Brooke's reflection in the polished steel, a cocky grin reflecting back. All she had to do was make it through lunch. She had put the final touches on the ending. Now she was ready to pass the story on to John and be done with it all.

Exiting into the lobby, Brooke noticed two women stand up as Luce moved closer to them. She stopped, spoke a few words to them, and then turned to Brooke.

"My car is this way."

The women followed close behind as they made their way out of the lobby and towards the parking lot. An extended black sedan pulled beside her and one of the women jumped to open the door for her. Assuming the car would be full, Brooke slid to the far side of the seat. Luce slid in practically next to Brooke as the car door shut behind her.

"Aren't they riding with us?" Brooke pointed to the small, empty seat across from her.

"Do you want them, too?"

"No, I mean, they do work for you, I assumed."

"They do, but they have the car behind me. You'll be safe with me. Relax, I won't let anything happen to you. If there is shooting I'll take the first bullet."

"That's not funny."

"I assure you I wasn't trying to be funny. Just practical."

"Chad, can you put up the privacy glass?"

"Yes, ma'am."

Brooke shook her head slightly as the black glass rose, cutting her off from the only other person in the car. Not that she thought he would do anything if she needed him, but it was worth a shot.

"What?" Luce questioned.

"Huh?"

"Why'd you shake your head?"

"You don't think for a moment that I believe we aren't being taped, do you?"

"Actually, if you're implying there's a camera or that the back seat is mic'd you'd be wrong. I conduct business back here and I don't want the world to know what I'm doing." She put a small bit of distance between them and turned towards Brooke, the tenor of her voice lowered. "Since we're on the question of cameras, did you like what you saw the first time you came to my house to interview me?"

Suddenly, the tension between them was so thick, even a knife couldn't cut through it. Brooke sat silently as she fumbled around in her head trying to put a coherent thought together. She'd been found out. There was no way to lie her way out of the question and she knew there'd be more. She thought for a moment longer before answering.

"First, let me say that it wasn't my intention to spy on you. Besides, it's all your fault."

"My fault, oh that's rich. You purport to blame me for sneaking around *my* house." Luce said, the frivolity in her voice lightened her tone.

"I didn't mean it quite that way. What I meant to say was that, the door was open and I was on my way to the bathroom when I heard a noise. By that time, it was too late. I mean I was afraid that you would hear me there and I…well. I just couldn't help myself," Brooke blurted out.

Staring down at her hands, she rubbed one of her nails, trying to ignore the laser-like stare she knew was being directed at her. The memories of that day were etched in her mind like the drive to work she took everyday. She could drive it everyday with her eyes closed, and when she closed her eyes at night, she saw Luce, tied-up. The red nylon rope bit into her delicate skin, leaving marks of the lash across her breasts, and finally Dr. Williams taking her to orgasm. The memories left an indelible mark on her brain that would never be replaced, not if she lived to be one hundred.

"But did you like it?"

"I—"

"Did it turn you on?"

"I mean—"

"Did it make you wet?"

The last question was said so close she could feel the warm, moist breath on her neck. Closing her eyes she leaned towards the feeling and waited.

"Tell me." Luce whispered.

"Yes." There, she'd said it.

Brooke finally admitted the experience was stimulating, erotic, and sensual. The silky wetness of Luce's tongue slid against the throbbing pulse in her neck. Her ear lobe was gently tugged into Luce's mouth. She bit it. Sharp needles of pleasure circled Brooke's nipples and ran through her body. Each sensation a prelude to a wave of pleasure that followed coursing through her body. The pressure of her hard nipples against her tight bra was exquisite. All she wanted to do was touch them, rub them roughly, and release them from their confines.

"We're here, Ms. Potter." The driver said through the intercom.

Luce keyed the mic. "Thank you, Chad." She grinned at Brooke. "Hungry?"

Chapter Twenty-seven

Disengaging from Brooke, Luce pulled herself together, straightened her jacket and studied Brooke, before she finally exited the car. The woman was a study in sensuality, the way she licked her lips when she was excited, the gentle caress of her tongue across the parted pink channel made Luce want to kiss them. Her closed eyes and soft moan, all clues that Luce was succeeding in her pursuit of this woman. After the night at the Dungeon, she had decided to entertain the idea of dating Brooke, The problem was, she didn't date. That wasn't quite true, she didn't have time for the normalities of dating. Then there was the issue of finding a woman who wasn't enraptured by her money, her position, or her lifestyle. Clearly, Brooke wasn't impressed with any of these things when it came to Luce and it intrigued her. Pulling away from the sexual tension between them, Luce cleared her throat and fixed her stare on Brooke.

"Ready," she said, frustrated.

"Oh, yes, of course."

Slipping out of the car, Luce reached for Brooke's hand and assisted her out. Holding on she gently pulled Brooke to the entrance of the restaurant without a word. The door magically open and a woman dressed in a kimono swept her hand wide.

"Kaida, *irasshaimase*." The gentle greeting was extended as the woman bowed.

"*Doumo.*"

"*Dou itashimashite,*" the petite woman said, bowing again. "Follow me please."

Still clutching Brooke's hand, Luce followed their hostess to the back of the restaurant. Kneeling down the hostess pulled a paper wall back, exposing a small room with a low table surrounded by pillows on the floor. Luce and the hostess exchanged words in Japanese before Luce slipped off her shoes and placed them by the door. Brooke automatically did the same and stepped into the room. The door behind them was closed with barely a sound. Luce took a seat on one of the pillows and motioned for Brooke to join her.

"This is my grandfather's favorite restaurant."

"It's beautiful in its simplicity."

"You think so?"

"I do."

Luce briefly remembered the day her grandfather brought her here to inform her of his decision to make her the head of the organization. It stood out as one of her most memorable moments in her life, so far. A waitress came in and spoke briefly to Luce, bowed, and quickly left.

"I hope you don't mind, I took the liberty of ordering for us," Luce said.

"Really?"

"I'm sorry, please," Luce said, embarrassed she had assumed she could order. "I'll call the waitress in and you can order whatever you like."

"It's fine." Brooke said, covering Luce's hand with her own. "I'm sorry, you invited me."

"No, no, I like a woman who knows what she

wants and isn't afraid to speak up."

"Really?"

"When I see something I want, I don't let anything stand in my way."

Oh yeah, she was definitely getting under Brooke's skin. The smoldering look Luce gave her made Brooke fidget. She could see that Brooke was struggling internally for self-control, darting her tongue out to wet her lips, then biting the corner of her mouth. If she only knew how that aroused Luce, she probably wouldn't do it again. A soft knock on the door drew Luce's attention away from the scene playing out in her mind.

"Come in," Luce said tensely.

A tray with wine and tea was placed on the low table. Before the drinks were poured, Luce waived off the waitress and nodded her agreement to a question asked.

Luce reached for the wine with an offer to pour. "This is a Fuji Apple sake," she explained. "It has a very mellow, but sweet taste. I hope you find it to your liking."

"Oh, I don't know if I should. I mean after the last time," Brooke protested.

"Please indulge me. I know it's still a work day. I promise not to get you drunk."

Watching Brooke gingerly take the glass, she poured herself a glass and waited. If the soft moan was any indication, Luce congratulated herself on the choice of wines. Now, if she played her cards right the wine wouldn't be the only good idea she had today.

"You're right it's very...refreshing." Brooke sipped again and then set the glass on the table. "Question."

"Answer."

"Why do you like to be tied up?"

Luce practically spit her mouthful of wine before she swallowed it with a resounding gulp. Wiping the corners of her mouth, she wiped her hands on a hot towel that accompanied the wine.

"You don't beat around the bush, so to speak," she said, chuckling at the double meaning.

"Since we've already established that I was there and what I witnessed, why 'beat around the bush' so to speak?"

"This isn't exactly polite dinner conversation now is it?"

"Good thing this isn't dinner." The look Brooke gave Luce practically melted her clothes off. If she thought she had Brooke pegged, she would have to think again, it seemed.

"Fair enough, but I get to ask you one intimate question."

"Is this the Japanese version of spin the bottle?"

Luce smiled and sipped from her glass again. Now, she was the one that was going to need the liquid courage it seemed. *Careful what you ask for Brooke,* she thought, studying her guest.

"I wouldn't know, I never played spin the bottle. Perhaps you'll show me one day."

"Now wouldn't that be interesting."

"Wouldn't it though?"

"So, back to my question, why?"

Trying to delay her answer, Luce pulled her jacket off and laid it beside her. She tugged at her blouse again, the heat pouring off her.

"Honestly," Luce said raising her eyebrows and smirking. "I don't do it that often, first off. Secondly, it isn't about sex as much as it's about allowing someone else to take control."

"But I saw you, I mean you–"

"Orgasm?"

Brooke blushed from her ears to her chest. Luce watched her hesitate and then drain the sweet liquid. Refilling the empty glass, Luce locked eyes with Brooke and smiled as long lashes dropped and hooded the dilated pupils. If Brooke wasn't careful she was giving off all the signs of being subservient to Luce's domination. The reaction wasn't only limited to the deepening blush and the lowered eyes. Brooke's blouse tented as her nipples hardened.

"Don't be embarrassed. I find it fascinating that you would go to such lengths to research a story. How did you like your time at the Dungeon?" Luce asked, knowing two could play this game.

Luce's fingertips casually stroked across the back of Brooke's hand tracing the raised veins. When Brooke didn't pull back she continued her path turning over Brooke's hand and caressing the palm and then the wrist. Brooke cleared her throat, drawing Luce's attention back to the now less than composed look on Brooke's face. Smiling, she waited, then cocked an eyebrow.

"So, the Dungeon."

"Oh, right. I would be lying if I said it wasn't…" Brooke's eyes searched Luce's face for the right word.

"Stimulating?"

"No."

"Sensual?"

"No."

"Titillating?"

"You're purposely trying to derail me, aren't you?"

"Can't blame a girl for trying can you?"

Another soft knock on the door broke the gaze they shared. The hostess entered again, only this time she had a stringed instrument with her. Bowing her head, she strummed the instrument and began to sing softly. Luce patted the seat next to her and whispered, "Sit over here so you can see."

Sliding next to Luce, Brooke watched intently as the geisha sang a low, melodic tune.

"What is she saying?"

"She's singing about a lost lover. His journey sent him away never to return."

"Do they do this for everyone?"

"No, this is usually reserved for male customers, but I asked her if she wouldn't mind indulging me, since my grandfather isn't here."

Wearing a dress, Brooke had to sit on her side with her legs together. Leaning on her arm put her closer to Luce, who was enjoying the close proximity they were sharing. Looking down at the head practically resting on her, Luce wanted to reach up and run her fingers through the soft brown mane, tumbling in front of her tauntingly. The soft fragrance of Brooke's perfume, mingled with her own spicy, warm scent, and Luce was having a hard time focusing on the singers voice. Her body trembled as she watched Brooke's gently sway towards her, then lean back slightly on her chest.

"Oh, sorry."

"No worries."

The song ended and the geisha gently closed the door behind her, leaving the pair barely touching. Reaching up, Luce threaded her fingers into the soft tresses and turned Brooke's head towards her. Her lips barely parted, she inhaled Brooke's scent and closed her eyes in solitude. Gently pulling Brooke's head back, she placed a delicate kiss on the waiting lips, savoring the sweet taste of sake that lingered. Her slick tongue glided over Brooke's lips begging for an invitation to enter. A soft moan vibrated through to Luce's tongue as it dueled with Brooke's for domination. She felt the warm touch of Brooke's hand cupping her breast, then thumb her rock hard nipple. A guttural moan escaped her own lips as she slipped further into Brooke's mouth. There was no way she could touch Brooke since she kept them both upright leaning on her arm. Frustrated, she broke the kiss and let her mouth slide down Brooke's throat claiming it for her own. Gently sucking, she remembered the love mark Brooke had left on her own neck and thought twice about leaving her own behind. Bending more she traveled down the front of Brooke's blouse, a faint wet stain followed the path to the one breast she could access. Tenderly, she bit the erect nipple through the satin blouse and lace bra.

She felt her head being pushed back briefly as Brooke unbuttoned her blouse and pulled her bra down, giving Luce access to the puckered nipple. Rolling her tongue around the areola, Luce heard a gasp and a low moan as she sucked it into her mouth. Brooke worked the pins out of her bun and she felt her hair fall forward shielding her face from view, as Brooke forced her down harder onto her breast. Pushing her head back, Luce let her teeth graze the tip and then pull it.

"Fuck."

Looking up, she stared into Brooke's glazed eyes. "I will if you'll let me."

"No, it's my turn," Brooke said pushing Luce backwards onto the bamboo mat. Leaning over Luce, Brooke brushed Luce's hands away and began to unbutton her blouse. Pulling it open from Luce's skirt, she smiled, seeing the black lace peak out from underneath. "Just when I think I have you figured out."

"Don't waste your time trying to figure me out. Fuck me."

"Oh I plan on it."

Luce felt her breast palmed over the lace. The coarse material roughened up her nipple, then suddenly was replaced with the warmth of Brooke's mouth. The tenderness of Brooke's touch sent a jolt to her clit. Her body arched in response. She felt the tip pinched as Brooke covered her mouth, her tongue probing urgently. Brooke's lips slowly worked their way down Luce's neck and back up to her ear where she whispered, "I wanna taste you."

The request was barely audible as the blood pounded erratically in Luce's ear. Before she could respond, Brooke lowered herself down her body. Brooke's naked breasts pressed against the length of her as she traveled down. Brooke pushed Luce's skirt up as she raised her hips.

"You're right, I shouldn't waste my time trying to figure you out," Brooke said. Wearing panties wasn't an option with Luce's tight skirt, so she'd opted to go without. "Thank god you didn't wear a pencil skirt."

"Thank god," Luce breathed out.

Pushing Brooke's head down, her warm breath caressed Luce's swollen clit making her jerk. The pressure of Brooke's tongue almost sent her over the edge before she had a chance to compose herself enough to enjoy the touch. Her body tensed at the contact. She tried to control her inner struggle with the orgasm taking root. Brooke flicked her clit back and forth, then assaulted it, flattening out her tongue against the hard surface. Threading both her hands into Brooke's hair, she rode out the orgasm that peaked, grinding herself against the slick tongue. Luce wanted to spread her legs to let Brooke enter her, but Brooke had wrapped her arms around her ass, forcing her hips up, pushing herself into Brooke's mouth. Just when she thought she could breathe, she felt Brooke start licking her again. This time Brooke pulled Luce open enough to get her tongue under her clit and rub her there. Her body reacted by pushing up and exposing more of herself, and suddenly she was on the peak of another orgasm. Every muscle bunched tighter as she spiraled out of control, jerking with each stroke of Brooke's tongue. She pushed Brooke's head and begged her to stop.

"Please."

Another flick of her tongue and Brooke raised her head, smiling. Reaching for the warm towels on the table, Luce watched as Brooke made a show of licking her lips and then wiping the moisture from her chin. Slowly, carefully, Brooke wiped at Luce's wetness, tapping her legs to open them so she could finish the job. The smirk on Brooke's face made Luce wish they had opted for lunch at her place, since there was no way lunch would wait.

Tossing the towel on the table, Brooke seductively crawled up to Luce and whispered, "I'm still hungry."

Chapter Twenty-eight

Her heart raced as she strode to the front door of the warehouse. Barking quick orders to Lyn and Sasha, she dispatched Lyn to the back and ordered Sasha to come with her. Blocking the noonday sun from her eyes, she scanned the periphery of the warehouse. Nothing. Looking down the street, the only cars were ones she recognized belonging to her associates.

"Let's go. If anything happens to me, kill anyone who isn't one of ours and get to my grandfather. He'll be waiting. Take him to the jet and get him to the island. I expect you to protect him with your life. Do you understand?"

"Of course, Kaida." Sasha pulled the heavy wooden door to the side, peered inside, and waited until Luce eased into the dark warehouse. The cold dampness was a welcome change from the heat of the day. She pulled on her leather gloves before drawing her semi-auto from her back. Luce flipped the safety switch, ready for combat. The muscles in her arms flinched as she tightened her grip on the gun and extended it out in front of her. She pivoted from left to right and back again, looking for anything that might be out of the ordinary as she made her way to the lit office. Getting closer she could hear a familiar voice booming inside.

"Fuck you, asshole."

She heard a thud and someone spitting and more

cursing. She crept closer to the door. A man was seated with three men standing over him. The familiar blonde hair made her grimace— JP. Sasha looked from the office to Luce, awaiting instructions. Tossing her head up, she motioned for Sasha to position herself above the office.

"You'll have a better vantage point from up there. Shoot anything that moves," Luce whispered.

Luce waited. Sasha nodded her agreement silently, and took up her position on the catwalk above the office. She visually checked around the warehouse once more, trying to ease her mind. JP wasn't to be trusted. Luce wouldn't put it past him to use himself as bait to catch her with her guard down. She walked into the office and all three men bowed. In unison they called out, "Oyabun".

"Aw, the old man is here."

"Sorry to disappoint you, JP."

Luce couldn't see the shocked look on his face, but she knew it was there and she relished in the knowledge that she was about to exact a little retribution tonight for her mother's death. Walking up to her father, she threaded her fingers through his thick hair and pulled his head back to stare down into his eyes.

"Well if it isn't my little girl. Hi, baby. How are you?"

The sickening sweet way he spoke made Luce want to puke. The last time he referred to her was at her mother's funeral. The 'slant eyed bitch' comment had been like a brand on her skin, something she would never be able to get rid of, no matter how hard she tried to forget. Seeing his face up close, she noticed he had aged around the eyes, the same green eyes she had, but now his were dull, almost lifeless. A small bruise had started to swell-up below his left eye on his cheek bone. Gray strands of hair were barely noticeable throughout his blond locks, but she could see them. Anger started to breed in her heart, facing the biological donor responsible for her birth. She wanted to wipe the arrogant smile off his face right now, but patience would prove her the better person, if she let it.

"Hello, JP." She saw the bruise on his face. "Who did this to him?" When no one answered, she looked at the three men and demanded, "Who. Did. This?"

Sammy cleared his throat and spoke. "I did Kaida. He swung at me and I defended myself. That's all."

"Hmm."

"Bullshit. The asshole, snuck up on me and hit me when I turned around."

"I doubt it. See his pinkie? He paid for not telling anyone when you were in one of my clubs, laughing it up, and drinking my beer. So, I doubt he would risk my wrath a second time."

Sammy held up his right hand so JP could see that he had paid for his first mistake. The bandage on the pinkie had a red tinge to it and made Luce wince inside. It was still tough to think she had witnessed the amputation, but she had an image to protect.

"Fuck, you're a brutal bitch," JP spat out as Luce kept his head pulled back.

"You have no idea. So, tell me why you were snooping around my businesses, again?"

"It isn't a crime to have a beer, is it?"

"It is when you're hanging out with the Russians and in one of my businesses."

Luce could see the muscles working as JP clenched his jaw tight. He was going to be a pain in her ass until she dealt with him, and she now had her grandfather's permission to handle the issue he brought upon her family. Looking down his chest she caught a glimpse of chrome pop out from under his jacket. Reaching for the chrome, she pulled a .357 revolver from a shoulder holster. She shot Sammy a look and shook her head. It pissed her off that he'd missed something so potentially dangerous. She would deal with that disappointment at another time. This time was reserved for a family reunion that wouldn't end well.

"You're such a fucking cowboy, JP. A chrome revolver, really? How come I'm not surprised?"

Hefting the weight in her hand, she noted the pearl handles. Her father was never a practical man from what she remembered and his choice in guns confirmed he still had an even bigger ego. Pushing his head forward as she released her grip on JP's head, she took a step back and turned the gun over in her hand. It was impractical, clunky, and more of a show piece than a working piece of equipment. Nothing like the .380 she strategically placed back in her waistband. Rolling the cylinder, the light reflected off the ridges of the spinning barrel. Pulling the catch she emptied the bullets. Luce made sure JP was watching as she slid a single bullet into one of the chambers. She made a show of closing the cylinder with the flick of her wrist. Hearing it lock, she spun the cylinder again. When it stopped she looked at her father.

"So, tell me again why you're here, JP."

Pointing the business end at her father, she cocked her head, squinted her eyes, and waited. If he was scared, he didn't show any sign of it. He looked down the barrel pointed at his forehead.

"You wouldn't dare."

"Oh, but I would. Now, let's try this again. What

are you doing here, and don't make me ask again."
Luce pulled the hammer back one click, feeling the hatch pattern on the hammer bite into her thumb. One more click back would make the gun ready to do what it was made to do, kill. Locking eyes with JP, her stoic features didn't change. In fact she hardened her stare at the one man she hated more than Petrov.

"I wasn't doing anything. I was having a drink in a club, relaxing. I didn't know it was one of your grandfather's."

"It isn't one of his. It's one of mine and I think you knew that, didn't you?"

"Since when do you have the money to own a club?"

"Since my grandfather made me Oyabun. I own everything now, JP."

"Well, this changes things now doesn't it?"

"Not for me."

Another click of the hammer, and it was ready to do her bidding. She was in control over her father's life and she liked the feeling. Her heart was beating so hard she could hear it pounding in her ears as the blood rushed through her body. She had waited for this moment for decades and she wasn't about to be denied. Putting the barrel against his thigh, she moved close enough that her nose was almost touching his. She wanted him to look her in the eyes when he lied, again.

"Last time, sure you don't want to change your story?"

"You won't shoot me, I'm your father."

Luce looked at her genetic maker and smiled wickedly. She hated him more than anything on this earth, and here he was toying with the idea that he could play the 'daddy' card. That somehow being his daughter, she would give him a pass for all the things he had said and done in her life. Oh, was he going to be disappointed. Luce pulled the trigger. The empty pop echoed through out the warehouse. It was his lucky day.

"I guess this is your lucky day. So far." Luce spun the cylinder.

"Are you crazy? Do you know who I am, you fucking bitch?"

"Aw, now that's the father I know and love. Welcome back, Daddy. Now back to my question, what were you doing in my club?"

"Nothing. I told you I was there to have a little fun. Now untie me, I'm your father, so show me some respect. You do know what that is, don't you?"

Pulling the hammer back once, she heard the click echo through the room. The second click caused JP's eyes to widen. His brow furrowed challenging his daughter. Luce chuckled, clearly he didn't know her anymore. That was to her advantage.

"I hate to disappoint you, but—" Her father screamed as the bullet passed through his thigh. The smell of cordite filtered up and scorched her nose, making her eyes water. "You being my father means nothing to me."

Luce stepped back while JP stomped his leg, trying to put the pain out of his mind. Tears rolled down his cheeks. He clamped his mouth shut, pressing his lips tight as if somehow it would lessen the pain. JP glared at Luce. Anger rolled off of him, and his body tensed against the waves of pain spreading through his rigid body.

"Let's try this once more." She dropped the empty

casing from the cylinder and replaced it with another bullet. She spun the cylinder again. Luce pressed the warm tip of the barrel against his other thigh. "What were you doing in my club?"

Their gazes locked. His challenging, hers questioning. She notched the hammer back one click and waited. JP's breathing labored. He gasped when Luce moved her face closer to his. Arching an eyebrow, she eased the hammer back to its final resting place, ready to be deployed, again. JP closed his eyes and waited. His lips sealed tight to suppress the scream on the verge of release.

"Nothing?"

Luce looked over at the three standing behind her. Their dispassionate faces fixed on hers as she looked at one and nodded towards the table. "Grab that rag and put it over his mouth. You." She pointed to another of her underlings. "Close the door and make sure no one's accidentally wandered into the warehouse to investigate, just in case Lyn or Sasha missed them."

Sammy stood silently by awaiting his orders. His hands trembled giving away his fear. Luce knew he worried this might blow back on him again. *Poor fellow.* She sighed. She would have to meet with him to put him back on track with the organization. Accidents happened. That's why they were called accidents, but in her organization they cost people their lives. Focusing back on her father, she pushed the nozzle of the barrel harder into his leg.

"Last chance, Father."

He closed his eyes, a signal that he wasn't going to give her what she wanted. This time when she pulled the trigger, his leg jerked as the bullet went through his thigh and out his heel. The agonized screams into the towel were slightly audible, but the man holding the towel pushed tighter on JP's mouth. "Take it off. Let him breathe." Luce said, casually opening the cylinder and dumping the spent cartridge into her hand. Inserting the four remaining bullets into the cylinder, she could smell the coppery odor of blood and cordite mixing, filling the room. She steeled herself for what was about to come. She owed her father nothing. The fact that he had contributed to her biology was a footnote on the long list of things she and her mother had to endure at his hand while they were a family. Some things couldn't be forgotten or forgiven, not to Luce. Remembering how at peace her mother looked as she lay in the mahogany casket, buffeted any feeling of empathy she might have for her father. No matter what she did, he would always be with her. She would never be able to forget him because every time she looked in the mirror, his eyes would stare back at her.

Blood pooled at JP's feet. She stepped back and ordered his legs wrapped with tourniquets. They would minimize the mess that the cleaning team would have to take care of later. The pallor of death covered JP's face. A grey tone replaced his normally pale coloring. His head flung forward as he passed out from the shock of being shot.

"Nuh, huh, you don't get off that easy, you bastard. Wakie, wakie. I want you to experience everything, Daddy. Like mom did when you hung her." Luce slapped his face to bring him around and ordered Sammy to bring her some water. Pouring it over his head, he pulled up, gasping as he breathed in the liquid. "Good, now are you taking me serious? Or would you like another example?"

"I told you—"

"Stop."

Luce slapped his face, a handprint appeared on his cheek as the water enhanced the stinging of the slap. She was losing patience with JP, and if he didn't know it yet, he soon would. She jerked back on his hair, and bent to whisper in his ear. "Listen to me. I know you're working with Petrov. In fact, I know you bragged about being able to deliver me, dead or alive. Now, the question is, do I deliver you to him, dead or alive?"

Releasing his head it slumped forward, his chin practically hitting his chest as it bounced. A maniacal laugh bubbled up from his despair, confusing Luce. Had he lost his mind, or was the pain so great that it clouded his judgment? Tossing his head back, he roared in laughter.

"You are so fucking screwed and don't even know it. You played right into our hands."

"What're you talking about?"

Luce stayed calm. She had seen JP try to weasel his way out of things through lying, so she wasn't playing along this time. Waiting, she absent-mindedly rolled the cylinder on the revolver, and the clicking echoed through the office. The muscles between her shoulders bunched together as tension filled her body. JP continued to laugh. She slammed the butt of the gun in his face, making him pause before shooting her a dirty look. Luce smiled at his dirty, tear soaked face. After tonight she would never it see again.

"Hmm, the way I see it, the only one screwed is you, JP. You have two holes..." Looking down at his legs, she corrected herself. "Make those three holes in your legs and the night isn't even over. So, if you even think you have any leverage here, you might want to reconsider your options."

"You're a little girl playing in a man's world, Luce. You have no idea what you've gotten yourself into do you?"

"God, you are so dramatic, JP."

Rolling the cylinder, she placed it against his temple and pulled the hammer back one click. Taking a deep breath, she steeled herself against the rage building deep inside, trying as hard as she could to temper it with patience, but it was no use. She closed her eyes and saw her mother's beautiful face. Her soft, almond shaped eyes seemed to close more when she smiled. Luce would often giggle and ask her mother if she could still see her when she smiled. Her mother's response was, *"Of course, Kaida. You are always in my mind."* Then she would bend down, cup her face, and kiss each of her pudgy cheeks. How she missed her mother, and thanks to the bastard sitting in front of her, taunting her, she would never see her again, never kiss her good night, never feel herself wrapped in a warm loving hug, ever. Her life had been replaced with the cold, hard reality that letting someone in might get them killed, so she adjusted her life accordingly. It was all *his* fault and she owed him nothing but her hatred. She felt tears threaten but swallowed her pain. She would be damned if he would see her cry, he didn't deserve that pleasure.

"Any last words?" The cold, dead tone in her voice made JP turn and look at her. If he thought he would find hope in her eyes he was wrong.

"Wait."

"You have no life lines, no friends to call, no one to help you, JP."

"Really?" He gasped. What about that little reporter you're seeing or your grandfather? Did you think I would be without options, Luce?"

"What're you talking about, old man? You have nothing to bargain with." Luce pressed the barrel harder into his temple.

"You really didn't think I would come alone did you?"

"Don't try and bullshit me. You don't have friends, JP, and it doesn't matter, you're going to die for what you did to my mother."

"Maybe you should listen to me for once, Luce. It could cost you, dearly."

Looking down at her watch she said, "You have five minutes."

Luce tossed the revolver on the table and took out her .380. She aimed it at JP. "Tick, tock, asshole."

"You know that old saying, keep your friends close and your enemies closer? Let's say that Frank's one of us."

Someone gasped behind her. Luce looked at the surprise evident on all three of the men's faces. They were as stunned by the revelation as Luce was. But why would Frank turn on her grandfather?

"That's bullshit. Frank's one of you? Don't make me laugh.

"Seems he didn't like the change in tradition. Actually, he was told to kill you, but I told 'em I would take care of you myself. Then you reassigned him to protect your grandfather, so they figured if you wouldn't come willingly, they could kill the old man. There's no love lost between me and the old man, but you, that's different."

Luce tried to wrap her mind around the idea that Frank had switched sides and that JP would be the one to save her life. The twists had her head spinning as she thought about all the things Frank was privy to, the dealings of the operation, the family connections, and her own grandfather's concerns about Frank. She had easily dismissed them, but now here she was being confronted with the very issue her grandfather had warned her about, insubordination.

"And the other person, you said there were two people to be killed. Who's the other one?"

"That reporter you've been getting real friendly with, what's her name? Brooke or something like that. Seems she dodged a bullet meant for her over in Europe. Petrov saw her at the charity ball and figured she's following him, so he wants her out of the way."

Wrong place, wrong time, it was all so coincidental now that Luce thought about it all. Looking over at Sammy, his head hanging, she knew something didn't make sense.

"Sammy, do you know anything about this?"

"Oyabun?"

"What do you know about all of this?"

"Nothing Oyabun, I followed orders. I'm sorry."

"What do you mean, you followed orders?"

"When you accused me of not reporting seeing JP at the club, I was told to admit that I had seen him." Sammy pointed at JP. "Frank told me to cover for him. I saw Frank talking to the Russian, but Frank said he was telling him to get out. That's all, *Oyabun*."

"And the ceremony, when my grandfather asked Frank to commit *seppuku*, you stood up for him again. You let him help you cut off your pinkie."

"He forced me to cut it off. I was going to tell you everything, but Frank said I would be the one to die after he committed suicide. He said that you would kill me."

"That bastard."

Her father had a smirk on his face that she wanted to knock off, but she was confused. Was he supposed to kill her or was he trying to save her? How could she have been so trusting of Frank? Trust was earned in their organization and Frank had earned his in spades. He was the perfect mole, no one would suspect such a high ranking member of the Yakuza family, not even Luce, who was raised to trust Frank. How could she have dismissed her grandfather's concerns about Frank, and then to make matters worse, have him protect the only thing that mattered to her? Tamiko.

Life was short for someone who betrayed their family. The rules were clear and if what JP said was true, Frank's life was over, but how would she notify her grandfather without arousing suspicion?

Chapter Twenty-nine

The phone call had been short and sweet: Meet Luce at her warehouse tonight. Looking back down at the directions she had hurriedly scribbled on the napkin, Brooke could barely make them out. Was she supposed to turn right on Cambridge or left on Seaboard? *Shit*, why hadn't she paid closer attention to the man's voice on the other end? She recognized it—at least she thought she did—as Luce's friend, Frank. He had said Luce wanted her to see how she did business, and that if she wanted to complete the story she was working on, she should meet her there at nine p.m. Her reporter mind went into overdrive after the phone call. Suddenly, Brooke felt like she was back in Orsha, behind the linen warehouse.

Her nerves were on alert as she weaved her way around the old, wooden warehouses. The pounding in her head only added to the anxiety she was feeling. Her gaze bobbed from one building to another, searching for something, anything familiar, but nothing looked familiar. The streetlights barely gave off enough light to see the numbers stamped on the exterior of the buildings, at least those that had them. A set of cars parked outside of a particular building down the street caught her attention. She slowed to turn down a side street and then made another turn, taking her off her course.

Killing her lights, she hugged the steering wheel

and squinted in the darkness, trying to make sure she didn't hit anything. The meeting wasn't supposed to take place for another hour, but something about the phone call didn't set well with Brooke. If Luce wanted her to go to a meeting to observe how she did business, why wasn't she the one to call? Secondly, they had seen each other earlier. Why didn't Luce say something then? Nothing was adding up, but she couldn't stop the reporter side of her from digging into whatever was going on.

Pulling up next to a deserted loading dock, Brooke shut her car off and looked around. Nothing moved as she checked her rearview mirror and her side mirrors. Pulling the hood of her sweatshirt on, she looked at her reflection in the mirror and smiled. Black wasn't her color. Worse was the big red "look at me" car she had driven to the warehouse district tonight.

"Oh well, you have to work with what you have," she said, quietly shutting the door to her Mercedes. She ran across the driveway, ducked behind a building, and slid along its side to the edge. Glancing around, she darted across to the next building and waited, listening for something, anything out of the ordinary. What that sounded like she wasn't sure, but she knew what footsteps sounded like. She didn't hear any. So far. Squatting down, she slid again along side the building and peeked around the corner. Light reflected off a car parked in front of one of the warehouses three buildings down. As she turned to run across the expanse between the buildings, a hand covered her mouth and held her back.

"Don't move."

Oh shit, oh shit, oh shit. Brooke had been set-up. Before she could do anything, she heard the soft *thwap* of a bullet shot through a silencer and then the thud of someone hitting the ground behind her. Being held still wouldn't have mattered, Brooke stood frozen in place. Fear anchored her where she stood until she heard movement behind her.

"Move." A woman pulled her arm in the direction of the warehouse. She crouched and Brooke followed her lead, crouching behind her. The woman peeked around a corner then popped her head back. Her finger up over her lips signaled for Brooke to be quiet. Her legs felt like jelly as she stood again. She followed the woman who shuffled quietly between the buildings. Brooke stopped against the side of a building. She felt herself starting to hyperventilate, and her erratic breathing and the wall were the only thing holding her upright.

"You need to keep moving. Come on." A soft feminine voice whispered. She didn't push Brooke. Looking from side to side, the woman rubbed Brooke's back, clearly she was aware of Brooke's struggle to breath. "I need to get you to a safe spot. Can you walk?"

Brooke nodded her head, standing slowly. She grabbed her knees to keep from falling forward. There was no way she was going anywhere and she knew it. Anxiety kept her frozen, glimpses of Mike laying in a pool of blood filled her vision. She felt her body picked up slung over the shoulder of the woman. Every step forced air from her lungs. Trying to time the steps, she sucked in a small breath each time the woman bounced in her stride. The ground passed by her as she tried to focus on each heel as it came into view. Counting the strides helped keep her mind occupied until finally she found herself deposited on the cement floor of a dark building.

"Who is it?"

"The woman, Kaida was with this week. I think her name is Brooke. Get the boss."

Brooke drifted in and out of consciousness, and the voices swirled around her, coming in and out of focus. A warm hand touched her face, and then she heard a familiar voice.

"What is she doing here? Brooke. Brooke, look at me."

Her eyelid was peeled back and a face, out of focus, came into her view. Pulling her head away, she squinted her eyes and tried to focus on Luce's face.

"What happened?" Luce said.

"I saw her enter the warehouse district. She went a few blocks over, probably thought she was staying out of sight. I made my way over to her and saw one of the Russian's following her. I don't think she knew he was back there."

"What happened to the Russian?"

Silence.

"I had to shoot him. He was almost on top of her by the time I got to her. There was no way I was going to let him get her."

"Good job Sasha. Lyn, get a team out here and clean up that body. Dump him on Petrov's door step."

Petrov. Brooke sucked in a breath at the mention of the Russian gangster's name. Brooke tried to sit-up, but felt her head spin, so she lay back down again.

"Calm down. You're safe. I'm not going to let anything happen to you." Her head was cradled against Luce's chest as Luce wrapped her arm around her shoulders. "What're you doing here, Brooke?"

She caught a whiff of blood on Luce's clothes and stiffened. "You're bleeding. What happened?"

"It's not my blood, don't worry."

"What's going on Luce?"

"First, tell me what you're doing here."

Rubbing her eyes, she pulled back and looked at Luce. Luce's cold stare frightened her. Something was wrong, very wrong and she suddenly wished she had listened to her inner voice and not the one on the phone.

"I got a phone call from some guy who told me that you wanted to see me here. He gave me directions to the warehouse and a time to meet you, but I came early. It didn't seem right, I thought if you wanted me to see your operation in action you would have told me earlier."

"What guy?"

"Your guy. You know that guy you always talk to on the phone. It sounded like him, so I said I'd meet you here. Like I said, he gave me directions and a time to meet you."

"What time did he say?"

Brooke heard the concern in Luce's voice as she quizzed her. "Nine p.m. What time is it now?"

Everyone looked at their watches and then looked at Luce. It was twenty minutes to nine.

"Get everyone and get the hell out of here. If they aren't already here they will be. Go!"

"What about you and JP?" Sasha said, helping Brooke up.

"You're dad's here?"

"Yeah, but not for long," she said, then looked at Sasha and Lyn. "I'll take Sammy, and Leo with me. You get Brooke to my house. Have Dr. Williams come over and look at her."

"No, I don't want to leave you. What about

Petrov? He'll hurt you, Luce," Brooke said.

"I can take care of myself, trust me." A quick kiss on Brooke's cheek and Luce barked another order. "Get her out of here, now. Wait, keys."

"Keys?" Sasha and Lyn said in unison.

"Her keys. Where are the keys to her car?"

Feeling around Brooke, Sasha found a set of keys and tossed them to Luce. "See you at the house. Be careful."

"I always am. Take care of her."

Brooke was pulled through the dark, cavernous warehouse, and out the back. Slipping outside into the darkness, she was pushed onto the floor of a black sedan that waited outside.

"Keep your head down."

She did as she was instructed. Gun shots echoed in the warehouse behind her. She popped her head up, but she was pushed back down. Unable to control her emotions anymore, Brooke covered her ears and started to cry.

"Guess you were a tad bit wrong about things, JP." Luce slapped the back of his head as she went by her father. "Sammy, we need to pack things up and get the hell out of here. I'm sure JP is ready for all of this to be over, aren't you, JP?"

His pale skin was cold and clammy and beads of sweat littered his upper lip. He wasn't looking good, not that it mattered to Luce. He was a dead man as far as she was concerned. Looking at the pitiful excuse for a father, she almost wished he had said something to save his sorry ass, but then people in hell want ice water, too.

Sliding her gun in her waistband holster, she grabbed her jacket and the revolver sitting on the desk.

"I want you to put the word out that I'm officially ordering a hit on Frank. He doesn't get out of this city alive. Understand?"

"Yes, Oyabun." Sammy and Leo bowed slightly and then went to their respective jobs cleaning up the office.

"Sammy, I want to talk to you for a minute."

"Yes, Oyabun."

Luce quickly went over some instructions with Sammy while Leo finished packing the duffle they had brought with them. Absentmindedly, she spun the cylinder of JP's revolver, watching the light bounce off the rotating chrome. She needed to apologize for what happened to Sammy because of Frank, but it wasn't something she was accustomed to doing. She wasn't good at humbling herself in front of her men, it didn't look good, but it needed to be said.

"I want to apologize for what Frank did, I'm sorry you lost your digit because of him."

"Oyabun, please don't apologize. You did what you had to do. I'm glad you didn't ask me to kill myself. My wife would have been devastated."

"Tell Kim I'll be over to see the new baby as soon as things calm down. I need to make sure my grandfather is safe, so can you take care of JP?"

"Of course."

"Once I get things in place with my grandfather, I want you to be his *Koban*."

"Kaida..." Sammy bowed and knew the honor she was bestowing on him couldn't be turned down. Her orders weren't to be questioned and she needed someone to take care of Tamiko as long as Frank was alive. Sammy was the logical choice, since he now had an axe to grind with Frank. He would make it his mission to protect her grandfather, find, and kill Frank, especially since he had dishonored Sammy's family and his name.

"It's done, Sammy."

"I'm honored that you would bestow such an honor. I won't let you down, Kaida."

"I know you won't Sammy. One more thing," she said, cupping her hand and whispering in his ear.

"I understand," he said, bowing.

"Okay, let's get this show on the road."

Luce clapped her hands and rushed through the office to her father's limp form. Pulling a pocketknife, she quickly sliced the bindings that held him, catching him as he pitched forward. Standing up with him, she suddenly felt him reach behind her, for her gun. Wrestling with JP, she grabbed his thigh and squeezed as hard as she could. He let out a piercing scream, so close to her ear that she tossed a shoulder into his chest, forcing him back into the chair.

"You stupid, bastard. You couldn't stop could you?"

"Fuck you."

"You couldn't be a good guy for once, could you?"

"Sammy, take care of him."

"You got it, Kaida."

"What you need one of your flunkies to do your dirty work?"

Luce turned towards her father and shook her head. He had to push all the way until the end didn't he? Lifting the revolver, she pointed it at JP and pulled the trigger. "No, I can take out the trash."

The sound of gunfire made Luce duck. Someone was shooting at them from the warehouse floor, and she had a pretty good idea who it was. A bullet broke a glass window and hit JP in the back spilling him on the floor.

"Sammy, I'll cover you. You guys get the hell out of here."

"We aren't leaving without you, Kaida."

The room was suddenly a mass of confusion. Sammy and Leo dodged and weaved, as glass and wood exploded everywhere around them. Luce crouched and crawled to the back door of the room.

"Come on let's go," she shouted at the men.

"Right behind you," Sammy yelled over the automatic fire peppering the walls.

Luce bolted for the open door and found herself face down in the dark hallway. A hand reached down and pulled her along towards the dim light at the bottom of the stairs. Looking up, she caught a glimpse of Leo as they pushed through the door and tumbled down the wooden stairs.

"We need to split up," Luce said. Gunfire still sprayed above her. Sammy ran down the stairs carrying the duffle bag that had been forgotten in the escape. "God, Sammy you could have left that, you almost got yourself killed."

"Lucky for me I'm quick. Here, this is for you." Sammy handed her a wadded piece of fabric. "I'll go by the Oyabun's and check on him."

Stuffing the wad of fabric in her pocket she yelled above the sporadic gunfire. "I'll call everyone tomorrow for a meeting. I want to get the word out about Frank as soon as possible."

The sound of gunfire drew closer, and they all

looked up to see the doorway splintering. It would only be a matter of seconds before the Russians were on top of them. Then it would be like shooting fish in a barrel from their vantage point above.

"Go, go!" she said, pushing the men away. She ran as fast as she could hitting the wall of the warehouse, and scooting along the side. Making her way towards Brooke's car, she had her .380 in one hand and JP's revolver in the other. Shooting her way to the red Mercedes, she circled around to the passenger side, pulled the keys, and slid into the tight confines.

"Geez, you need a fucking shoe horn to get into this thing."

Trying her best to watch and move, she gingerly forced herself into the driver's seat, struggling to wedge her long body into the cramped compartment. A bullet hit the rear quarter panel as she gunned the engine and stomped on the gas. Glass flew around her. Luce looked in the rearview mirror to see a lone gunman trying to get a bead on her. A quick jerk of the wheel and she was zipping between the last two warehouses before she hit the main intersection.

"Great," she said looking around the interior of the car. "She's gonna kill me when she sees this."

Chapter Thirty

I'm glad you're all right, Grandfather. No, I can't believe it either."

Luce rubbed her eyes and yawned.

"Yes, I've taken care of everything. No, I'm afraid he's dead."

"Thanks, but I wish I felt bad for him. I know, I know."

"I'll call you in the morning, Grandfather. Goodnight. I love you, too."

Luce tossed the cell phone on the couch next to her as she thought about the events of the night. It had been tougher than she thought it would be seeing JP up close. Even now, she couldn't believe he had forced her to kill him. He played the role of asshole until the end. He had to know she would kill him, especially after what he did to her mother. She couldn't let that debt go unpunished. He had earned his date with death tonight and she was glad she was there to see it.

The hot shower helped to clear the night's events from her body, but she doubted it would do anything for her weary soul. Pulling her robe closed, she thought about how growing the organization into a legitimate business was harder each day, but now she had to worry about Petrov and Frank working together. Frank knew things that could create problems for her, so she needed to find him and kill him. Tomorrow, the promise of another day would give her what she needed. The word was out. Frank was a marked man. It was only a matter of time before she had him. Patience was her friend, not her enemy, and she needed to remember that. Right now she needed to check in on her houseguest.

Pouring two fingers of bourbon, she took a slow sip and let it linger in her mouth. The earthy taste burned as it went down, so she took a sip of water. After a few more sips she felt herself relax and let her mind linger on Brooke. The lunch they had shared the day before flashed in front of her. Brooke's sensual curves and softness of her skin burned across Luce's body as she laid on top of her. The impatient way she brushed Luce's hands aside when she took her blouse off made Luce blush all over again. She could still feel the bamboo mat under her as Brooke forced her back and parted her thighs, smiling in surprise when she found out that Luce wasn't wearing panties. Somewhere in all of that, Luce wanted to tell Brooke she was her new boss, but it didn't seem quite the time for an employer/employee meeting.

Pouring another bourbon, Luce walked to the guest room and peeked in on her guest. If she was right, Dr. Williams had probably prescribed something to help Brooke's anxiety, which would mean she would be sleeping soundly until morning. The soft light on the nightstand had been left on, probably by Brooke, casting its glow around her. Crossing the room to the big leather wingback, Luce slid into its inviting comfort. She looked at Brooke, her hair splayed out around her, arms and legs everywhere. Thinking about the future, she wasn't sure what she could offer Brooke, but if she could promise anything it would be time. It would take time to get to know each other, time to explore, and time to understand how things would work between them. Was she ready to add a new dimension to her life?

"Hey." A soft voice ripe with sleep whispered.

"Hey yourself."

Brooke sat up on her elbows, watching Luce. From what Luce could see a T-shirt was the only thing Brooke was wearing. This had been a bad idea. She should have gone to her own room and left Brooke alone, but she wanted to make sure she was all right. At least that was what she told herself earlier.

"I was worried."

"Were you? Why?"

"There were people with guns trying to kill you. Does that happen all the time?"

"Not normally. Usually I get them before they get me."

"Really."

"No, not really," Luce lied.

She didn't want Brooke worrying. For some reason it mattered what Brooke thought. Sinking further back in the chair, she took a sip of her bourbon, contemplating how much she wanted to tell Brooke about tonight. Would she tell her about JP and how he was dead? Would she tell her she had been the one to make sure JP had paid his debt to her family, or would she gloss over the events of the night? It wasn't in her to lie, but she had never been in a situation like this, possibly having someone that mattered. Starting off with a lie would mean that they had no boundaries, no rules about truth, and no foundation on which to build something. If Brooke asked, she would tell the truth, she hoped Brooke wouldn't ask.

"Were you hurt?"

Luce shook her head. She had been lucky. In fact her whole crew had been lucky, no one was hurt or killed.

"Were you scared?"

Luce shook her head again.

"I was scared."

"Come here," Luce said, her tone husky.

Brooke slipped out of bed and it was almost too much for Luce as she walked toward her in only a T-shirt. Her sensual curves were driving Luce crazy already and they hadn't even touched. Taking one last sip of her bourbon, she set it on the table and patted her lap. Grabbing Brooke's curvy ass she nestled it in tight, turning her so her legs hung over the arm of the chair. Luce put her arm around her back and pulled her close. Brooke laid her head on Luce's shoulder, and nuzzled her neck.

"Careful of what you get started."

"Hmm."

"Didn't Dr. Williams give you something for your anxiety?"

"I didn't take it," she mumbled against Luce's neck. "I wanted to be awake when you got here."

Turning her head toward the whisper, Luce kissed Brooke's waiting lips. Soft, warm, and inviting, Luce indulged as Brooke parted her lips, and slipped her tongue inside. Her body still tense from the night's events, it wouldn't take much to push her into the abyss she found herself slipping towards. Wavering on its edge, Luce found she wanted to forget, to get lost in Brooke's arms and fall headlong into a night filled with making love. Brooke must have read her mind. She grabbed Luce's hand and slipped it under her T-shirt. Luce played with a taut nipple before palming the breast.

She loved the heft of Brooke's breasts in her hands and showered them with attention when she made love to her. Scooting to the edge of the chair, she lifted Brooke up and carried her to the bed. Luce dropped Brooke's legs and she slid down Luce's firm body, her T-shirt rolling up. Brooked pulled on the belt and the robe fell open, exposing Luce to her touch.

"Turn around" Luce commanded.

Doing as she was instructed, Brooke pushed her ass against Luce's groin. Sliding her hands down Luce's hips, she grabbed them and wiggled against Luce. Luce kissed Brooke's neck, finding her raging pulse and sucking on it. Tonight, Brooke would wear her brand as she had worn Brooke's earlier. Reaching around she let her hands roam over Brooke's breasts, caressing the nipples, feeling them pucker against her finger and thumb. She gently pulled the tips, rotating and tugging them again. Sliding one hand down to cup Brooke's warm center, she slipped a finger between the slick folds and stroked her. Wetness coated her finger as she continued to play with Brooke. Unable to stand it anymore, Brooke spread her legs, reached down and pushed Luce's hand deeper into her. Brooke's muscles tightened around her fingers signaling Brooke's impending orgasm, but she stopped her movements. She didn't want Brooke to come like this, not tonight.

"Lay down on the bed."

"Okay." Her body primed and ready, Brooke waited for Luce's next command.

Stripping her robe off, she climbed in behind Brooke and let the weight of her body slowly cover Brooke's. Gently, she pushed her groin against the hard ass under her. The resistance was enough that she felt her clit begin to throb as the movement continued. She slid her hands under Brooke's arms and grabbed her wrists, essentially trapping her. If Brooke protested she would release her grip, but she was getting off on the dominance position and it took all of her strength to stay on her elbows and her knees on either side of Brooke's ass. She didn't want to smother or scare her so she gently, but firmly rubbed her breast against her back and her groin undulated across Brooke's ass. Slowly she began to buck her hips against Brooke's ass, as if she were fucking her. With each buck she heard Brooke groan, spurring her on. The tips of her nipples moved across her back, stimulating Luce further. She was about to come undone when she heard Brooke say something.

"What?"

"Blindfold me," Brooke pleaded.

"What? Are you sure?"

"I want to feel what you feel when you're blindfolded."

"Do you trust me?"

The silence lingered as both women hovered somewhere between ecstasy and orgasm. Luce knew she was close, but wanted to give Brooke what she wanted, if she truly wanted to be blindfolded.

"Yes." The whispered answer finally came.

Reaching into the nightstand, Luce pulled out a scarf and wrapped Brooke's eyes. Tonight would put them on a different road sexually and Luce hoped Brooke was ready. Still straddling Brooke's hips, she ran her nails down Brooke's back. The faint red marks rose instantly.

"Turn over and put your hands above your head. Don't move them. If you do, I'll stop. Do you understand?"

Brooke nodded her head and Luce smiled. She already understood the rules. Pulling her hips she positioned Brooke in the center of the bed.

"Spread your legs," Luce commanded. "This position is called the Eiffel tower. It usually is done in binding, but I'm trusting you'll stay put until I tell you to move. Can you do that?"

Brooke nodded her head again in consent. Luce could see that she was already struggling internally with her instructions. Her body rigid, every muscle on alert as Luce ran her tongue down the center of Brooke's slender body. Her muscles twitched as she ran her mouth over her ribs. If Brooke thought she was being tortured, she hadn't experienced anything yet. Spreading her legs more, Luce settled her shoulders between them and started to kiss her inner thighs, watching her hands tighten and release as each kiss moved closer to their destination. Luce stopped briefly and inhaled deeply. The musky smell of Brooke sent a tingle through her body, as if tiny fingers were under the skin moving to her pussy. Parting Brooke's lips, she was finally able to study the woman as she opened her further. Wetting a finger, Luce stroked it across her clit and watched her jump at the stroke. Slowly and methodically, Luce stroked the swollen nub until Brooke moaned. Luce stopped and the moans stopped. Brooke wiggled her hips as if begging for more contact.

"Don't stop please."

"Please what?"

"Oh god, please…"

"Tell me what you want, Brooke," she urged.

"I want you to make me come, please."

Smiling, Luce reached up and tweaked a nipple, pulling the tip and then releasing it. Moving back to her original job, she licked across the hard clit, feeling it flick as she lifted her tongue off it. Lapping at it she watched Brooke's pussy start to flinch with each stroke of her tongue. Adjusting her weight, she slid a finger, then two into the tight space and began stroking in and out as she licked the hard ridge. Without warning, Brooke's body began to spasm as she reached orgasm.

"Oh, fuck. Oh fuck," she grunted out.

Reaching up Luce flicked a nipple and continued to pump in and out of Brooke, prolonging her orgasm. A brief pause made Luce work more on the wet center, moving her tongue furiously over Brooke's clit. She felt the ebb and flow of another orgasm taking root and worked it until Brooke's body jerked and spasmed again.

"Stop, please stop. I'm not sure I can take anymore."

A final flick of her tongue finished her off. Sliding up the vibrating body, Luce pulled Brooke on top of her and sighed. Another jerk and Brooke finally relaxed, yanking the blindfold off.

"That was amazing."

A smug smile crossed Luce's face as she looked at the content woman on top of her. "I know."

"Glad to see you're not humble."

"Hey, when you got it, you got it."

Sliding down into the crook of Luce's arm, Brooke slapped at her breast. "You'll be happy to know you got it," she said, sticking her tongue out at the arrogance of her lover.

"Careful, I'm going to put that to use in a minute."

"Hmm, I wish. You'll probably fall asleep."

"Hmm."

"So how do you like your fringe benefits?" Luce questioned.

"What? What'd you mean?"

"You slept with the boss."

"My boss? Okay, color me clueless."

"I bought the magazine."

"Shut-up. You didn't," she said wondering. "Did you? When?"

"About two weeks ago. That's why I was there the other day, to speak to John."

"When you came to the club and interviewed my grandfather, I had finalized it that day."

"Holy shit, that's what John meant when he said he needed to tell me something important."

The room became silent as both women considered whether it would change their relationship.

"So does this mean you want me to dump the story?"

"This doesn't change anything, if you don't want it to."

Brooke rested her chin on Luce's chest. Luce rested her head on her hands and waited for a response from Brooke. Maybe she should have waited for a better moment, but things were moving so fast. If she didn't tell Brooke now, chances were pretty good the cat would be out of the bag when she went back to work. The financial and legal documents she had to file would be public knowledge by Monday morning, and there was no way to delay them.

"Your turn," Brooke said as she straddled Luce's hips.

Chapter Thirty-one

"Here ya go." Petrov said, passing the man a tip.

"Thanks, Buddy. Have a good one."

Shutting the door without a response, Petrov took the package into the office. Looking at the return address on the box, he recognized it as one of the banks he did business with in the Ukraine.

"Who was it?" Frank said, sipping his coffee as he walked over to the desk.

"I don't know. It looks like a delivery from one of my banks." Petrov turned the package over and inspected the label again. "What did you hear about last night?"

"Not much, it seems that they shot the place up and they shot someone, but the police arrived before they could see who it was. JP should be coming by this afternoon to give us an update."

Pulling out his pocketknife, Petrov sliced the tape on the box and slid the contents out on the table. A lacquer box and a scroll dropped out onto the table with a thud. Both men froze as they studied the contents, neither wanting to touch them.

"Shit," Frank said tensely.

"What? What is it?"

Frank reached over and flipped the top open.

Inside the satin lined box sat a finger with a signet ring on it. Not just any finger, but a pinkie with all three digits. Bending down Frank looked closer at the signet ring, recognizing it instantly.

"Shit."

"What the fuck is that?"

"It's JP's ring."

"Are you kidding me?"

"I don't kid about shit like this," Frank said, picking up the scroll.

Popping off the wax seal, Frank opened it looking at the Kanji writing. It was for Frank's eyes only, but he read it aloud.

"You're traitorous ways will be richly rewarded, my friend. Signed, Tamiko Yoshida, Oyabun."

"Fuck."

Coming 2013

American Yakuza
The Lies That Bind

About the Author

Award winning author Isabella, lives in California with her wife and three sons. In June 2011, Isabella's first novel, Always Faithful, won a GCLS award in the Traditional Contemporary Romance category. She was also a finalist in the International Book Awards and an Honorable Mention in the 2010 Rainbow awards

She is a member of Gold Crown Literary Society, Romance Writers of America, and IBPA. She has written several short stories, and is now working on her next novel, Executive Disclosure due out in Summer 2012.

Other Titles Available at Sapphire Books

Award winning novel - Always Faithful - By Isabella   ISBN - 978-09828608-0-9

Major Nichol "Nic" Caldwell is the only survivor of her helicopter crash in Iraq. She is left alone to wonder why she and she alone. Survivor's guilt has nothing on the young Major as she is forced to deal with the scars, both physical and mental, left from her ordeal overseas. Before the accident, she couldn't think of doing anything else in her life.

Claire Monroe is your average military wife, with a loving husband and a little girl. She is used to the time apart from her husband. In fact, it was one of the reasons she married him. Then, one day, her life is turned upside down when she gets a visit from the Marine Corps.

Can these two women come to terms with the past and finally find happiness, or will their shared sense of honor keep them apart?

GCLS Nominated - Scarlet Masquerade - By Jett Abbott ISBN - 978-09828608-1-6

What do you say to the woman you thought died over a century ago? Will time heal all wounds or does it just allow them to fester and grow? A.J. Locke has lived over two centuries and works like a demon, both figuratively and literally. As the owner of a successful pharmaceutical company that specializes in blood research, she has changed the way she can live her life. Wanting for nothing, she has smartly compartmentalized her life so that when she needs to, she can pick up and start all over again, which happens every twenty years or so.

Clarissa Graham is a university professor who has lived an obscure life teaching English literature. She has made it a point to stay off the radar and never become involved with anything that resembles her past life. She keeps her personal life separate from her professional one, and in doing so she is able to keep her secrets to herself. Suddenly, her life is turned upside down when someone tries to kill her. She finds herself in the middle of an assassination plot with no idea who wants her dead.

Broken Shield - By Isabella - ISBN - 978-09828608-2-3

Tyler Jackson, former paramedic now firefighter, has seen her share of death up close. The death of her wife caused Tyler to rethink her career choices, but the death of her mother two weeks later cemented her return to the ranks of firefighter. Her path of self-destruction and womanizing is just a front to hide the heartbreak and devastation she lives with every day. Tyler's given up on finding love and having the family she's always wanted. When tragedy strikes her life for a second time she finds something she thought she lost.

Ashley Henderson loves her job. Ignoring her mother's advice, she opts for a career in law enforcement. But, Ashley hides a secret that soon turns her life upside down. Shame, guilt and fear keep Ashley from venturing forward and finding the love she so desperately craves. Her life comes crashing down around her in one swift moment forcing her to come clean about her secrets and her life.

Can two women thrust together by one traumatic event survive and find love together, or will their past force them apart?